SECRET STORIES

Tales from the Secret History of the World

by

F. Paul Wilson

CONTENTS

Secret Stories

Copyright © 2019 by F. Paul Wilson

First published in 2019

INTRODUCTION

The preponderance of my work deals with a history of the world that remains undiscovered, unexplored, and unknown to most of humanity. Some of this Secret History has been revealed in the Adversary Cycle, some in the Repairman Jack novels, and bits and pieces in other, seemingly unconnected works. Taken together, even these millions of words barely scratch the surface of what has been going on behind the scenes, hidden from the workaday world.

Here I've gathered some of the shorter pieces of the Secret History and placed them for convenience between a single set of covers. I've left off the pieces available as stand-alones or collected in *Quick Fixes*, and concentrated on those published in scattered collections and anthologies over the years. To each I've added commentary as to how it earned its place in the Secret History.

For a more comprehensive overview, may I suggest *Scenes from the Secret History* which is free on Smashwords.com.

F. Paul Wilson
The Jersey Shore
February 2019

DEMONSONG

Here you have one of the cornerstones of the Secret History.

By the mid-1970s I'd read most of the original Conan stories by Robert E. Howard and decided to try my hand at a little sword and sorcery myself. But I didn't want simply to rehash Howard. I decided to put my own stamp on it by writing a sword and sorcery tale in which the barbarian warrior never draws his sword. Gary Hoppenstand took it for his semi-pro-zine, *Midnight Sun* but returned it with a kill fee when he had to discontinue the magazine. (Now *that's* class.)

Soon afterward I placed it with Gerald Page's *Heroic Fantasy* from DAW Books. The barbarian was named Glaeken and the evil wizard he faced called himself Rasalom. I forgot about those two until a few years later when I needed to cast two ancient foes for a novel I planned to call *The Keep*.

Demonsong

A tale of the First Age

"*H*o, outlander!" *cried the burlier of the two men-at-arms stationed before the city's newsboard. His breath steamed in the chill post-dawn haze. "You look stout of arm, poor of cloak, and lame of brain – this notice from the prince should interest you!"*

"He'd have to be an outlander to be interested," his companion muttered through a gap-toothed leer. "No one from around here's going to take the prince up on it."

The first scowled. "The prince ought to go himself! Then maybe we'd get a real man on the throne. Musicians and pretty-boys!" He spat. 'The palace is no longer a fit place for a warrior. Wasn't like that like that during his father's reign."

The other nodded and the pair walked off without a backward glance.

The outlander hesitated, then approached the elaborately hand-written notice. He ran long fingers through his dusty red hair as he stared it. The language was fairly new to him and, although he spoke it passably, reading was a different matter. The gist of the notice was an offer of 10.000 gold grignas to the man who would undertake a certain mission for Prince Iolon. Inquiries should be made at the palace.

The outlander fingered his coin pouch; a few measly coppers rattled within. He didn't know the weight of a grigna, but if it was gold and there were 10,000 of them...money would not be a problem for quite some time. He shrugged and turned toward the palace.

*

The streets of Kashela, the commercial center of Prince Iolon's realm, were alive at first light. Not so the palace. It was well-nigh midday before Glaeken was allowed entrance. The huge antechamber was empty save for an elderly blue-robed official sitting behind a tiny desk, quill in hand, a scroll and ink-well before him.

"State your business," he said in a bored tone, keeping his eyes on the parchment.

"I've come to find out how to earn those 10,000 grignas the prince is offering."

The old man's head snapped up at Glaeken's unfamiliar accent. He: saw a tall, wiry, red-headed man – that hair alone instantly labeled him a foreigner – with high coloring and start-lingly blue eyes. He wore leather breeches, a shirt of indeter-minate color girded by a broad belt that held a dirk and longs-word; he carried a dusty red cloak over his left shoulder.

"Oh. A northerner, eh? Or is it a westerner?"

"Does it matter?"

"No...no, I suppose not. Name?"

"Glaeken,"

The quill dipped into the well, then scratched out strange black letters on the scroll. "Glaeken of what?"

"How many Glaekens do you have in this city?"

"None. It's not even in our tongue."

"Then Glaeken alone will do."

The air of finality to the statement caused the official to re-gard the outlander with more careful scrutiny. He saw a young man not yet out of his third decade who behaved with an assur-ance beyond his years.

A youth with oiled locks and dressed in a clinging white robe entered the antechamber then. He gave Glaeken a frankly appraising stare as he sauntered past on his way to the inner chambers.

"Captain of the palace guard, I presume," Glaeken said blandly after the epicene figure had passed from sight.

"Your humor, outlander, could cost you your head should any of the guard hear such a remark."

"What does the prince want done?" he said, ignoring the caveat.

"He wants someone to journey into the eastern farmlands and kill a wizard."

"He has an army, does he not?"

The official suddenly became very interested in the scroll. "The captains have refused to send their men."

Glaeken mulled this. He sensed an air of brooding discontent in palace, an undercurrent of frustration and hostility perilously close to the surface.

"No one has tried to bring in this wizard then? Come, old man! The bounty surely didn't begin at 10,000 gold pieces."

"A few squads were sent when the problem first became apparent, but they accomplished nothing."

"Tell me where these men are quartered. I'd like to speak to them."

"You can't." The official's eyes remained averted. "They never came back."

Glaeken made no immediate reply. He fingered his coin pouch, then tapped the heel of his right hand against the butt of his longsword.

Finally: "Get a map and show me where I can find this wizard."

*

Glaeken dallied in one of those nameless little inns that dot the back streets on any commercially active town. His sat by the window. The shutters were open to let out the sour stench of last night's spilled ale, and the late morning sunlight glinted off the hammered tin goblet cheap wine that rested on the table before him. The harlot in the corner eyed him languidly...this foreigner might prove interesting. A little early in the day for her talents, but perhaps if he stayed around a little longer...

A commotion arose on the street and Glaeken peered out the window to find its source. A squat, burly, misshapen hillock of a man with a square protruding jaw was trudging by, a large, oddly shaped leather case clutched with both arms against his chest. Behind him and around him ran the local gang of street youths, pushing, shoving and calling. The wooden heels of their crude boots clacked as they scampered about; all wore a make-shift uniform of dark green shirts and rough brown pants.

"Ho, Ugly One!" cried a youth who seemed to be the leader, a lean, black-haired adolescent with a fuzzy attempt at a beard shading his cheeks. "What've y'got in that case? Give us a look! It truly must be something to behold if you're clutching it so tightly. Give us a look!"

The man ignored the group, but this only incited them to greater audacity. They began pummeling him and trying to trip him, yet the man made no attempt to protect himself. He merely clutched the case closer and tighter. Glaeken wondered at this as he watched the scene. This "Ugly One's" heavy frame and thickly muscled arms certainly appeared strong enough to handle the situation. Yet the well-being of the leather case seemed his only concern.

The leader gave a signal and he and his followers leaped upon the man. The fellow kept his footing for a while and even managed to shake a few of the attackers off his back, but their numbers soon drove him to the ground. Glaeken noted with a smile of admiration that the man twisted as he fell so that he landed on his back with the case unharmed. Only a matter of a few heartbeats, however, before the case was torn from his grasp.

With the loss of his precious possession, the little man became a veritable demon, cursing, gnashing his teeth, and struggling with such ferocity that it took the full strength of eight of the rowdies to hold him down.

"Be still, Ugly One!" the leader commanded as he stood near Glaeken's window and fumbled with the clasps on the case. "We only want to see what you've got here."

As the last clasp gave way, the case fell open and from it the leader pulled a double-barreled harmohorn. The shouts and scuffling ceased abruptly as all in sight, rowdy and bystander alike, were captured by the magnificence of the instrument. The intricate hand-carved wood of the harmohorn glistened in

6

the sun under countless coats of flawlessly applied lacquer. A reed instrument, rare and priceless; in the proper hands it was capable of producing the most subtle and devious harmonies known to man. The art of its making had long been lost, and the musician fortunate enough to possess a harmohorn was welcomed – nay, sought – by all the royal courts of the world.

The squat little man redoubled his efforts against those restraining him.

"Damage that horn and I'll have your eyes!" he screamed.

"Don't threaten me, Ugly One!" the leader warned.

He raised the instrument aloft at if to smash it on the stones at his feet. In doing so he brought the horn within Glaeken's reach. To this point the outlander had been neutral, refusing to help a man who would not help himself. But now he knew the reason for the man's reluctance to fight, and the sight of the harmohorn in the hands of street swine disturbed him.

The horn abruptly switched hands.

The leader spun in surprise and glared at Glaeken.

"You!" he yelled, leaning in the window. "Return that before I come in and get it!"

"You want to come it?" Glaeken said with a tight smile. "Then by all means waste no time!"

He grabbed the youth by his shirt and pulled him half way through the window.

"Let go of me, red-haired dog!" he screeched.

"Certainly." And Glaeken readily replied, but not without enough of a shove to ensure that the youth would land sprawled in the dust.

Scrambling to his feet, the leader turned to his pack. "After him!"

They forgot the man they were holding and charged the inn door. But Glaeken was already there, waiting and ready.

He smiled as he met their attack and laughed as it moved out to the street where he darted among them, striking and kicking and wreaking general havoc upon their ranks. But these youths were hardly novices at street brawls, and when they realized that their opponent, too, was well experienced in the dubious art, they regrouped and began to stalk him.

"Circle him!" said the leader and his followers responded with dispatch. Before the menacing ring could close, however, the pack found itself harassed from an unexpected quarter.

"Ugly One" was upon them. Having regained his feet and sized up the situation, the little man charged into the pack with the roar of an angry bull. He was enraged to the point of madness and a smiling Glaeken stepped back to watch as the street youths were hurled and scattered about like jackstraws. A complete rout seemed inevitable. It was then that Glaeken glanced at the leader and saw him pull a dirk from within his shirt and lunge.

The blade never found its target. Glaeken moved and yanked the pack leader off his feet by his long hair; he pulled the knife from his grasp and extended his grimy neck over his knee. All fighting stopped as everyone watched the tableau of Glaeken and the pack leader.

"You should be slain outright," Glaeken said, toying with the dirk over the terrified youth's vulnerable throat. "And no one would miss you or mourn you."

"No!" he cried as he saw the cold light in Glaeken's eyes. "I no meant harm!"

Glaeken used the point to scratch an angry, ragged red line ear to ear across the leader's throat.

"A good street brawl is one thing, my young friend, but if I see you show your steel to the back of an unarmed man again, I'll finish the job this scratch has begun."

So saying, he lifted the youth by his hair and shoved him toward his companions. The green-shirted pack and its frightened leader wasted no time then in fleeing the scene.

"Ugly One" turned to Glaeken and extended his hand. "I thank you, outlander. I am called Cragjaw, although I assure you I was not given that name by my parents."

"No thanks called for," Glaeken said, clasping the hand. "A street brawl at midday is a good spirit-lifter." He did offer his own name in return.

"I'm prefer quieter ways to amuse myself," Cragjaw muttered as he stooped to pick up the empty leather case.

The barmaster was sheathing a dirk of his own as they re-entered. The contested musical instrument lay on the bar before him.

"I guarded the harmohorn well while you were out on the street!" he shouted to Cragjaw.

"And what would you have done with it if he hadn't been able return to claim it?" Glaeken asked with a knowing grin.

The barmaster shrugged and eyed the horn as Cragjaw returned it to its case.

"I suppose I would have had to sell it to someone... I have no talent for such an instrument."

Glaeken threw a coin on the bar. "That's for the wine," he said turned toward the door.

Cragjaw laid a hand on his arm. "At least let me buy you cup before you go."

"Thanks, no. I'm riding the East Road and already I've tarried long."

"The East Road? Why, I must travel that way, too. Would you mind a companion for a ways?"

"The roads are free," said Glaeken.

*

Glaeken's mount, a stallion called Stoffral, took him eastward from Kashela at an easy walk. Cragjaw ambled beside him on a chestnut mare.

"You're a Northerner, aren't you?" the shorter man observed.

"In a way, yes."

"You never told me your name."

"It is Glaeken."

Glaeken..." Cragjaw paused before continuing. "Stories circulate among the wine cups in the back rooms of the court of Prince Iolon – in whose service I am presently employed as a musician – and in the taverns about a man named Glaeken. He's said to live in the Western Isles and is supposedly young and

F. Paul Wilson

flame-haired like yourself."

"Interesting," Glaeken remarked. "And what are these tales?"

"Well, he is called Glaeken-the-Laugher by some and it is said that he once led the dreaded Nightriders who pillage vast areas of the Western Isles."

Glaeken nodded for his companion to continue.

"I know only what I've heard, but 'tis said that each of these raiders rides a monstrous bat with a body the size of a horse and wings like ketch sails that sweep the night. The tales tell of an evil king named Marag who was the favorite target of the Nightriders and who sent many champions against them with the quest to bring back the head of the Nightrider lord. But shortly after each set out, a monster bat would fly over Marag's hold and drop the latest champion's body into the courtyard.

"Finally, a man named Glaeken, who had refused to be the king's champion for many years, was called into Marag's court. And there in a steel cage suspended from the ceiling sat the damsel in whose company this Glaeken had been often seen. Now, they say that Glaeken had no serious future plans for the young lady but felt somewhat responsible for her present predicament. So he traveled to the pinnacle fortress of the Nightriders where he challenged and beat their lord in a contest of swords."

"And did he bring the head to Marag?" Glaeken asked.

"That and more, for it seems that by tradition the Nightriders must claim as leader the man who fairly defeats the reigning lord. This Glaeken returned with his new followers and taught Marag a grisly lesson." Cragjaw glanced at his companion. "Could you be that Glaeken?"

"A good tale, my friend, but how could I and this bat-rider be one and the same? How could I be pillaging the Western Isles at night and ride the East Road in Prince Iolon's domain with you today? Quite impossible."

"Not so," said Cragjaw with a sly grin. "For it is also said that after a year or two with the Nightriders, the man named Glaeken grew restless and dissatisfied. He left them to their own devices and no one knows where he travels now." The

10

squat little man made a point of clearing his throat. "Where travel you now, Glaeken?"

"To Elder Cavern in the eastern farmlands."

"Elder Cavern! Why, that's in the very center of the plague area. Nothing out there but dying farms and..." Cragjaw's voice faded as he seemed to remember something. "Oh, I see. You must have answered the Prince's notice."

Glaeken nodded. "It seems that the mystery of the region's woes has been cleared up. They've discovered that a sorcerer named Rasalom – a giant of a man, I'm told – entered the cavern nearly two years ago. Not too long thereafter the crops, the cattle, and the farmers in the area began to sicken. Rasalom has been neither seen nor heard from since, and the Prince's advisors seem certain that he's still in the cavern."

"So the infamous Rasalom is behind it all," Cragjaw muttered. "We've long thought it to be a plague of some sort, released from the cavern after eons of sleep."

"The prince's advisors were rather vague about the plague," Glaeken said. "Do you know what it's like?"

"Stories vary, but most agree that the victims complain of a throbbing in the head and ears and slowly begin to lose their strength, becoming very lethargic. Soon they cannot get out of bed and eventually they waste away and die. But what puzzled the court physicians was the curious fact that all victims seem to improve and recover when moved out of the area. No one could give a reason for this...but sorcery explains it well: Rasalom has laid a curse of some sort on the region."

"So it would seem," Glaeken agreed.

"But what purpose could he have? Why would he want to lay waste the eastern farmlands – for not only do people sicken and die out there, but cattle and crops as well."

Glaeken shrugged. "Why is not my concern. I admit that I'm somewhat curious, but my task is merely to bring back Rasalom himself, or some proof of his demise, such as his Ring of Chaos, whatever that may be."

"'Tis rumored to be the most potent focus of power for black sorcery this side of the Netherworld. You will have to slay Rasalom to gain it, and that will not be easy." He shuddered. "Not only does that wizard have the black arts at his command, but he is said to stand half again as tall as a tall man, and be three times as broad in the shoulders. No wonder Iolon has to send an outlander! No local man would set foot in Elder Cavern! I hope the prince is paying you well."

"I seldom take on a gainless task." Glaeken replied.

"If that's true, then why did you aid me against those street thugs?"

Glaeken smiled. "I was quite willing to let them have their fun with you until I saw the harmohorn. I have a weakness for music and consequently a respect for musicians."

They came to a crossroads when and Cragjaw turned his horse to the north.

"We part here, Glaeken," he said. "I go to the prince's summer quarters to prepare entertainment for the arrival of his entourage tomorrow. I would bid you ride south and have no further thought of Elder Cavern, but I know you'll not heed me. So instead I bid you luck and hope to see you at the summer palace soon with either Rasalom or his ring. One word of warning though: travel quickly. Few who venture into that land nowadays are ever seen again."

Glaeken waved and headed east. He did not quicken his pace.

*

The land was arid and vegetation generally scarce in Iolon's domain, but as Glaeken penetrated into the eastern farmlands he became aware of an almost total lack of greenery. Bark-shedding trees lifted their dry, stunted, leafless branches skyward in silent supplication for surcease of – what? And the further east he moved, the darker became the sky; gray clouds slid by, twisting, churning, writhing, and rolling as if suffering from an agony of their own as they passed over the region.

Long-rotted cattle carcasses dotted the fields on both sides of the road, the hides dried and matted and close-fitting in death, perfectly outlining the skeleton within. Glaeken saw no evidence that scavengers had been at the carrion, and then realized that he had not seen a single trace of beast or fowl since he'd entered the region. Even vultures shunned this place.

The motionless air became thick and heavy as he pushed on, his lungs labored at their task. As evening consolidated the gray of the sky to black, Glaeken was glad to dismount. He built a fire not too far off the road between a dead tree and a large stone. He gave Stoffral free rein to find what nourishment he could in the lifeless, desiccated grasses nearby, but the horse seemed to have lost all appetite. Glaeken, too, felt no hunger, unusual after half a day's ride, but managed to force down some dried beef and stale wine

He was strangely tired and this gave him some concern. He had never been one to believe in sorcerers and evil magic, considering them little more than tales designed to frighten children. The only magic he'd ever seen had been the work of charlatans. Yet for a man of his age and fitness to feel so lethargic after a mere six hours on horseback was decidedly unnatural. Maybe there was something to this curse after all.

He moved away from the heat of the fire and sat with his back against the rock. The oppressive silence made him uneasy. Even the nightbugs were quiet. He glanced about...no pairs of feral eyes reflected the firelight from the darkness around his little camp. That, too, was unusual. Slowly, his eyes grew heavy. Against his better judgment he allowed himself to doze.

...the sound grows in his brain by imperceptible degrees, a ghastly, keening, wailing cacophony of madness that assaults his sanity with murderous intensity...and as the volume increases there appear wild, distorted visages of evil, countless blank-eyed demons howling with mindless joy, screaming louder and louder until he is sure he must go mad...

Glaeken found himself awake and on his feet, sweat coursing along his skin in runnels. The fire had burned down to a fitful glow and all was quiet. He shook his head to clear it of the dream and glanced around for Stoffral. Gone!

Fully alert to danger now, Glaeken began shouting the horse's name. Stoffral was too loyal a beast to desert him. His third shout was answered by a faint whinny from behind the rock. Glaeken cautiously peered into the darkness and saw the dim form of his mount on the ground. He ran to its side and made a careful check. The horse had suffered no harm and Glaeken concluded that Stoffral must be a victim of the same lethargy afflicting his master.

He slapped the horse's flanks in an effort to rouse the beast back to its feet but to no avail. Stoffral's strength seemed completely drained. Glaeken remembered the cattle carcasses along the road and swore that his steed would not suffer a similar fate. He stalked to the fire and lifted a branch that had been only partially consumed. Fanning it in the air until the tip glowed cherry with heat, he applied the brand to Stoffral's right hindquarter. Amid the whiff of singed hair and the hiss of searing flesh, the horse screamed in pain and rose on wobbly legs.

Glaeken could not help but cast a fearful glance over his shoulder as he steadied his mount; horses were rare and highly valued creatures in the land where he had been raised, and any man caught doing harm to one was likely to be attacked by an angry mob. But pain or not, scar or not, Stoffral was on his feet now and somewhat revived. That was all that mattered at the moment. And the horse seemed to know instinctively that the act had been done without malice.

Replacing the saddle on Stoffral's back, he packed it with everything but the jerked beef, the waterskin, and the half-dozen torches he had fashioned before leaving Kashela. Then he shouted and slapped the horse's flanks and chased him back down the road. Hopefully, Stoffral would await his master beyond the zone of danger.

Glaeken waited a moment, then shouldered his pack and began walking in the opposite direction. He'd have preferred to wait until morning...travel would be easier in the light. But Glaeken's doubts about the supposed curse on the eastern farmlands had been thoroughly shaken. Perhaps something truly evil was afoot in the region. For all he knew, morning might prove too late if he waited for it. So he traveled in darkness.

*

Dawn lightened the perpetual overcast as Glaeken stood before the high arched entrance to Elder Cavern. He felt as if his eyes had been tom out and replaced with heated coals. His head buzzed and hummed; his sword had become a drag anchor. The very air weighed upon him like a stone. He stood swaying, questioning the wisdom of entering the opening before him. His strength had steadily declined during the night and he was now so weakened that he seriously entertained thoughts of abandoning his mission.

Everything seemed so hopeless. With barely strength enough to stand, he'd be insane to challenge a giant in stature and sorcery such as Rasalom. Yet he forced himself to stagger toward the cavern maw.

Part of his fogged brain screamed to turn back, but he kept pushing forward. He could not turn back, for he would never make it to the crossroads; he'd end up like the rotting cattle he'd had passed yesterday.

Why not simply lay down and die then?

Because he could not pass up the slim chance that he might find a way to outwit Rasalom. And of course the golden reward was a lure, as was his need to learn what lay behind the curse that weighed upon this region like a plague. And beneath it all, driving him like a whip, was that peculiar aspect of his nature that insisted he see a task through to its finish.

As he was engulfed by the darkness within, Glaeken paused, removed the tinderbox from his sack and ignited one of the torches. The flame flickered light off the walls and made marching armies of the stalactite and stalagmite shadows as he moved. His shuffling feet kicked up smelly clouds of dust that irritated his nose. He knew the odor well – bat dung, and none of it fresh. Even the bats were gone.

The tunnel sloped at a steep angle and the roof bore down on him until he had to walk in a slight crouch. The walls glistened with moisture as he plunged deeper and deeper into the earth, and his torch would hiss as it brushed against them. The odd, persistent humming in his brain grew louder and more distracting as he moved. He could only hope that the tunnel would lead him directly to Rasalom.

The passage broadened into a wider, higher chamber and Glaeken cursed as the torchlight revealed the problem he had hoped not to meet: three other tunnels opened into this same chamber. As he slumped against the wall in near complete exhaustion, his torch sagged and dipped into a brackish puddle. In sudden total darkness he fumbled for the tinderbox to light a fresh torch, then froze. Down the tunnel to the right trickled the faintest hint of illumination.

Glaeken forgot about torch and tinderbox and stumbled along the passage toward the beckoning tendrils of light. Rounding a corner he found himself in a dim, long-shadowed room. The walls were smooth and bare except for a few oil lamps flickering in sconces. A huge, throne-like chair rested in a dark corner, otherwise the room was empty.

Wary, Glaeken started to draw his broadsword as he moved further into the room, but the weight of it seemed so enormous to his weakened muscles that he let it slide back into its scabbard. He rested his hand instead on the handle of his dirk.

A massive door appeared to be cut into the wall to his right. Eyes darting constantly about the room, Glaeken approached it. He saw no latch, no ring, no handle, but the arcuate scratches on the floor before it were proof that the door did in some way swing open. Yet try as he might, he could not see how.

A voice rasped behind him: "There's a hidden latch."

The nape of his neck tingling with fear and surprise, Glaeken wheeled and peered closely at the massive chair in the corner. The seat lay immersed in Stygian shadow. He moved closer and faintly made out a human outline. Grabbing an oil lamp from the wall, he held it high.

As the shadows receded Glaeken saw that he faced a lank-haired skeleton of a man dressed in a robe once richly embroidered but now tattered and torn, foul and filthy.

"You must be strong-willed to have come this far," said the seated figure in a voice like rats' feet scurrying over dried corn husks.

"Who are you?" Glaeken demanded.

"I am called Rasalom."

"I was told Rasalom is a giant of a man, not a mere bag of bones."

"I am he, nevertheless," Rasalom replied with a grin that was horrible to behold. "You no doubt started on your journey with visions of a terrible struggle against a huge, sword-wielding wizard. You foresaw a mighty battle with flashes of steel and shouts of fury. Yet look at us now: you can barely stand and I have not the strength to cast the most elementary of weirds." He barked a harsh laugh. "What a comedy we play!"

But Glaeken could see no humor in the situation. He spoke with desperate determination.

"I've come in the name of Prince Iolon to put an end to this curse you've laid on the land."

"I know all about Iolon and his reward," Rasalom snarled. "He wants you to bring back Rasalom or his ring." He fumbled within his robe and withdrew a large ring of intricately worked gold. It was set with a small, spherical black stone, so black that it seemed to absorb all light, appeared to be a rent in the very fabric of existence, a tiny portal to the nothingness beyond. The ring dangled from a golden chain.

"You wish the Ring of Chaos?" he said. "Here...take it. It no longer fits me and I have no further need of it."

Glaeken stiffened visibly at the offer.

Rasalom smiled again. "No trick, I assure you. For why should I want to keep a mere Ring of Chaos when soon I shall be an integral part of Chaos itself?" The warlock's eyes began to glow as he spoke. "I, Rasalom, have called forth the twelve hundred idiot demons of the Amphitheater! It took two years to complete the task. Each of the twelve hundred had to be summoned by a separate spell, and each spell took its toll. I was once as you were told – a huge, robust man. Look at me now! But I care not. Eternity is mine!"

Glaeken's expression mirrored his doubts about Rasalom's sanity.

"I don't blame you for thinking me mad. But beyond that stone door you tried so futilely to move lies the Amphitheater of Chaos, and therein are assembled the twelve hundred idiot demons... the Choir of Chaos. They exist only to sing. There is no curse on the land... only their singing. For they sing to Chaos itself and the vibration of their song strikes discord in the life processes of all living things."

"But you–"

"I am protected, for I am performing The Task. And what a task it is! The Lords of Chaos are wise. They know that to extend their domain they must occasionally accept new blood into their ranks. But the newcomer must prove beyond all doubt that he is worthy. So The Task was set, an ordeal that only a practitioner of the greatest skill and stamina could hope to accomplish. For each of the twelve hundred demons of the choir sucks a little bit of life from the one who calls it forth. I have raised them all and yet I still live! I am wasted but I have succeeded!"

"If this is success," Glaeken said, "what would be failure?"

"Ah, but you see, within the Amphitheater the embryo of my new form gestates, slowly incorporating my being into its own as it matures. The time for parturition draws nigh. Soon I shall be eternal and all this world my domain!"

Glaeken remained unconvinced. "Your sorcery has wasted your mind as well as your body, Rasalom. Lift your curse and give me the ring and I shall leave you to your delusions. Refuse and my blade will end everything for you."

"You doubt my word?" the wizard rasped. "I tell you there is no curse! The Choir of Chaos sings and its song is slow death to all within reach of it! You are dying as we speak, my foolish interloper. And you cannot threaten me with death, for that would only accelerate the embryo's progress. I welcome death at this moment – it will bring my rebirth that much closer!"

Glaeken shook his head in dismay. How do you deal with a madman?

"Go!" Rasalom cried. "See for yourself! Pull the handle on the lamp by the door. The passage leads to the Amphitheater. View the Choir of Chaos. See my masterwork, and die!"

Wordlessly, wearily, Glaeken shuffled to the door. If Rasalom were mad, this would prove it. If sane, then Glaeken's life – nay, his whole world – was in grave danger.

He pulled down on the lamp handle. It moved easily. Behind the wall he heard the clank of weights as they were released. Slowly, the door swung open to reveal a narrow passage lit with oil lamps similar to those in the room. The throbbing hum was louder here. Glaeken moved into the passage and saw another stone door at its end. This one was equipped with a ring latch. He grasped the ring and pulled on it, doubting very much that he had strength left to budge it. But the hinges were perfectly balanced and the stone slab swung toward him.

He repeated this procedure with the three identical subsequent doors and each time the hum increased in volume until at the final door it had risen to a muted scream. This door was doubly thick and vibrated with the intensity of the sound behind it. But it swung as easily as the others when Glaeken pulled on the ring.

The sound was a physical thing, washing over him with a volume and intensity that drove him to his knees. He crouched on the edge of a precipice and before him lay the Amphitheater of Chaos, an inverted cone, mistily illuminated by light that filtered up from the unguessed depths below. Carved into the rounded walls that sloped upward to the pointed roof were twelve hundred niches, and in each of those niches huddled one of the twelve hundred idiot demons.

Blank-eyed and mindless they were, shaped in every deformity imaginable and unimaginable. Faces suffused with an insane, malignant glee, they howled and caterwauled in tones that ranged from far below to far above those audible to the human ear. No two tones harmonized, all was discord and conflict. Glaeken now knew the origin of his dream the night before...the Choir of Chaos was assembled and at work.

His gaze shifted from the howling demons to the ebon sphere that floated in the center of the Amphitheater. It appeared to be a thin-membraned ball of inky fluid, suspended above and before him by no visible means. The eyes of each of the twelve hundred were fixed steadily upon it.

Glaeken noticed a slight swirling movement within the sphere and recoiled at a fleeting glimpse of a dark, nameless shape and two glowing malevolent eyes.

The embryo of Rasalom's new form floated there in its inky amnion, suspended on a placenta of sound from the Choir of Chaos. Rasalom was not mad – he had been telling the truth.

Suddenly Glaeken gave in to a sudden urge to sing. He had no idea where it came from. Perhaps it was a feeble effort to counteract the effect of the sound that pressed down on him with such ferocity...perhaps the glimpse of those eyes in the sac had pushed him to the brink of madness and the song offered a tenuous link to sanity. He didn't know, he simply began singing.

He lifted his voice in the hymn of praise to the goddess Eblee, a sweet simple song known the world over. And his effort did not go unnoticed. The demons of the Choir pulled their gaze away from the amniotic sac and glared at him with unrestrained fury. Perhaps the merest trace of coherent melody within the Amphitheater interfered with the gestative process, for Glaeken noticed a slight ripple coursing over the membranous surface of the sac.

In response, the twelve hundred increased their volume and Glaeken was knocked flat. Vision and awareness blurred as every fiber of his being screamed in anguish. Still he sang, clinging to the melody as a last thread to sanity; but he was fading, losing his grip on consciousness. His hoarse tones grew fainter as the Choir of Chaos attacked him with unwavering vocal fury.

And then Glaeken heard another sound, as out of place as the sun in a starry sky: the dulcet tones of a harmohorn had joined him in song. Blinking his eyes into focus, he turned his head and there behind him stood Cragjaw. Eyes closed, bathed in sweat, the squat little man was leaning against the wall and blowing a perfect modal harmony to Glaeken's song. Glaeken found new strength then and redoubled his vocal efforts.

Something began to happen in the Amphitheater. The flawless acoustics permeated the new sound throughout the huge chamber. If a touch of coherence had proved slightly disruptive before, the harmony of man-made instrument and human voice began to have a shattering effect. The twelve hundred demons became agitated, thrashing in their niches, their voices faltering. And this in turn had its effect on the embryo. The tortured membrane stretched and bulged from the rolling convulsions of the thing within. The glowing eyes pressed against the sac wall, glaring in unearthly rage.

Then came a weakening, a thinning, a tiny puncture, a rent – the membrane ruptured in an explosion of inky fluid as its contents burst free into the air. The sac and its partially formed occupant fell swiftly and silently into the mists below.

A howling scream of agony rose from the Choir of Chaos. The idiot demons ceased their song and flew into fits of rage, slamming themselves against the walls of their niches and finally hurtling over the edges and down. One by one, then in groups, and finally in a hellish rain, they followed the embryo back to the hell of their origin. And then...

Silence.

Glaeken had almost given up hope of ever experiencing it again. He remained prone and reveled in the lack of sound as strength and sanity surged back into his body.

"Ho, Cragjaw," he said finally, rising to his feet. "What brought you to this concert?"

Cragjaw sighed exhaustedly as he slipped the harmohorn back into its case. "I owed you a service so I came after you. Seems a good thing I did."

Together they stumbled back down the passage toward the antechamber.

F. Paul Wilson

"We are more than even, my friend," Glaeken said. "I did but aid you in a street brawl – and enjoyed it, too. You risked your life just by entering this region."

They arrived then in the antechamber and found Rasalom stretched out on the floor halfway between the throne chair and the doorway. Dead.

Glaeken reached into the withered sorcerer's robe, pulled out the Ring of Chaos, and snapped the chain.

"That cannot be Rasalom!" Cragjaw exclaimed. "And where did he come from? I didn't see him when I passed through!"

"It's Rasalom, all right. The curse is broken but I suppose Iolon will want to have the ring before he gives me the reward."

Cragjaw started to speak as they headed for the surface, hesitated, then started again.

"Ah, Glaeken, I fear I bring bad news. When I reached the summer palace I learned that Iolon had been overthrown by his army. There will be no reward, I'm afraid."

Glaeken took this news in silence and continued walking. Receiving no reply, Cragjaw continued.

"I too am out of work. The generals have no liking for the harmohorn. Their tastes in music are a bit coarse for my skills, running more to naked girls with tambourines and bells. Knowing they would not honor Iolon's promise of a reward, I traveled to warn you that you would be imperiling yourself for naught. I found your horse on the way – he is well – and thought you might be in some I danger, so I rode my own horse nearly into the ground and ran the rest of the way on foot in an effort to catch you before you entered the cavern. I was too late. But I heard this awful caterwauling within and followed the sound. You know the rest."

Glaeken nodded appreciatively. "But what made you bring the harmohorn?"

"You don't think I'd leave it unguarded, do you?" Cragjaw replied indignantly. "It never leaves my side!"

"I suppose you sleep with it, too?"

"Of course!"

22

Glaeken smiled and tucked the Ring of Chaos into his belt. "Ah, well, the quest has been rewarding in one way if not another. I may not come away a rich man but at least I've found a friend among you strange easterners."

"Strange easterners, are we?" Cragjaw said with a gleam in his eyc as they reached the mouth of the cavern. "Then you must be from the Western Isles after all!"

With the late morning sun warm on his face, Glaeken offered only a good-natured laugh in reply.

ARYANS AND ABSINTHE

A key episode in the Secret History.

Early in the summer of 1993 Douglas E. Winter called to tell me about his idea for an anthology of novellas, each centering on some apocalyptic event in the twentieth century. I picked the 1920s – Weimar Germany, specifically. The arts were flourishing there but the economic chaos and runaway inflation of the times were so surreal, so devastating to everyone's day-to-day life that people – Jew and gentile alike – were looking for a savior. A foppish little guy named Hitler came to prominence presenting himself as that savior.

I did extensive research for "Aryans and Absinthe" because I wanted to get the details *right* so I could make you feel you were *there*. I was pretty high on it when I finished – still am. I think I captured the tenor and tempo of the times to convey an apocalyptic experience.

And into this chaos I inserted the enigmatic figure of Ernst Drexler. He plays at being a bon vivant, but if you listen closely you might decide he has a very definite agenda he's keeping under wraps. I offered no explanation in "Aryans…" but years later I decided he was a high-up member of a sinister brotherhood known as Septimus. I introduced his son, Ernst Drexler II, to thirteen-year-old Jack in the Teen Trilogy. Just recently, in "Wardenclyffe," I traveled back to 1903 to see what Ernst's father Rudolph was up to.

Aryans and Absinthe

T oday it takes 40,000 marks to buy a single US dollar.
Volkischer Beobachter, May 4, 1923

Ernst Drexler found the strangest things entertaining. That was how he always phrased it: *entertaining*. Even inflation could be entertaining, he said.

Karl Stehr remembered seeing Drexler around the Berlin art venues for months before he actually met him. He stood out in that perennially scruffy crowd with his neatly pressed suit and vest, starched collar and tie, soft hat either on his head or under his arm, and his distinctive silver-headed cane wrapped in black rhinoceros hide. His black hair swept back sleek as linoleum from his high forehead; the bright blue eyes that framed his aquiline nose were never still, always darting about under his dark eyebrows; thin lips, a strong chin, and tanned skin, even in winter, completed the picture. Karl guessed Drexler to be in his mid-thirties, but his mien was that of someone older.

For weeks at a time he would seem to be everywhere, and never at a loss for something to say. At the Paul Klee show where Klee's latest, "The Twittering Machine," had been on exhibition, Karl had overheard his sarcastic comment that Klee had joined the Bauhaus not a moment too soon. Drexler was always at the right places: at the opening of *Dr. Mabuse, der Spieler*, at the cast party for that Czech play *R.U.R.*, and at the secret screenings of Murnau's *Nosferatu*, to name just a few.

And then he'd be nowhere. He'd disappear for weeks or a month without a word to anyone. When he returned he would pick up just where he'd left off, as if there'd been no hiatus. And when he was in town he all but lived at the Romanisches Cafe where nightly he would wander among the tables, glass in hand, a meandering focus of raillery and bavardage, dropping dry, witty, acerbic comments on art and literature like ripe fruit. No one seemed to remember who first introduced him to the cafe. He more or less insinuated himself into the regulars on his own. After a while it seemed he had always been there. Everyone knew Drexler but no one knew him well. His persona was a strange mixture of accessibility and aloofness that Karl found intriguing.

They began their friendship on a cool Saturday evening in the spring. Karl had closed his bookshop early and wandered down Budapesterstrasse to the Romanisches. It occupied the corner at Tauentzien across from the Gedachtniskirche: large for a cafe, with a roomy sidewalk area and a spacious interior for use on inclement days and during the colder seasons.

Karl had situated himself under the awning, his knickered legs resting on the empty chair next to him; he sipped an aperitif among the blossoming flower boxes as he reread *Siddartha*. At the sound of clacking high heels he'd glance up and watch the "new look" women as they trooped past in pairs and trios with their clinging dresses fluttering about their knees and their smooth tight caps pulled down over their bobbed hair, their red lips, mascara'd eyes, and coats trimmed in fluffy fur snuggled around their necks.

Karl loved Berlin. He'd been infatuated with the city since his first sight of it when his father had brought him here before the war; two years ago, on his twentieth birthday, he'd dropped out of the University to carry on an extended affair with her. His lover was the center of the art world, of the new freedoms. You could be what you wanted here: a free thinker, a free lover, a communist, even a fascist; men could dress like women and women could dress like men. No limits. All the new movements in music, the arts, the cinema, and the theatre had their roots here. Every time he turned around he found a new marvel.

Night was upon Karl's mistress when Ernst Drexler stopped by the table and introduced himself.

"We've not formally met," he said, thrusting out his hand.

"Your name is Stehr, I believe. Come join me at my table. There are a number of things I wish to discuss with you."

Karl wondered what things this man more than ten years his senior could wish to discuss, but since he had no other plans for the evening, he went along.

The usual crowd was in attendance at the Romanisches that night. Lately it had become the purlieu of Berlin bohemia – all the artists, writers, journalists, critics, composers, editors, directors, scripters, and anyone else who had anything to do with the avante garde of German arts, plus the girlfriends, the boyfriends, the mere hangers on. Some sat rooted in place, others roved ceaselessly from table to table. Smoke undulated in a muslin layer above a gallimaufry of scraggly beards, stringy manes, bobbed hair framing black-rimmed eyes, homburgs, berets, monocles, pince nez, foot-long cigarette holders, baggy sweaters, dark stockings, period attire ranging from the Helenic to the pre-Raphaelite.

"I saw you at *Siegfried* the other night," Drexler said as they reached his table in a dim rear corner, out of the peristaltic flow. Drexler took the seat against the wall where he could watch the room; he left the other for Karl. "What do you think of Lang's latest?"

"Very Germanic," Karl said as he took his seat and reluctantly turned his back to the room. He was a people watcher.

Drexler laughed. "How diplomatic! But how true. Deceit, betrayal, and backstabbing – in both the figurative and literal sense. Germanic indeed. Hardly Neue Sachlichkeit, though."

"I think New Realism was the furthest thing from Lang's mind. Now, *Die Strasse*, on the other hand–"

"Neue Sachlichkeit will soon join Expressionism in the mausoleum of movements. And good riddance. It is shit."

"Kunst ist Scheisse?" Karl said, smiling. "Dada is the deadest of them all."

Drexler laughed again. "My, you are sharp, Karl. That's why I wanted to talk to you. You're very bright. You're one of the few people in this room who will be able to appreciate my new entertainment."

"Really? And what is that?"

"Inflation."

Before Karl could ask what he meant, Drexler flagged down a passing waiter.

"The usual for me, Freddy, and–?" He pointed to Karl, who ordered a schnapps.

"Inflation? Never heard of it. A new card game?"

Drexler smiled. "No, no. It's played with money."

"Of course. But how–"

"It's played with real money in the real world. It's quite entertaining. I've been playing it since the New Year."

Freddy soon delivered Karl's schnapps. For Drexler he brought an empty stemmed glass, a sweaty carafe of chilled water, and a small bowl of sugar cubes. Karl watched fascinated as Drexler pulled a silver flask from his breast pocket and unscrewed the top. He poured three fingers of clear green liquid into the glass, then returned the flask to his coat. Next he produced a slotted spoon, placed a sugar cube in its bowl, and held it over the glass. Then he dribbled water from the carafe, letting it flow over the cube and into the glass to mix with the green liquid... which began to turn a pale yellow.

"Absinthe!" Karl whispered.

"Quite. I developed a taste for it before the War. Too bad it's illegal now – although it's still easily come by."

Now Karl knew why Drexler frequently reserved this out-of-the-way table. Instinctively he glanced around, but no one was watching.

Drexler sipped and smacked his lips. "Ever tried any?"

"No."

Karl had never had the opportunity. And besides, he'd heard that it drove you mad.

Drexler slid his glass across the table. "Take a sip."

Part of Karl urged him to say no, while another pushed his hand forward and wound his fingers around the stem of the glass. He lifted it to his lips and took a tiny sip.

The bitterness rocked his head back and puckered his cheeks.

"That's the wormwood," Drexler said, retrieving his glass. "Takes some getting used to."

Karl shuddered as he swallowed. "How did that ever become a craze?"

"For half a century, all across the continent, the cocktail hour was known as *l'heure verte* after this little concoction." He sipped again, closed his eyes, savoring. "At the proper time, in the proper place, it can be... revelatory."

After a moment, he opened his eyes and motioned Karl closer.

"Here. Move over this way and sit by me. I wish to show you something."

Karl slid his chair around to where they both sat facing the crowded main room of the Romanisches.

Drexler waved his arm. "Look at them, Karl. The cream of the city's artists attended by their cachinating claques and coteries of epigones and acolytes, mixing with the city's lowlifes and lunatics. Morphine addicts and vegetarians cheek by jowl with Bolsheviks and boulevardiers, arrivistes and anarchists, abortionists and anti-vivisectionists, directors and dilettantes, doyennes and demimondaines."

Karl wondered how much time Drexler spent here sipping his absinthe and observing the scene. And why. He sounded like an entomologist studying a particularly interesting anthill.

"Everyone wants to join the parade. They operate under the self-induced delusion that they're in control: 'What happens in the Berlin arts today, the rest of the world copies next week.' True enough, perhaps. But this is the Masque of the Red Death, Karl. Huge forces are at play around them, and they are certain to get crushed as the game unfolds. Germany is falling apart – the impossible war reparations are suffocating us, the French and Belgians have been camped in the Ruhr Valley since January, the communists are trying to take over the north, the right wingers and monarchists practically own Bavaria, and the

Reichsbank's answer to the economic problems is to print more money."

"Is that bad?"

"Of course. It's only paper. It's been sending prices through the roof."

He withdrew his wallet from his breast pocket, pulled a bill from it, and passed it to Karl.

Karl recognized it. "An American dollar."

Drexler nodded. "'Good as gold,' as they say. I bought it for 10,000 marks in January. Care to guess what the local bank was paying for it today?"

"I don't know. Perhaps..."

"Forty thousand. Forty thousand marks."

Karl was impressed. "You quadrupled your money in four months."

"No, Karl," Drexler said with a wry smile. "I've merely quadrupled the number of marks I control. My buying power is exactly what it was in January. But I'm one of the very few people in this storm-tossed land who can say so."

"Maybe I should try that," Karl said softly, admiring the elegant simplicity of the plan. "Take my savings and convert it to American dollars."

"By all means do. Clean out your bank account, pull every mark you own out from under your mattress and put them into dollars. But that's mere survival – hardly entertainment."

"Survival sounds good enough."

"No, my friend. Survival is never enough. Animals limit their concerns to mere survival; humans seek entertainment. That is why we must find a way to make inflation entertaining. Inflation is here. There's nothing we can do about it. So let's have some fun with it."

"I don't know..."

"Do you own a house?"

"Yes," Karl said slowly, cautiously. He didn't know where this was leading. "And no."

"Really. You mean it's mortgaged to the hilt?"

"No. Actually it's my mother's. A small estate north of the city near Bernau. But I manage it for her."

Father had died a colonel in the Argonne and he'd left it to her. But Mother had no head for money, and she hadn't been quite herself in the five years since Father's death. So Karl took care of the lands and the accounts, but spent most of his time in Berlin. His bookstore barely broke even, but he hadn't opened it for profit. He'd made it a place where local writers and artists were welcome to stop and browse and meet; he reserved a small area in the rear of the store where they could sit and talk and sip the coffee he kept hot for them. His dream was that someday one of the poor unknowns who partook of his hospitality would become famous and perhaps remember the place kindly – and perhaps someday stop by to say hello with Thomas Mann or the reclusive Herman Hesse in tow. Until then Karl would be quite satisfied with providing coffee and rolls to starving scribblers.

But even from the beginning, the shop had paid non-pecuniary dividends. It was his entree to the literati, and from there to the entire artistic caravan that swirled through Berlin.

"Any danger of losing it?"

"No." The estate produced enough so that, along with Father's Army pension, his mother could live comfortably.

"Good. Then mortgage it. Borrow to the hilt on it, and then borrow some more. Then turn all those marks into US dollars."

Karl was struck dumb by the idea. The family home had never had a lien on it. Never. The idea was unthinkable.

"No. I – I couldn't."

Drexler put his arm around Karl's shoulder and leaned closer. Karl could smell the absinthe on his breath.

"Do it, Karl. Trust me in this. It's an entertainment, but you'll see some practical benefits as well. Mark my words, six months from now you'll be able to pay off your entire mortgage with a single US dollar. A single coin."

"I don't know..."

"You must. I need someone who'll play the game with me.

It's much more entertaining when you have someone to share the fun with."

Drexler straightened up and lifted his glass.

"A toast!" He clinked his glass against Karl's. "By the way, do you know where glass clinking originated? Back in the old days, when poisoning a rival was a fad among the upper classes, it became the practice to allow your companion to pour some of his drink into your cup, and vice versa. That way, if one of the drinks were poisoned, you'd both suffer."

"How charming."

"Quite. Inevitably the pouring would be accompanied by the clink of one container against another. Hence, the modern custom." Once again he clinked his absinthe against Karl's schnapps. "Trust me, Karl. Inflation can be very entertaining – and profitable as well. I expect the mark to lose fully half its value in the next six weeks. So don't delay."

He raised his glass. "To inflation!" he cried and drained the absinthe.

Karl sipped his schnapps in silence.

Drexler rose from his seat. "I expect to see you dollar rich and mark poor when I return."

"Where are you going?"

"A little trip I take every so often. I like to swing up through Saxony and Thuringia to see what the local Bolsheviks are up to – I have a membership in the German Communist Party, you know. I subscribe to *Rote Fahne*, listen to speeches by the Zentrale, and go to rallies. It's very entertaining. But after I tire of that – Marxist rhetoric can be *so* boring – I head south to Munich to see what the other end of the political spectrum is doing. I'm also a member of the National Socialist German Workers Party down there and subscribe to their *Volkischer Beobachter*."

"Never heard of them. How can they call themselves 'National' if they're not nationally known?"

"Just as they can call themselves Socialists when they are stridently fascist. Although frankly I, for one, have difficulty discerning much difference between either end of the spectrum

– they are distinguishable only by their paraphernalia and their rhetoric. The National Socialists – the call themselves Nazis – are a power in Munich and other parts of Bavaria, but no one pays too much attention to them up here. I must take you down there sometime to listen to one of their leaders. Herr Hitler is quite a personality. I'm sure our friend Freud would love to get him on the couch."

"Hitler? Never heard of him, either."

"You really should hear him speak sometime. Very entertaining."

Today it takes 51,000 marks to buy a single US dollar.
Volkischer Beobachter, May 21, 1923

A few weeks later, when Karl returned from the bank with the mortgage papers for his mother to sign, he spied something on the door post. He stopped and looked closer.

A mezuzah.

He took out his pocket knife and pried it off the wood, then went inside.

"Mother, what is this?" he said, dropping the object on the kitchen table.

She looked up at him with her large, brown, intelligent eyes. Her brunette hair was streaked with gray. She'd lost considerable weight immediately after Father's death and had never regained it. She used to be lively and happy, with an easy smile that dimpled her high-colored cheeks. Now she was quiet and pale. She seemed to have shrunken, in body and spirit.

"You know very well what it is, Karl."

"Yes, but haven't I warned you about putting it outside?"

"It belongs outside."

"Not in these times. Please, Mother. It's not healthy."

"You should be proud of being Jewish."

"I'm not Jewish."

They'd had this discussion hundreds of times lately, it

seemed, but Mother just didn't want to understand. His father, the Colonel, had been Christian, his mother Jewish. Karl had decided to be neither. He was an atheist, a skeptic, a free-thinker, an intellectual. He was German by language and by place of birth, but he preferred to think of himself as an international man. Countries and national boundaries should be abolished, and someday soon would be.

"If your mother is Jewish, *you* are Jewish. You can't escape that. I'm not afraid to tell the world I'm Jewish. I wasn't so observant when your father was alive, but now that he's gone..."

Her eyes filled with tears.

Karl sat down next to her and took her hands in his.

"Mother, listen. There's a lot of anti-Jewish feeling out there these days. It will die down, I'm sure, but right now we live in an inordinately proud country that lost a war and wants to blame someone. Some of the most bitter people have chosen Jews as their scapegoats. So until the country gets back on an even keel, I think it's prudent to keep a low profile."

Her smile was wan. "You know best, dear."

"Good." He opened the folder he'd brought from the bank. "And now for some paperwork. These are the final mortgage papers, ready for signing."

Mother squeezed his hands. "Are you sure we're doing the right thing?" "Absolutely sure."

Actually, now that the final papers were ready, he was having second thoughts.

Karl had arranged to borrow every last pfennig the bank would lend him against his mother's estate. He remembered how uneasy he'd been at the covetous gleam in the bank officers' eyes when he'd signed the papers. They sensed financial reverses, gambling debts, perhaps, a desperate need for cash that would inevitably lead to default and subsequent foreclosure on a prime piece of property. The bank president's eyes had twinkled over his reading glasses; he'd all but rubbed his hands in anticipation.

Doubt and fear gripped Karl now as his mother's pen

hovered over the signature line. Was he being a fool? He was a bookseller and they were financiers. Who was he to presume to know more than men who spent every day dealing with money? He was acting on a whim, spurred on by a man he hardly knew.

But he steeled himself, remembering the research he'd done. He'd always been good at research. He knew how to ferret out information. He'd learned that Rudolf Haverstein, the Reichsbank's president, had increased his orders of currency paper and was running the printing presses at full speed on overtime.

He watched in silence as his mother signed the mortgage papers.

He'd already taken out personal loans, using Mother's jewelry as collateral. Counting the mortgage, he'd now accumulated 500 million marks. If he converted them immediately, he'd get 9,800 US dollars at today's exchange rate. Ninety-eight hundred dollars for half a billion marks. It seemed absurd. He wondered who was madder – the Reichsbank or himself.

Today it takes 500,000,000 marks to buy a single US dollar.
Volkischer Beobachter, September 1, 1923

"To runaway inflation," Ernst Drexler said, clinking his glass of cloudy yellow against Karl's clear glass of schnapps.

Karl sipped a little of his drink and said nothing. He and Drexler had retreated from the heat and glare of the late summer sun on the Romanisches Cafe's sidewalk to the cooler, darker interior.

Noon on a Saturday and the Romanisches was nearly empty. But then, who could afford to eat out these days?

Only thieves and currency speculators.

Four months ago Karl hadn't believed it possible, but for a while they had indeed had fun with inflation.

Now it was getting scary.

Less than four months after borrowing half a billion marks,

his 9,800 US dollars were worth almost five trillion marks. Five *trillion*. The number was meaningless. He could barely imagine even a billion marks, and he controlled five thousand times that amount.

"I realized today," Karl said softly, "that I can pay off all of my half-billion-mark debt with a single dollar bill."

"Don't do it," Drexler said quickly.

"Why not? I'd like to be debt free."

"You will be. Just wait."

"Until when?"

"It won't be long before the exchange rate will be billions of marks to the dollar. Won't it be so much more entertaining to pay off the bankers with a single American coin?"

Karl stared at his glass. This game was no longer "entertaining." People had lost all faith in the mark. And with good reason. Its value was plummeting. In a mere thirty days it had plunged from a million to the dollar to half a *billion* to the dollar. Numbers crowded the borders of the notes, ever-lengthening strings of ever more meaningless zeros. Despite running at twenty-four hours a day, the Reichsbank presses could not keep up with the demand. Million-mark notes were now being over-stamped with *TEN MILLION* in large black letters. Workers had gone from getting paid twice a month to weekly, and now to daily. Some were demanding twice-daily pay so that they could run out on their lunch hour and spend their earnings before they lost their value.

"I'm frightened, Ernst."

"Don't worry. You've insulated yourself. You've got nothing to fear."

"I'm frightened for our friends and neighbors. For Germany."

"Oh, that."

Karl didn't understand how Drexler could be so cavalier about the misery steadily welling up around them like a rain-engorged river. It oppressed Karl. He felt guilty, almost ashamed of being safe and secure on his high ground of foreign currency. Drexler drained his absinthe and rose, his eyes bright.

"Let's go for a walk, shall we? Let's see what your friends and neighbors are up to on this fine day."

Karl left his schnapps and followed him out into the street. They strolled along Budapesterstrasse until they came upon a bakery.

"Look," Drexler said, pointing with his black cane. "A social gathering."

Karl bristled at the sarcasm. The long line of drawn faces with anxious, hollow eyes – male, female, young, old – trailing out the door and along the sidewalk was hardly a social gathering. Lines for bread, meat, milk, any of the staples of life, had become so commonplace that they were taken for granted. The customers stood there with their paper bags, cloth sacks, and wicker baskets full of marks, shifting from one foot to the other, edging forward, staying close behind the person in front of them lest someone tried to cut into the line, constantly turning the count of their marks in their minds, hoping they'd find something left to buy when they reached the purchase counter, praying their money would not devalue too much before the price was rung up.

Karl had never stood in such a line. He didn't have to. He needed only to call or send a note to a butcher or baker listing what he required and saying that he would be paying with American currency. Within minutes the merchant would come knocking with the order. He found no pleasure, no feeling of superiority in his ability to summon the necessities to his door, only relief that his mother would not be subject to the hunger and anxiety of these poor souls.

As Karl watched, a boy approached the center of the line where a young woman had placed a wicker basket full of marks on the sidewalk. As he passed her he bent and grabbed a handle on the basket, upended it, dumping out the marks. Then he sprinted away with the basket. The woman cried out but no one moved to stop him – no one wanted to lose his place in line.

Karl started to give chase but Drexler restrained him.

"Don't bother. You'll never catch him."

Karl watched the young woman gather her scattered marks into her apron and resume her long wait in line, weeping. His heart broke for her.

"This has to stop. Someone has to do something about this."

"Ah, yes," Drexler said, nodding sagely. "But who?"

They walked on. As they approached a corner, Drexler suddenly raised his cane and pressed its shaft against Karl's chest.

"Listen. What's that noise?"

Up ahead at the intersection, traffic had stopped. Instead of the roar of internal combustion engines, Karl heard something else. Other sounds, softer, less rhythmic, swelled in the air. A chaotic tapping and a shuffling cacophony of scrapes and draggings, accompanied by a dystonic chorus of high-pitched squeaks and creaks.

And then they inched into view – the lame, the blind, the damaged, dismembered, demented, and disfigured tatterdemalions of two wars: The few remaining veterans of the Franco-Prussian War of 1870 – stooped, wizened figures in their seventies and eighties who had besieged Paris and proclaimed Wilhelm of Prussia as Emperor of Germany in the Hall of Mirrors at Versailles – were leading the far larger body of pathetic survivors from the disastrous Great War, the War To End All Wars, the valiant men whose defeated leaders five years ago had abjectly agreed to impossible reparations in that same Hall of Mirrors.

Karl watched aghast as a young man with one arm passed within a few meters of him dragging a wheeled platform on which lay a limbless man, hardly more than a head with a torso. Neither was much older than he. The Grand Guignol parade was full of these fractions of men and their blind, deaf, limping, stumbling, hopping, staggering companions. Karl knew he might well be among them had he been born a year or two earlier.

Some carried signs begging, pleading, demanding higher pensions and disability allowances; they all looked worn and defeated, but mostly *hungry*. Here were the most pitiful victims of the runaway inflation.

Karl fell into line with them and pulled Drexler along.

"Really," Drexler said, "this is hardly my idea of an entertaining afternoon."

"We need to show them that they're not alone, that we haven't forgotten them. We need to show the government that we support them."

"It will do no good," Drexler said, grudgingly falling into step beside him. "It takes time for the government to authorize a pension increase. And even if it is approved, by the time it goes into effect, the increase will be meaningless."

"This can't go on! Someone has got to do something about this chaos!"

Drexler pointed ahead with his black cane. "There's a suggestion."

At the corner stood two brown-shirted men in paramilitary gear and caps. On their left upper arms were red bands emblazoned with a strange, black twisted cross inside a white circle. Between them they held a banner:

COME TO US, COMRADES!
ADOLF HITLER WILL HELP YOU!

"Hitler," Karl said slowly. "You mentioned him before, didn't you?"

"Yes. The Austrian Gefreiter. He'll be at that big fascist rally in Nuremberg tomorrow to commemorate something or other. I hope to get to hear him again. Marvelous speaker. Want to come along?"

Karl had heard about the rally – so had all the rest of Germany. Upward of two hundred thousand veterans and members of every right-wing volkisch paramilitary group in the country were expected in the Bavarian town to celebrate the anniversary of the Battle of Sedan in the Franco-Prussian War.

"I don't think so. I don't like big crowds. Especially a big crowd of fascists."

"Some other time, then. I'll call you when he's going to address one of the beer hall meetings in Munich. He does that a lot.
That way you'll get the full impact of his speaking voice. Most
entertaining."

Adolf Hitler, Karl thought as he passed the brown-shirted
men with the strange armbands. Could he be the man to save
Germany?

"Yes, Ernst. Do call me. I wish to hear this man."

Today it takes 200 billion marks to buy a single US dollar.
Volkischer Beobachter, October 22, 1923

"It's like entering another country," Karl murmured as he
stood on the platform of the Munich train station.

Ernst Drexler lounged beside him as they waited for a por-
ter to take his bags.

"Not another country at all. Merely an armed camp filled
with people as German as the rest of us. Perhaps more so."

"People in love with uniforms."

"And what could be more German than that?"

Drexler had sent him a message last week, scrawled in
his reverse-slanted script on the blank back of a 100-million-
-mark note. Even with all its overworked presses running at
full speed, the Reichsbank found itself limited to printing the
new marks on only one side in order to keep up with the
ever-increasing demand for currency. Drexler seemed to find it
amusing to use the blank sides of the smaller denominations as
stationery. And this note had invited Karl south to hear Herr
Hitler.

Karl now wished he'd ignored the invitation. A chill had
come over him as the train crossed into Bavaria; it began in the
pit of his stomach, then encircled his chest and crept up his
spine to his neck where it now insinuated icy fingers around
his throat. Uniforms... military uniforms everywhere, lolling

about the train station, marching in the streets, standing on the corners, and none of them sporting the comfortably familiar field gray of regular Reichswehr troops. Young men, middle-aged men, dressed in brown, black, blue, and green, all with watchful, suspicious eyes and tight, hostile faces.

Something sinister was growing here in the south, something unclean, something dangerous.

It's the times, he told himself. Just another facet of the chaotic Zeitgeist.

No surprise that Bavaria was like an armed camp. Less than three weeks ago its cabinet, aghast at what it saw as Berlin's cowardly submission to the continuing Franco-Belgian presence in the Ruhr Valley, had declared a state of emergency and suspended the Weimar Constitution within its borders. Gustav von Kahr had been declared Generalstaatskommissar of Bavaria with dictatorial powers. Berlin had blustered threats but so far had made no move against the belligerent southern state, preferring diplomatic avenues for the moment.

But how long would that last? The communists in the north were trying to ignite a revolution in Saxony, calling for a "German October," and the more radical Bavarians here in the south were calling for a march on Berlin because of the government's impotence in foreign and domestic affairs, especially in finance and currency.

Currency...when the mark had sunk to five billion to the dollar two weeks ago, Karl had paid off the mortgage on the estate plus the loans against his mother's jewelry with a US ten-cent piece – what the Americans called a "dime."

Something had to happen. The charges were set, the fuse was lit. Where would the explosion occur? And when?

"Think of them as human birds," Drexler said, pointing to their left at two groups in different uniforms. "You can tell who's who by their plumage. The gray are soldaten... regular Reichswehr soldiers, of course. The green are Bavarian State Police. And as we move through Munich you'll see the city's regular police force, dressed in blue."

F. Paul Wilson

"Gray, green, blue," Karl murmured.

"Right. Those are the official colors. The *unofficial* colors are brown and black. They belong in varying mixes to the Nazi S.A. – their so-called storm troopers – and the Reichskriegs-flagge and Bund Oberland units."

"So confusing."

"It is. Bavaria has been a hotbed of fascism since the war, but mostly it was fragmented thing – more feisty little para-military groups than you could count. But things are different these days. The groups have been coalescing, and now the three major factions have allied themselves into something called the Kampfbund."

"The 'Battle Group'?"

"Precisely. And they're quite ready for battle. There are more caches of rifles and machine guns and grenades hidden in cellars or buried in and around Munich than Berlin could imagine in its worst nightmares. Hitler's Nazis are the leading faction of the Kampfbund, and right now he and the Bavarian government are at odds. Hitler wants to march on Berlin, General Commissioner Kahr does not. At the moment, Kahr has the upper hand. He's got the Green Police, the Blue Police, and the Reichswehr regulars to keep the Kampfbund in line. The question is, how long can he hold their loyalty when the hearts of many of his troops are in the Nazi camp, and Hitler's speeches stir more and more to the Nazi cause?"

Karl felt the chill tighten around his throat. He wished Drexler hadn't invited him to Munich. He wished he hadn't accepted.

"Maybe now is not a good time to be here."

"Nonsense! It's the *best* time! Can't you feel the excitement in the air? Don't you sense the huge forces at work around us? Stop and listen and you'll hear the teeth of cosmic gears grind-ing into motion. The clouds have gathered and are storing their charges. The lightning of history is about to strike and we are near the ground point. I know it as surely as I know my name."

"Lightning can be deadly."

Drexler smiled. "Which makes it all the more entertaining."

*

"Why a beer hall?" Karl asked as they sat in the huge main room of the Burgerbraukeller.

A buxom waitress set a fresh pair of liter steins of lager on the rough planked table before them.

Drexler waved a hand around. "Because Munich is the heart of beer-drinking country. If you want to reach these people, you speak to them where they drink their beer."

The Burgerbraukeller was huge, squatting on a sizable plot of land on the east side of the Isar River that cut the city in two. After the Zirkus Krone, it was the largest meeting place in Munich. Scattered inside its vast complex were numerous separate bars and dining halls, but the centerpiece was the main hall. All its 3,000 seats were filled tonight, with latecomers standing in the aisles and crowded at the rear.

Karl quaffed a few ounces of lager to wash down a mouthful of sausage. All around him were men in black and various shades of brown, all impatient for the arrival of their Fuhrer. He saw some in business suits, and even a few in traditional Bavarian lederhosen and Tyrolean hats. Karl and Drexler had made instant friends with their table neighbors by sharing the huge platter of cheese, bread and sausage they had ordered from the bustling kitchen. Even though they were not in uniform, not aligned with any Kampfbund organization, and wore no armbands, the two Berlin newcomers were now considered komraden by the locals who shared their long table. They became even more welcome when Drexler mentioned that Karl was the son of Colonel Stehr who'd fought and died at Argonne.

Far better to be welcomed here as comrades, Karl thought, than the opposite. He'd been listening to the table talk, the repeated references to Adolf Hitler in reverent tones as the man who would rescue Germany from all its enemies, both within and without, and lead the Fatherland back to the glory it deserved. Karl sensed that even the power of God might not be enough to save a man in this crowd who had something to say against Herr Hitler.

The hazy air was ripe with the effluvia of any beer hall: spilled hops and malt, tobacco smoke, the garlicky tang of steaming sausage, sharp cheese, sweaty bodies, and restless anticipation. Karl was finishing off his latest stein when he heard a stir run through the crowd. Someone with a scarred face had arrived at the rostrum on the bandstand. He spoke a few words into the increasing noise and ended by introducing Herr Adolf Hitler.

With a thunderous roar the crowd was on its feet and shouting "Heil! Heil!" as a thin man, about five-nine or so, who could have been anywhere from mid-thirties to mid-forties in age, ascended the steps to the rostrum. He was dressed in a brown wool jacket, a white shirt with a stiff collar, and a narrow tie, with brown knickers and stockings on his short, bandy legs. Straight brown hair parted on the right and combed across his upper forehead; sallow complexion, almost yellow; thin lips under a narrow brush of a mustache. He walked stooped slightly forward with his head canted to the left and his hands stuffed into his jacket pockets.

Karl could hardly believe his eyes.

This is the man they call Fuhrer? He looks like a shop-keeper, or a government clerk. This is the man they think is going to save Germany? Are they all mad or drunk... or both?

As Hitler reached the rostrum and gazed out over the cheering audience, Karl had his first glimpse of the man's unforgettable eyes. They shone like beacons from their sockets, piercing the room, staggering Karl with their startling pale blue fire. Flashing, hypnotic, gleaming with fanaticism, they ranged the room, quieting it, challenging another voice to interrupt his.

And then he began to speak, his surprisingly rich baritone rising and falling like a Wagnerian opus, hurling sudden gutturals through the air for emphasis like fist-sized cobblestones.

For the first ten minutes he spoke evenly and stood stiffly

with his hands trapped in his jacket pockets. But as his voice rose and his passion grew, his hands broke free, fine, graceful, long-fingered hands that fluttered like pigeons and swooped like hawks, then knotted into fists to pound the top of the rostrum with sledgehammer blows.

The minutes flew, gathering into one hour, then two. At first Karl had managed to remain aloof, picking apart Hitler's words, separating the carefully selected truths from the half-truths and the outright fictions. Then, in spite of himself, he began to fall under the man's spell. This Adolf Hitler was such a passionate speaker, so caught up in his own words that one had to go along with him; whatever the untruths and specious logic in his oratory, no could doubt that this man believed unequivocally every word that he spoke, and somehow transferred that fervent conviction to his audience so that they too became unalterably convinced of the truth of what he was saying.

He was never more powerful than when he called on all loyal Germans to come to the aid of a sick and failing Germany, one not merely financially and economically ill, but a Germany on its intellectual and moral deathbed. No question that Germany was sick, struck down by a disease that poultices and salves and cathartics could not cure. Germany needed radical surgery: The sick and gangrenous parts that were poisoning the rest of the system had to be cut away and burned before the healing could begin. Karl listened and became entranced, transfixed, unmindful of the time, a prisoner of that voice, those eyes.

And then this man, this Adolf Hitler, was standing in front of the rostrum, bathed in sweat, his hair hanging over his forehead, waving his arms, calling for all loyal Germans who truly cared for their Fatherland to rally around the Nazi Party and demand a march on Berlin where they would extract a promise from the feeble Weimar republicans to banish the Jews and the communists from all positions of power and drive the French and Belgian troops from the Ruhr Valley and once again make the Fatherland's borders inviolate, or by God, there would be a new government in power in Berlin, one that would bring Germany to the greatness that was her destiny. German misery must be broken by German iron. Our day is here! Our time is *now*!

The main hall went mad as Hitler stepped back and let the frenzied cheering of more than three thousand voices rattle the walls and rafters around him. Even Karl was on his feet, ready to shake his fist in the air and shout at the top of his lungs. Suddenly he caught himself.

What am I doing?

*

"Well, what did you think of the Gefreiter?" Drexler said. "Our strutting lance corporal?"

They were out on Rosenheimerstrasse, making their way back to the hotel, and Karl's ears had finally stopped ringing. Ahead of them in the darkness, mist rising from the Isar River sparkled in the glow of the lights lining the Ludwig Bridge.

"I think he's the most magnetic, powerful, mesmerizing speaker I've ever heard. Frighteningly so."

"Well, he's obviously mad – a complete loon. A master of hyperbolic sophistry, but hardly frightening."

"He's so...so...so anti-Semitic."

Drexler shrugged. "They all are. It's just rhetoric. Doesn't mean anything."

"Easy for you to say."

Drexler stopped and stood staring at Karl. "Wait. You don't mean to tell me you're...?"

Karl turned and nodded silently in the darkness.

"But Colonel Stehr wasn't–"

"His wife was."

"Good heavens, man! I had no idea!"

"Well, what's so unusual? What's wrong with a German officer marrying a woman who happens to be Jewish?"

"Nothing, of course. It's just that one becomes so used to

these military types and their–"

"Do you know that General von Seeckt, commander of the entire German army, has a Jewish wife? So does Chancellor Stresemann."

"Of course. The Nazis point that out at every opportunity."

"Right! We're everywhere!" Karl calmed himself with an effort. "Sorry, Ernst. I don't know why I got so excited. I don't even consider myself a Jew. I'm a human being. Period."

"Perhaps, but by Jewish law, if the mother is Jewish, then so are the children."

Karl stared at him. "How do you know that?"

"Everybody knows that. But that doesn't matter. The locals we've met know you as Colonel Stehr's son. That's what will count here in the next week or so."

"Next week or so? Aren't we returning to Berlin?"

Drexler gripped his arm. "No, Karl. We're staying. Things are coming to a head. The next few days promise to be *most* entertaining."

"I shouldn't–"

"Come back to the hotel. I'll fix you an absinthe. You look like you could use one."

Karl remembered the bitter taste, then realized he could probably do with a bit of oblivion tonight.

"All right. But just one."

"Excellent! Absinthe tonight, and we'll plan our next steps in the morning."

Today it takes 4 trillion marks to buy a single US dollar.
Volkischer Beobachter, November 8, 1923

"Herr Hitler's speaking in Freising tonight," Drexler said.

They strolled through the bright, crisp morning air, past onion-cupolaed churches and pastel house fronts that would have looked more at home along the Tiber than the Isar.

"How far is that?"

"About twenty miles north. But I have a better idea. Gustav

F. Paul Wilson

von Kahr, Bavaria's honorable dictator, is speaking at the Burgerbraukeller tonight."

"I'd rather hear Hitler."

Already more than a week into November and Karl was still
in Munich. He'd expected to be home long ago but he'd found
himself too captivated by Adolf Hitler to leave. Such a strange
attraction, equal parts fascination and revulsion. Here was a
man who might pull together Germany's warring factions and
make them one, yet then might wreak havoc upon the freedoms
of the Weimar Constitution. But where would the Constitution
be by year's end with old mark notes now being over-printed
with *EINE BILLION*?

Karl felt like a starving sparrow contemplating a viper's
offer to guard her nest while she hunts for food. Surely her nest
would be well protected from other birds in her absence, but
could she count on finding any eggs left when she returned?

He'd spoken to a number of Jews in Munich, shopkeepers
mostly, engaging them in casual conversation about the Kampfbund groups, and Herr Hitler in particular. The seismic up-
heavals in the economy had left them frazzled and desperate,
certain that their country would be in ruins by the end of the
year unless somebody did something. Most said they'd support
anyone who could bring the economic chaos and runaway inflation under control. Hitler and his Nazis promised definitive so-
lutions. So what if the country had to live under a dictatorship
for a while? Nothing – *nothing* – could be worse than this.

After all, they said, hadn't the Kaiser been a dictator? And
they'd certainly done better under him than with this Weimar
Republic with its Constitution that guaranteed so many freedoms. What good were freedom of the press and speech and
assembly if you were starving? As for the antisemitism, most
of the Munich Jews echoed Drexler's dismissal: mere rhetoric.
Nothing more than tough talk to excite the beer drinkers.

Still uneasy, Karl found himself drawn back again and again
to hear Hitler speak – in the Zirkus Krone, and in the Burgerbraukeller and other beer halls around the city – hoping each time

48

the man would say something to allay his fears and allow him to embrace the hope the Nazis offered.

Absinthe only added to the compulsion. Karl had taken to drinking a glass with Drexler before attending each new Hitler speech, and as a result he had acquired a taste for the bitter stuff.

Because Herr Hitler seemed to be speaking all the time.

Especially since the failed communist putsch in Hamburg. It failed because the German workers refused to rally to the red flag and Reichswehr troops easily put down the revolution in its second day. There would be no German October. But the attempt had incited the Kampfbund groups to near hysteria. Karl saw more uniforms in Munich's streets than he'd seen in Berlin during the war. And Herr Hitler was there in the thick of it, fanning the sparks of patriotic fervor into a bonfire wherever he found an audience.

Karl attended his second Hitler speech while under the influence of absinthe, and there he experienced his first hallucination. It happened while Hitler was reaching his final crescendo: The hall wavered before Karl, the light dimmed, all the color drained from his sight, leaving only black and white and shades of gray; he had the impression of being in a crowded room, just like the beer hall, and then it passed. It hadn't lasted long enough for Karl to capture any details, but it had left him shivering and afraid.

The following night it happened again – the same flash of black and white, the same aftershock of dread.

An absinthe effect, he was sure. He'd heard it caused delirium and hallucinations and even madness in those who overused it. But Karl did not feel he was going mad. No, this was something else. Not madness, but a different level of perception. He had a sense of a hidden truth, just beyond the grasp of his senses, beckoning to him, reaching for him. He felt he'd merely grazed the surface of that awful truth, and that if he kept reaching he'd soon seize it.

And he knew how to extend his reach: more absinthe.

Drexler was only too glad to have another enthusiast for his favorite libation.

"Forget Herr Hitler tonight," Drexler said. "Kahr will be better. Bavaria's triumvirate will be there in person – Kahr, General Lossow, and Colonel von Seisser. Rumor has it that Kahr is going to make a dramatic announcement. Some say he's going to declare Bavaria's independence. Others say he's going to return Crown Prince Rupprecht to the throne and restore the Bavarian monarchy. You don't want to miss this, Karl."

"What about Hitler and the rest of the Kampfbund?"

"They're frothing at the mouth. They've been invited to attend but not to participate. It's clear, I think, that Kahr is making a move to upstage the Kampfbund and solidify his leadership position. By tomorrow morning, Hitler and his cronies may find themselves awash in a hysterical torrent of Bavarian nationalism. This will be worse than any political defeat – they'll be... irrelevant. Think of their outrage, think of their frustration." Drexler rubbed his palms with glee. "Oh, this will be *most* entertaining!"

Reluctantly, Karl agreed. He felt he was getting closer and closer to that elusive vision, but even if Generalstaatskommissar Kahr tried to pull the rug out from under the Kampfbund, Karl was sure he would have plenty of future opportunities to listen to Herr Hitler.

*

Karl and Drexler arrived early at the Burgerbraukeller, and a good thing too. The city's Blue Police had to close the doors when the hall filled to overflowing. This was a much higher class audience than Hitler attracted. Well-dressed businessmen in tall hats and women in long dresses mingled with military officers and members of the Bavarian provincial cabinet; the local newspapers were represented by their editors rather than mere reporters. Everyone in Munich wanted to hear what Generalstaatskommissar Kahr had to say, and those left in the cold drizzle outside protested angrily.

They were the lucky ones, Karl decided soon after Gustav von Kahr began to speak. The squat, balding royalist had no earth-shaking announcement to make. Instead, he stood hunched over the rostrum, with Lossow and Seisser, the other two-thirds of the ruling triumvirate, seated on the bandstand behind him, and read a dull, endless anti-Marxist treatise in a listless monotone.

"Let's leave," Karl said after fifteen minutes of droning.

Drexler shook his head and glanced to their right. "Look who just arrived."

Karl recognized the figure in the light tan trench coat standing behind a pillar near the rear of the hall, chewing on a fingernail.

"Hitler! I thought he was supposed to be speaking in Freising."

"That's what the flyers said. Apparently he changed his mind. Or perhaps he simply wanted everyone to think he'd be in Freising." Drexler's voice faded as he turned in his seat and scanned the audience. "I wonder..."

"Wonder what?"

He leaned close and whispered in Karl's ear. "I wonder if Herr Hitler might not be planning something here tonight."

Karl's intestines constricted into a knot. "A putsch?"

"Keep your voice down. Yes. Why not? Bavaria's ruling triumvirate and most of its cabinet are here. If I were planning a takeover, this would be the time and place."

"But all those police outside."

Drexler shrugged. "Perhaps he'll just take over the stage and launch into one of his speeches. Either way, history could be made here tonight."

Karl glanced back at Hitler and wondered if this was what the nearly-grasped vision was about. He nudged Drexler.

"Did you bring the absinthe?"

"Of course. But we won't be able to fix it properly here." He paused. "I have an idea, though."

He signaled the waitress and ordered two snifters of cognac.

She looked at him strangely, but returned in a few minutes and placed the glasses on the table next to their beer steins. Drexler pulled his silver flask from his pocket and poured a more than generous amount of absinthe into the cognac.

"It's not turning yellow," Karl said.

"It only does that in water." Drexler lifted his snifter and swirled the greenish contents. "This was Toulouse-Lautrec's favorite way of diluting his absinthe. He called it his 'earthquake.'" Drexler smiled as he clinked his glass against Karl's. "To earth-shaking events."

Karl took a sip and coughed. The bitterness of the wormwood was enhanced rather than cut by the burn of the cognac. He washed it down with a gulp of ale. He would have poured the rest of his "earthquake" into Drexler's glass if he hadn't felt he needed every drop of the absinthe to reach the elusive vision. So he finished the entire snifter, chasing each sip with more ale. He wondered if he'd be able to walk out of here unassisted at the night's end.

He was just setting down the empty glass when he heard shouting outside. The doors at the rear of the hall burst open with a shattering bang as helmeted figures charged in brandishing sabers, pistols, and rifles with fixed bayonets. From their brown shirts and the swastikas on their red arm bands Karl knew they weren't the police.

"Nazi storm troopers!" Drexler said.

Pandemonium erupted. Some men cried out in shock and outrage while others shouted "Heil!" Some were crawling under the tables while others were climbing atop them for a better view. Women screamed and fainted at the sight of a machine gun being set up at the door. Karl looked around for Hitler and found him charging down the center aisle holding a pistol aloft. As he reached the bandstand he fired a shot into the ceiling.

Sudden silence.

Hitler climbed up next to General Commissioner von Kahr and turned toward the crowd. Karl blinked at the sight of him. Hitler had shed the trench coat and was wearing a poorly cut morning coat with an Iron Cross pinned over the left breast. He looked... ridiculous, more like the maître d' in a seedy restaurant than the savior of Germany.

Drexler snickered. "The Gefreiter looks like a waiter who's led a putsch against the restaurant staff."

But then the pale blue eyes cast their spell and the familiar baritone rang through the hall announcing that a national revolution had broken out in Germany. The Bavarian cities of Augsburg, Nuremberg, Regensburg, and Wurzburg were now in his control; the Reichswehr and State Police were marching from their barracks under Nazi flags; the Weimar government was no more. A new national German Reich was being formed. Hitler was in charge.

Drexler muttered something about "exaggeration" but Karl barely heard him. The vision was coming... close now... the absinthe, fueled by the cognac and ale, was drawing it nearer than ever before... the room was flickering about him, the colors draining away...

And then the Burgerbraukeller was gone and he was in blackness... silent, formless blackness... but not alone. He detected movement around him in the palpable darkness...

And then he saw them.

Human forms, thin, pale, bedraggled, sunken cheeked and hollow eyed, dressed in rags or dressed not at all, and thin, so painfully thin, like parchment-covered skeletons through which each rib and each bump and nodule on the pelvis and hips could be touched and numbered, all stumbling, sliding, staggering, shambling, groping toward him out of the dark. At first he thought it a dream, a nightmare reprise of the march of the starving disabled veterans he'd witnessed in Berlin, but these... people... were different. No tattered uniforms here. The ones who had clothing were dressed in striped prison pajamas, and there were so many of them. With their ranks spanning to the right and left as far as Karl could see, and stretching and fading off into the distance to where the horizon might have been, their number was beyond counting... thousands, hundreds of thousands, millions...

And all coming his way.

They began to pick up speed as they neared, breaking into a staggering run like a herd of frightened cattle. Closer, now... their gaunt faces became masks of fear, pale lips drawn back over toothless mouths, giving no sign that they saw him... he could see no glint of light in the dark hollows of their eye sockets... but he gasped as other details became visible.

They had been mutilated – branded, actually. A six-pointed star had been carved into the flesh of each. On the forehead, between the breasts, on the belly – a bleeding Star of David. The only color not black, white, or gray was the red of the blood that oozed from each of those six-pointed brands.

But why were they running? What was spurring the stampede?

And then he heard a voice, shouting, faint and far off at first, then louder: *"Alle Juden raus!"* Over and over: *"Alle Juden raus! Alle Juden raus!"* Louder and louder as they approached until Karl had to clasp his hands over his ears to protect them.

"ALLE JUDEN RAUS! ALLE JUDEN RAUS!"

And then they were upon him, mobbing him, knocking him to his knees and then flat on his face in their panicked flight through the darkness, oblivious as they stepped on him and tripped over him in their blind rush to nowhere. He could not regain his feet; he did not try. He had no fear of being crushed because they weighed almost nothing, but he could not rise against their numbers. So he remained face down in the darkness with his hands over his head and listened to that voice.

"ALLE JUDEN RAUS! ALLE JUDEN RAUS!"

After what seemed an eternity, they were past. Karl lifted his head. He was alone in the darkness. No... not alone. Someone else... a lone figure approaching. A naked woman, old, short, thin, with long gray hair, limping his way on arthritic knees. Something familiar about her–

"Mother!"

He stood paralyzed, rooted, unable to turn from her nakedness. She looked so thin, and so much older, as if she'd aged twenty years. And into each floppy breast had been carved a Star of David.

He sobbed as he held his arms out to her.

"Dear God, Mother! What have they done to you?"

But she took no notice of him, limping past as if he did not exist.

"Mother, I—!"

He turned, reaching to grab her arm as she passed, but froze in mute shock when he saw the mountain.

All the gaunt living dead who had rushed past were piled in a mound that dwarfed the Alps themselves, carelessly tossed like discarded dolls into a charnel heap that stretched miles into the darkness above him.

Only now they had eyes. Dead eyes, staring sightlessly his way, each with a silent plea... *help us... save us... please don't let this happen...*

His mother – she was in there. He had to find her, get her out of there. He ran toward the tower of wasted human flesh, but before he reached it the blacks and whites began to shimmer and melt, bleeding color as that damned voice grew louder and louder... *"ALLE JUDEN RAUS! ALLE JUDEN RAUS!"*

And Karl knew that voice. God help him, he knew that voice.

Adolf Hitler's.

Suddenly he found himself back in the Burgerbraukeller, on his feet, staring at the man who still stood at the rostrum. Only seconds had passed. It had seemed so much longer.

As Hitler finished his proclamation, the triumvirate of Kahr, Lossow, and Seisser were marched off the stage at gunpoint. And Hitler stood there with his feet spread and his arms folded across his chest, staring in triumphant defiance at the shocked crowd mingling and murmuring before him.

Karl now understood what he had seen. Hitler's hate wasn't mere rhetoric. This madman meant what he said. Every word of it. He intended the destruction of German Jewry, of Jews everywhere. And now, here in this beer hall, he was making a grab for the power to do just that. And he was succeeding!

He had to be stopped!

As Hitler turned to follow the captured triumvirate, Karl staggered forward, his arm raised, his finger pointing, ready to accuse, to shout out a denunciation. But no sound came from his throat. His lips were working, his lungs pumping, but his vocal cords were locked. Hoarse, breathy hisses were the only sounds he could make.

But those sounds were enough to draw the attention of the Nazi storm troopers. The nearest turned and pointed their rifles at him. Drexler leaped to his side and restrained him, pulling his arm down.

"He's not well. He's been sick and tonight's excitement has been too much for him."

Karl tried to shake free of Drexler. He didn't care about the storm troopers or their weapons. These people had to hear, had to know what Hitler and his National Socialists planned. But then Hitler was leaving, following the captured triumvirate from the bandstand.

In the frightened and excited confusion that followed, Drexler steered Karl toward one of the side doors. But their way was blocked by a baby-faced storm trooper.

"No one leaves until the Fuhrer says so."

"This man is sick!" Drexler shouted. "Do you know who his father was? Colonel Stehr himself! This is the son of a hero of the Argonne! Let him into the fresh air immediately!"

The young trooper, certainly no more than eighteen or nineteen, was taken aback by Drexler's outburst. It was highly unlikely that he'd ever heard of a Colonel Stehr, but he stepped aside to let them pass.

The drizzle had turned to snow, and the cold air began to clear Karl's head, but still he had no voice. Pulling away from Drexler's supporting arm, he half ran, half stumbled across the grounds of the Burgerbraukeller, crowded now with exuberant members of the Kampfbund. He headed toward the street, wanting to scream, to cry out his fear and warn the city, the country, that a murderous lunatic was taking over.

When he reached the far side of Rosenheimerstrasse, he found an alley, leaned into it, and vomited. After his stomach was empty, he wiped his mouth on his sleeve and returned to where Drexler waited on the sidewalk.

"Good heavens, man. What got into you back there?"

Karl leaned against a lamppost and told him about the vision, about the millions of dead Jews, and Hitler's voice and what it was shouting.

Drexler was a long time replying. His eyes had a faraway look, almost glazed, as if he were trying to see the future Karl had described.

"That was the absinthe," he said finally. "Lautrec's earthquake. You've been indulging a bit much lately and you're not used to it. Lautrec was institutionalized because of it. Van Gogh cut off one of his ears under the influence."

Karl grabbed the front of Drexler's overcoat. "No! The absinthe is responsible, I'll grant that, but it only opened the door for me. This was more than a hallucination. This was a vision of the future, a warning. He's got to be stopped, Ernst!"

"How? You heard him. There's a national revolution going on, and he's leading it."

A steely resolve, cold as the snow falling around them, was taking shape within Karl.

"I've been entrusted with a warning," he said softly. "I'm not going to ignore it."

"What are you going to do? Flee the country?"

"No. I'm going to stop Adolf Hitler."

"How?"

"By any means necessary."

Germany is having a nervous breakdown. There
is nothing sane to report.

F. Paul Wilson

Ben Hecht, 1923

The rest of the night was a fearful phantasm, filled with shouts, shots, and conflicting rumors – yes, there was a national revolution; no, there were no uprisings in Nuremberg or the other cities.

One thing was clear to Karl: A revolution was indeed in progress in Munich. All through the night, as he and Drexler wandered the city, they crossed paths again and again with detachments of brown-shirted men marching under the swastika banner. And lining the sidewalks were men and women of all ages, cheering them on.

Karl wanted to grab and shake each one of them and scream into their faces, *You don't know what you're doing! You don't know what they're planning!*

No one was moving to stop the putsch. The Blue Police, the Green Police, the Reichswehr troops were nowhere in sight. Drexler led Karl across the river to the Reichswehr headquarters where they watched members of the Reichskriegsflagge segment of the Kampfbund strutting in and out of the entrance.

"It's true!" Karl said. "The Reichswehr troops are with them!"

Karl tried to call Berlin to see what was happening there but could not get a phone connection. They went to the offices of the *Munchener Post*, a newspaper critical of Hitler in the past, but found its offices ransacked, every typewriter gone, every piece of printing equipment destroyed.

"The putsch is not even a day old and they've started already!" Karl said, standing on the glass-littered sidewalk in the wan dawn light and surveying the damage. "Crush anyone who disagrees with you."

"Yes!" a voice cried behind them. "Crush them! Grind them under your heel!"

They turned to see a bearded middle-aged man waving a bottle of champagne as he joined them before the *Post* offices. He wore a swastika armband over a tattered army coat.

"It's our time now!" The man guzzled some of the champagne and held it aloft. "A toast! Germany for the Germans, and damn the Jews to hell!" He thrust the bottle at Karl. "Here! Donated by a Jew down the street."

Icy spikes scored the inner walls of Karl's chest.

"Really?" he said, taking the half-full bottle. "Donated?"

"Requisitioned, actually." He barked a laugh. "Along with his watch and his wife's jewelry... after they were arrested!"

Uncontrollable fury, fueled by the growing unease of the past two weeks and the horror of his vision in the beer hall, exploded in Karl. He reversed his grip on the bottle and smashed it against the side of the man's head.

"My God, Karl!" Drexler cried.

The man stiffened and fell flat on his back in the slush, coat open, arms and legs akimbo.

Karl stared down at him, shocked by what he'd done. He'd never struck another man in his life. He knelt over him.

"He's still breathing."

Then he saw the pistol in the man's belt. He gripped the handle and pulled it free. He straightened and cradled the weapon in his trembling hands as he turned toward Drexler.

"You asked me before how I was going to stop Hitler. Here is the answer."

"Have you gone mad?"

"You don't have to come along. Safer for you if you return to the hotel while I search out Herr Hitler."

"Don't insult me. I'll be beside you all the way."

Karl stared at Drexler, surprised and warmed by the reply.

"Thank you, Ernst."

Drexler grinned, his eyes bright with excitement. "I wouldn't miss this for the world!"

*

Throughout the morning, conflicting rumors traveled up and down the Munich streets with the regularity of the city trolleys.

The triumvirate has thrown in with Hitler...the triumvirate is free and planning countermoves against the putsch... the Reichswehr has revolted and is ready to march on Berlin behind Hitler... the Reichswehr is marching on Munich to crush this putsch just as it crushed the communist attempt in Hamburg last month... Hitler is in complete control of Munich and its armed forces... support for the putsch is eroding among some police units and the young army officers...

Karl chased each rumor, trying to learn the truth, but truth seemed to be an elusive commodity in Munich. He shuttled back and forth across the river, between the putsch headquarters in the Burgerbraukeller on the east bank and the government offices around Marianplatz on the west, his right hand thrust into his coat pocket, clutching the pistol, searching for Hitler. He and Drexler had separated, figuring that two searchers could cover more ground apart than together.

By noon Karl began to get the feeling that Hitler might not have as much control as he wished people to think. True, the putschists seemed to have an iron grip on the city east of the river, and a swastika flag still flew from a balcony of the New City Hall on the west side, but Karl had noticed the green uniforms of the Bavarian State Police gathering at the west ends of the bridges across the Isar. They weren't blocking traffic, but they seemed to be on guard. And Reichswehr troops from the Seventh Division were moving through the city. Reichswehr headquarters on the west bank was still held by units of the Kampfbund, but the headquarters itself was now surrounded by two Reichswehr infantry battalions and a number of artillery units.

The tide is turning, Karl thought with grim satisfaction.

Maybe he wouldn't have to use the pistol after all.

He was standing on the west side of the Ludwig Bridge, keeping his back to the wind, when he saw Drexler hurrying toward him from the far side.

"They're coming this way!" he shouted, his cheeks red with

the excitement and the cold.

"Who?"

"Everyone! All the putschists – thousands of them. They've begun a march through the city. And Hitler's leading them."

No sooner had Drexler spoken than Karl spied the front ranks of the march – brown-shirted Nazis carrying the red and white flags that whipped and snapped in the wind. Behind them came the rest, walking twelve abreast, headed directly toward the Ludwig Bridge. He spotted Hitler in the front ranks wearing his tan trench coat and a felt hat. Beside him was General Ludendorf, one of the most respected war heroes in the nation.

A crowd of putsch supporters and the merely curious gathered as the Green Police hurried across to the east side of the bridge to stop the marchers. Before they could set up, squads of storm troopers swarmed from the flanks of the march, surrounding and disarming them.

The march surged across the bridge unimpeded.

Karl tightened his grip on the pistol. He would end this here, now, personal consequences be damned. But he couldn't get a clear view of Hitler through the throng surrounding him. To his dismay, many bystanders from the crowd joined the march as it passed, further swelling its ranks.

The march streamed into the already crowded Marianplatz in front of City Hall where it was met with cheers and cries of adulation by the thousands mobbed there. A delirious rendition of "Deutschland Uber Alles" rattled the windows all around the plaza and ended with countless cries of "Heil Hitler!"

At no time could Karl get within a hundred yards of his target.

And now, its ranks doubled, the march was off again, this time northward up Wienstrasse.

"They're heading for Reichswehr headquarters," Drexler said.

"It's surrounded. They'll never get near it."

Drexler shrugged. "Who's going to stop them? Who's going to fire with General Ludendorf at Hitler's side and all those civilians with them?"

Karl felt his jaw muscles bunch as the memory of the vision surged through his brain, dragging with it the image of his elderly, withered, unclothed, bleeding mother.

"I am."

He took off at a run along a course parallel to the march, easily outdistancing the slow-moving crowd. He calculated that the marchers would have to come up Residenzstrasse in order to reach the Reichswehr building. He ducked into a doorway of the Feldherrnhalle, near the top of the street and crouched there, panting from the unaccustomed exertion. Seconds later, Drexler joined him, barely breathing hard.

"You didn't have to come."

Drexler smiled. "Of course I did. We're witnessing the making of history."

Karl pulled the pistol from his coat pocket. "But after today someone other than Adolf Hitler will be making it."

At the top of Residenzstrasse, where it opened into a plaza, Karl saw units of the Green Police setting up barricades.

Good. They'd slow the march, and that would be his moment.

"Here they come," Drexler said.

Karl's palms began to sweat as he searched the front ranks for his target. The pistol grip was slippery in his hand by the time he identified Hitler. This was it. This was his moment in history, to turn it from the horrors the vision had shown him.

Doubt gripped the base of his throat in a stranglehold. What if the vision was wrong? What if it had been the absinthe and nothing more? What if he was about to murder a man because of a drunken hallucination?

He tore free of the questions.

No. No doubts. No hesitation. Hitler has to die. Here. Now. By my hand.

As he'd predicted, the march slowed when it neared the barricades and the storm troopers approached the Green Police shouting, "Don't shoot! We are your comrades! We have General

Ludendorf with us!"

Karl raised the pistol, waiting for his chance.

And then a passage opened between him and Hitler's trench-coated form.

Now! It has to be now!

He took aim, cautiously, carefully. He wasn't experienced with pistols. His father had taken him hunting with a rifle or a shotgun as a young man, but he'd never found much pleasure in it. Just as he found no pleasure in this, only duty. But he knew how to aim, and he had the heart of this strutting little monster in his sights. He remembered his father's words...

Squeeze, don't pull... squeeze... be surprised by the shot...

And while Karl waited for his surprise, he imagined the tapered lead cylinder blasting from the muzzle, hurtling toward Hitler, plunging into his chest, tearing through lung and heart, ripping the life from him before he could destroy the lives of the hapless, helpless, innocent millions he so hated. He saw Hitler twist and fall, saw a brief, violent spasm of rage and confusion as the milling putschists fired wildly in all directions, rioting until the Green Police and the regular army units closed in to divide their ranks, arrest their leaders, and disperse the rest. Perhaps another Jew hater would rise, but he would not have this man's unique combination of personal magnetism and oratory power. The future Karl had seen would never happen. His bullet would sever the link from this time and place to that future.

And so he let his sweat-slick forefinger caress the curve of the trigger... *squeezing...*

But just as the weapon fired, something brushed against his arm. The bullet coughed into the chill air, high, missing Hitler.

Time stopped. The marchers stood frozen, some in mid stride. All except for Hitler. His head was turned Karl's way, his pale blue eyes searching the doorways, the windows. And then those eyes fixed on Karl's. The two men stared at each other for an instant, an eternity... then... Hitler smiled.

And with that smile time resumed its course as Karl's single shot precipitated a barrage of gunfire from the Green Police and the Kampfbund troops. Chaos erupted on Residenzstrasse. Karl watched in horror as people ran in all directions, screaming, bleeding, falling, and dying. The pavement became red and slick with blood. He saw Hitler go down and stay down. He prayed that someone else's bullet had found him.

Finally the shooting stopped. The guns were silent but the air remained filled with the cries of the wounded. To Karl's shock he saw Hitler struggle to his feet and flee along the sidewalk, holding his arm. Before Karl could gather his wits and take aim again with his pistol, Hitler had jumped into a yellow Opel sedan that sped him away.

Karl added his own shouts to those of the wounded. He turned to Drexler.

"It was you! Why did you hit my arm? I had him in my sights and you... you made me miss!"

"Terribly sorry," Drexler said, avidly scanning the carnage on the street before them. "It was an accident. I was leaning over for a look and lost my balance. Not to worry. I think you accomplished your goal: This putsch is over."

> The Munich putsch definitely eliminates Hitler
> and his National Socialist followers.
> *New York Times*, November 9, 1923

Karl was overjoyed when Adolf Hitler was captured by the Green Police two days later, charged with high treason, and thrown into jail. His National Socialist Party was disbanded and declared illegal. Adolf Hitler had lost his political firmament, his freedom, and because he was an Austrian, there was a good possibility he would be deported after his trial.

While waiting for the trial, Karl reopened his bookstore and tried to resume a normal routine in Berlin. But the vision and specter of Adolf Hitler haunted him. Hitler was still alive, might still wreak the horrors Karl had seen. He hungered for the trial, to see Hitler humiliated, sentenced to a minimum of twenty years. Or deported. Or best yet: shot as a traitor.

He saw less and less of Drexler during the months leading to the trial. Drexler seemed bored with Berlin. New, gold-backed marks had brought inflation under control, the new government seemed stable; with no new putsches in the works, life was far less "entertaining."

*

They met up again in Munich on the day of Hitler's sentencing. Like the trial, the sentencing was being held in the main lecture hall of the old Infantry School because the city's regular courtrooms could not accommodate the huge crowds. Karl had been unable to arrange a seat inside; nor, apparently, had Drexler. Both had to be content to stand outside under the bright midday sky and wait for the news along with the rest of their fellow citizens.

"I can't say I'm surprised to see you here," Drexler said as they shook hands.

"Nor I you. I suppose you find all this amusing."

"Quite." He pointed with his cane. "My, my. Look at all the people."

Karl had already studied them, and they upset him. Thousands of Germans from all over the country swarmed around the large brick building, trying in vain to get into the courtroom. Two battalions of Green Police were stationed behind barbed wire barriers to keep the crowds at bay. During the 25 days of the trial, Karl had moved among them and had been horrified at how many spoke of Hitler in the hushed tones of adoration reserved for royalty, or a god.

Today the women had brought bouquets of flowers for their god, and almost everyone in the huge throng wore ribbons of red, white, and black – the Nazi colors.

"He's a national figure now," Drexler said. "Before the putsch no one had ever heard of him. Now his name is known all over

F. Paul Wilson

the world."

"And that name will soon be in jail," Karl said vehemently.

"Undoubtedly. But he's made excellent use of the trial as a national soap box."

Karl shook his head. He could not understand why the judges had allowed Hitler to speak at such length from the witness box. For days – *weeks* – he went on, receiving standing ovations in the courtroom while reporters transcribed his words and published them for the whole country to read.

"But today it comes to an end. Even as we speak, his sentence is being pronounced. Today Adolf Hitler goes to prison for a long, long time. Even better: Today he is deported to Austria."

"Jail, yes," Drexler said. "But I wouldn't count on deportation. He is, after all, a decorated veteran of the German Army, and I do believe the judges are more than a little cowed by the show of support he has received here and in the rest of the country."

Suddenly shouts arose from those of the huge crowd nearest the building, followed by wild cheering as word of the sentencing was passed down: five years in Landau Prison... but eligible for parole in six months.

"Six months!" Karl shouted. "No, this can't be! He's guilty of treason! He tried to overthrow the government!"

"Hush, Karl," Drexler said. "You're attracting attention."

"I will *not* be silenced! The people have to know!"

"Not these people, Karl."

Karl raised his arms to the circle of grim faces that had closed about him. "Listen to me! Adolf Hitler is a monster! They should lock him up in the deepest darkest hole and throw away the key! He–"

Sudden agony convulsed through his back as someone behind him rammed a fist into his right kidney. As Karl staggered forward another man with wild, furious eyes and bared teeth punched him in the face. He slumped to the ground with cries of "Communist!" and "Jew!" filling his ears. The circle closed about

66

him and the sky was shut out by enraged, merciless faces as heavy boots began to kick at his back and belly and head.

Karl was losing his last grip on consciousness when the blows suddenly stopped and blue sky appeared above him again.

Through blurry eyes he saw Drexler leaning over him, shaking his head in dismay.

"Good God, man! Do you have a death wish? You'd be a bloody pulp now if I hadn't brought the police to your aid!"

Painfully, Karl raised himself on one elbow and spit blood. Scenes from the dark vision began flashing before his eyes.

"It's going to happen!" he sobbed.

He felt utterly alone, thoroughly defeated. Hitler had a national following now. He'd be back on the streets and in the beer halls in six months, spreading his hatred. Instead of the end of him, this trial was the beginning. It had catapulted him into the national spotlight. He was on his way. He was going to take over.

And the vision would become reality.

"Damn you, Drexler! Why did you have to knock off my aim?"

"I told you, Karl. It was an accident."

"Really?" During the months since that cold fall day, Karl's thoughts had returned often to the perfectly-timed nudge that had made him miss. "I wonder about that 'accident,' Ernst. I can't escape the feeling that you did it on purpose."

Drexler's face tightened as he rose and stood towering over Karl.

"Believe what you will, Karl. But I can't say I'm sorry. I, for one, am convinced that the next decade or two will be far more entertaining *with* Herr Hitler than without him." His smile was cold, but his eyes were bright with anticipation. "I am rather looking forward to the years to come. Aren't you?"

Karl tried to answer, but the words would not come. If only Drexler knew...

Then he saw the gleam in Drexler's eyes and the possibility

struck Karl like a hob-nailed boot: Perhaps he *does* know.

Drexler touched the brim of his hat with the silver head of his cane. "If you will excuse me now, Karl, I really must be off. I'm meeting a friend – a new friend – for a drink."

He turned and walked away, blending with the ever-growing crowd of red and white, black and brown.

DAT-TAY-VAO

The mysterious force known in modern times by its Vietnamese name, *Dat-tay-vao*, spans the entire Secret History, from the First Age (perhaps even *before* the First Age) right up through *Nightworld*.

I'd originally intended to use a much shorter version of "Dat-tay-vao" as either a flashback or a prologue in *The Touch*, but no matter how I tried to work it in, it simply wouldn't fit. Used early on, it gave away too much of the mystery of what would be happening to Alan Bulmer in the body of the novel; inserted later, it seemed redundant. So I scrapped it.

After the novel was finished I fleshed it out as a stand-alone prequel to *The Touch*. It appeared in the March 1987 issue of *Amazing Stories* and was voted a finalist for the Stoker Award (but didn't win). The story takes place in March, 1968... right about the time of *Reborn*, another novel in the Secret History of the World.

Consider: In February-March of 1968, Rasalom is reincarnated into the baby conceived by Carol and Jim Stevens in *Reborn*. Around the same time, on the other side of the world, the *Dat-Tay-Vao* (as detailed in this story) enters Army Medic Walter Erskine and heads for America. Coincidence? What have I told you about coincidences?

In 1970, Walt Erskine receives his medical discharge from the Army after treatment for a mental condition at Northport V.A. Hospital. He's diagnosed as a paranoid schizophrenic – guy thinks he can heal people. Two years later he joins a faith-healing tent show in the South but is kicked off the tour because he's never sober. In 1974 he moves in with sister in Johnson, NJ,

F. Paul Wilson

hometown of the boy who will become Repairman Jack.

Finally, in the summer before *Nightworld*, the *Day-Tay-Vao* migrates from poor, homeless, booze-ravaged Walter Erskine to Dr. Alan Bulmer and sets course to help prevent the end of the world as we know it.

But here's how Walt became involved…

Dat-Tay-Vao

1

Patsy cupped his hands gently over his belly to keep his intestines where they belonged. Weak, wet, and helpless, he lay on his back in the alley and looked up at the stars in the crystal sky, unable to move, afraid to call out. The one time he'd yelled loud enough to be heard all the way to the street, loops of bowel had squirmed against his hands, feeling like a pile of Mom's slippery-slick homemade sausage all gray from boiling and coated with her tomato sauce. Visions of his insides surging from the slit in his abdomen like spring snakes from a novelty can of nuts had kept him from yelling again.

No one had come.

He knew he was dying. Good as dead, in fact. He could feel the blood oozing out of the vertical gash in his belly, seeping around his fingers and trailing down his forearms to the ground. Wet from neck to knees. Probably lying in a pool of blood... his very own homemade marinara sauce.

Help was maybe fifty feet away and he couldn't call for it. Even if he could stand the sight of his guts jumping out of him, he no longer had the strength to yell. Yet help was out there... the nightsounds of Quang Ngai streetlife... so near...

Nothing ever goes right for me. Nothing. Ever.

It had been such a sweet deal. Six keys of Cambodian brown. He could've got that home to Flatbush no sweat and then he'd have been set up real good. Uncle Tony would've known what to do with the stuff and Patsy would've been made. And he'd never be called Fatman again. Only the grunts over here called him Fatman. He'd be Pasquale to the old boys, and Pat to the younger guys.

And Uncle Tony would've called him Kid, like he always did.

Yeah. Would have. If Uncle Tony could see him now, he'd call him Shit-for-Brains. He could hear him now:

Six keys for ten G's? Whatsamatta witchoo? Din't I always tell you if it seems too good to be true, it usually is? Ay! Gabidose! Din't you smell no rat?

Nope. No rat smell. Because I didn't want to smell a rat. Too eager for the deal. Too anxious for the quick score. Too damn stupid as usual to see how that sleazeball Hung was playing me like a hooked fish.

No Cambodian brown.

No deal.

Just a long, sharp K-bar.

The stars above went fuzzy and swam around, then came into focus again.

The pain had been awful at first, but that was gone now. Except for the cold, it was almost like getting smashed and crashed on scotch and grass and just drifting off. Almost pleasant. Except for the cold. And the fear.

Footsteps... coming from the left. He managed to turn his head a few degrees. A lone figure approached, silhouetted against the light from the street. A slow, unsteady, almost staggering walk. Whoever it was didn't seem to be in any hurry. Hung? Come to finish him off?

But no. This guy was too skinny to be Hung.

The figure came up and squatted flatfooted on his haunches next to Patsy. In the dim glow of starlight and streetlight he saw a wrinkled face and a silvery goatee. The gook babbled something in Vietnamese.

God, it was Ho Chi Minh himself come to rob him.

Too late. The money's gone. All gone.

No. Wasn't Ho. Couldn't be. Just an old papa-san in the usual black pajamas. They all looked the same, especially the old ones. The only thing different about this one was the big scar across his right eye. Looked as if the lids had been fused closed over the socket.

The old man reached down to where Patsy guarded his intestines and pushed his hands away. Patsy tried to scream in protest but heard only a sigh, tried to put his hands back up on his belly but they'd weakened to limp rubber and wouldn't move.

The old man smiled as he singsonged in gooktalk and pressed his hands against the open wound in Patsy's belly. Patsy screamed then, a hoarse, breathy sound torn from him by the searing pain that shot in all directions from where the old gook's hands lay. The stars really swam around this time, fading as they moved, but they didn't go out.

By the time his vision cleared, the old gook was up and turned around and weaving back toward the street. The pain, too, was sidling away.

Patsy tried again to lift his hands up to his belly, and this time they moved. They seemed stronger. He wiggled his fingers through the wetness of his blood, feeling for the edges of the wound, afraid of finding loops of bowel waiting for him.

He missed the slit on the first pass. And missed it on the second. How could that happen? It had been at least a foot long and had gaped open a good three or four inches, right there to the left of his belly button. He tried again, carefully this time…

…and found a thin little ridge of flesh.

But no opening.

He raised his head – he hadn't been able to do that before – and looked down at his belly. His shirt and pants were a bloody mess, but he couldn't see any guts sticking out. And he couldn't see any wound, either. Just a dark wet mound of flesh.

If he wasn't so goddamn fat he could see down there! He rolled onto his side – God, he was stronger! – and pushed himself up to his knees to where he could slump his butt onto his heels, all the time keeping at least one hand tight over his belly. But nothing came out, or even pushed against his hand. He pulled his shirt open.

The wound was closed, replaced by a thin, purplish vertical line.

Patsy felt woozy again. What's going on here?

He was in a coma – that had to be it. He was dreaming this.

But everything was so *real* – the rough ground beneath his

knees, the congealing red wetness of the blood on his shirt, the sounds from the street, even the smell of the garbage around him. All so real...

Bracing himself against the wall, he inched his way up to his feet. His knees were wobbly and for a moment he thought they'd give out on him. But they held and now he was standing.

He was afraid to look down, afraid he'd see himself still on the ground. Finally, he took a quick glance. Nothing there but two clotted puddles of blood, one on each side of where he'd been lying.

He tore off the rest of the ruined shirt and began walking – very carefully at first – toward the street. Any moment now he would wake up or die, and this craziness would stop. No doubt 'bout that. But until then he was going to play out this little fantasy to the end.

2

By the time he made it to his bunk – after giving the barracks guards and a few wandering night owls a story about an attempted robbery and a fight – Patsy had begun to believe that he was really awake and walking around.

It was so easy to say it had all been a dream, or maybe hallucinations brought on by acid slipped into his after-dinner coffee by some wise-ass. He managed to convince himself of that scenario a good half dozen times. And then he would look down at the scar on his belly, and at the blood on his pants...

Patsy sat on his rack in a daze.

It really happened! He just touched me and closed me up!

A hushed voice in the dark snapped him out of it.

"Hey! Fatman! Got any weed?"

It sounded like Donner from two bunks over, a steady customer.

"Not tonight, Hank,"

"What? Fatman's never out of stock!"

"He is tonight"

"You shittin' me?"

"Good night, Hank."

Actually, he had a bunch of bags stashed in his mattress, but Patsy didn't feel like dealing tonight. His mind was too numb to make change. He couldn't even mourn the loss of all his cash – every red cent he'd saved up from almost a year's worth of chickenshit deals with guys like Donner. All he could think about, all he could see, was that old one-eyed gook leaning over him, smiling, babbling, and touching him.

He'd talk to Tram tomorrow. Tram knew everything that went on in this goddamn country. Maybe he'd heard something about the old gook. Maybe he could be persuaded to look for him.

One way or another, Patsy was going to find that old gook. He had plans for him. Big plans.

3

Somehow he managed to make it through breakfast without perking the powdered eggs and scrambling the coffee.

It hadn't been easy. He'd been late getting to the mess hall kitchen. He'd got up on time but had stood in the shower staring at that purple line up and down his belly for he didn't know how long, remembering the cut of Hung's knife, the feel of his intestines in his hands.

Did it really happen?

He knew it had. Accepting it and living with it was going to be the problem.

Finally he'd pulled on his fatigues and hustled over to the kitchen. Rising long before sunup was the only bad thing about being an army cook. The guys up front might call him a pogue but it sure beat hell out of being a stupid grunt in the field. *Anything* was better than getting shot at. Look what happened in Hue last month, and the whispers about My Lai. Only gavones got sent into the field. Smart guys got mess assignments in nice safe towns like Quang Ngai.

At least smart guys with an Uncle Tony did.

Patsy smiled as he scraped hardened scrambled egg off the

griddle. He'd always liked to cook. Good thing too. Because in a way, the cooking he'd done for Christmas last year had kept him out of the fight this year.

As always, Uncle Tony had come for Christmas dinner. At the table Pop edged around to the big question: What to do about Patsy and the draft. To everyone's surprise, he'd passed his induction physical...

...another example of how nothing ever went right for him. Patsy had learned that a weight of 225 pounds would keep a guy his height out on medical deferment. Since he wasn't too many pounds short of that, he gorged on everything in sight for weeks. It would've been fun if he hadn't been so desperate. But he made the weight: On the morning of his induction physical the bathroom scale read 229.

But the scale they used downtown at the Federal Building read 224.

He was in and set to go to boot camp after the first of the year.

Pop finally came to the point: Could Uncle Tony maybe...?

Patsy could still hear the disdain in Uncle Tony's voice as he spoke around a mouthful of bread.

"You some kinda peacenik or somethin'?"

No, no, Pop had said, and went on to explain how he was afraid that Patsy, being so fat and so clumsy and all, would get killed in boot camp or step on a mine his first day in the field. You know how he is.

Uncle Tony knew. Everybody knew Patsy's fugazi reputation. Uncle Tony had said nothing as he poured the thick red gravy over his lasagna, gravy Patsy had spent all morning cooking. He took a bite and pointed his fork at Patsy.

"Y'gotta do your duty, kid. I fought in the big one. You gotta fight in this here little one." He swallowed. "Say, you made this gravy, dincha? It's good. It's real good. And it gives me an idea of how we can keep you alive so you can go on making this stuff every Christmas."

So Uncle Tony pulled some strings and Patsy wound up an

army cook.

He finished with the cleanup and headed downtown to the central market area, looking for Tram. He smelled the market before he got to it – the odors of live hens, *thit heo*, and roasting dog meat mingled in the air.

He found Tram in his usual spot by his cousin's vegetable stand, wearing his old ARVN fatigue jacket. He'd removed his right foot at the ankle and was polishing its shoe.

"Nice shine, yes, Fatman?" he said as he looked up and saw Patsy.

"Beautiful." He knew Tram liked to shock passersby with his plastic lower leg and foot. Patsy should have been used to the gag by now, but every time he saw that foot he thought of having his leg blown off…

"I want to find someone."

"American or gook?" He crossed his right lower leg over his left and snapped his foot back into place at the ankle. Patsy couldn't help feeling uncomfortable about a guy who called his own kind gooks.

"Gook."

"What name?"

"Uh, that's the problem. I don't know."

Tram squinted up at him. "How I supposed to find somebody without a name?"

"Old papa-san. Looks like Uncle Ho."

Tram laughed. "All you guys think old gooks look like Ho!"

"And he has a scar across his eye" – Patsy put his index finger over his right eye–"that seals it closed like this."

4

Tram froze for a heartbeat, then snapped his eyes back down to his prosthetic foot. He composed his expression while he calmed his whirling mind.

Trinh…Trinh was in town last night! And Fatman saw him!

He tried to change the subject. Keeping his eyes down, he said, "I am glad to see you still walking around this morning. Did

Hung not show up last night? I warned you – he number ten bad gook."

After waiting and hearing no reply, Tram looked up and saw that Fatman's eyes had changed. They looked glazed.

"Yes," Fatman finally said, shaking himself. "You warned me." He cleared his throat. "But about the guy I asked you about–"

"Why you want find this old gook?"

"I want to help him."

"How?"

"I want to do something for him."

"You want do something for old gook?"

Fatman's gaze wandered away as he spoke. "You might say I owe him a favor."

Tram's first thought was that Fatman was lying. He doubted this young American knew the meaning of returning a favor.

"Can you find him for me?" Fatman said.

Tram thought about that. And as he did, he saw Hung saunter out of a side street into the central market. He watched Hung's jaw drop when he spotted Fatman, watched his amber skin pale to the color of boiled bean curd as he spun and hurriedly stumbled away.

Tram knew in that instant that Hung had betrayed Fatman last night in a most vicious manner, and that Trinh had happened by and saved Fatman with the *Dat-tay-vao*.

It was all clear now.

On impulse, Tram said, "He lives in my cousin's village. I can take you to him."

"Great" Fatman said, grinning and clapping him on the shoulder. "I'll get us a jeep!"

"No jeep," Tram said. "We walk."

"Walk?" Fatman's face lost much of its enthusiasm. "Is it far?"

"Not far. Just a few klicks on the way to Mo Due. A fishing village. We leave now."

"Now? But–"

"Could be he not there if we wait."

This wasn't exactly true, but he didn't want to give Fatman too much time to think. Tram watched reluctance and eagerness battle their way back and forth across the American's face. Finally...

"All right. Let's go. Long as it's not too far."

"If not too far for man with one foot, not too far for man with two."

5

As Tram led Fatman south toward the tiny fishing village where Trinh had been living for the past year, he wondered why he'd agreed to bring the two of them together. His instincts were against it, yet he'd agreed to lead the American to Trinh.

Why?

Why was a word too often on his mind, it seemed. Especially where Americans were concerned. Why did they send so many of their young men over here? Most of them were either too frightened or too disinterested to make good soldiers. And the few who were eager for the fight hadn't the experience to make them truly valuable. They did not last long.

He wanted to shout across the sea: Send us seasoned soldiers, not your children!

But who would listen?

And did age really matter? After all, hadn't he been even younger than these American boys in the fight against the French at Dien Bien Phu fifteen years ago? But he and his fellow Vietminh had had a special advantage on their side. They had all burned with a fiery zeal to drive the French from their land.

Tram had been a communist then. He smiled at the thought as he limped along on the artificial foot, a replacement for the real one he'd lost to a Cong booby trap last year. Communist... he had been young at Dien Bien Phu and the constant talk from his fellow Vietminh about the glories of class war and revolution had drawn him into their ideological camp. But after the fighting was over, after the partition, what he saw of the birth

F. Paul Wilson

pangs of the glorious new social order almost made him long for French rule again.

He'd come south then and had remained here ever since. He'd willingly fought for the South until the finger-charge booby trap had caught him at the knee; after that he found that his verve for any sort of fight had departed with his leg.

He glanced at Fatman, sweating so profusely as he walked beside him along the twisting jungle trail. He'd come to like the boy, but he could not say why. Fatman was greedy, cowardly, and selfish, and he cared for no one other than himself. Yet Tram had found himself responding to the boy's vulnerability. Something tragic behind the bluff and bravado. With Tram's aid, Fatman had gone from the butt of many of the jokes around the American barracks to their favored supplier of marijuana. Tram could not deny that he'd profited well by helping him gain that position. He'd needed the money to supplement his meager pension from the ARVN, but that had not been his only motivation. He'd felt a need to help the boy.

And he *was* a boy, no mistake about that. Young enough to be Tram's son. But Tram knew he could never raise such a son as this.

So many of the Americans he'd met here were like Fatman. No values, no traditions, no heritage. Empty. Hollow creatures who had grown up with nothing expected of them. And now, despite all the money and all the speeches, they knew in their hearts that they were not expected to win this war.

What sort of parents provided nothing for their children to believe in, and then sent them halfway around the world to fight for a country they had never heard of?

And that last was certainly a humbling experience – to learn that until a few years ago most of these boys had been blithely unaware of the existence of the land that had been the center of Tram's life since he'd been a teenager.

"How much farther now?" Fatman said.

Tram could tell from the American's expression that he was uneasy being so far from town. Perhaps now was the time to ask.

"Where did Hung stab you?" he said.

Fatman staggered as if Tram had struck him a blow. He stopped and gaped at Tram with a gray face.

"How…?"

"There is little that goes on in Quang Ngai that I do not know," he said, unable to resist an opportunity to enhance his stature. "Now, show me where."

Tram withheld a gasp as Fatman pulled up his sweat-soaked shirt to reveal the purple seam running up and down to the left of his navel. Hung had gut cut him, not only to cause an agonizing death, but to show his contempt.

"I warned you…"

Fatman pulled down his shirt. "I know, I know. But after Hung left me in the alley, this old guy came along and touched me and sealed it up like magic. Can he do that all the time?"

"Not all the time. He has lived in the village for one year. He can do it some of the time every day. He will do it many more years."

Fatman's voice was a breathy whisper. "Years! But how? Is it some drug he takes? He looked like he was drunk."

"Oh, no. *Dat-tay-vao* not work if you drunk."

"What won't work?"

"*Dat-tay-vao*… Trinh has the touch that heals."

"Heals what? Just knife wounds and stuff?"

"Anything."

Fatman's eyes bulged. "You've got to get me to him!" He glanced quickly at Tram. "So I can thank him… reward him."

"He requires no reward."

"I've got to find him. How far to go?"

"Not much." He could smell the sea now. "We turn here."

As he guided Fatman left into thicker brush that clawed at their faces and snagged their clothes, he wondered again if he'd done the right thing by bringing him here. But it was too late to turn back.

Besides, Fatman had been touched by the *Dat-tay-vao*. Surely that worked some healing changes on the spirit as well as the body. Perhaps the young American truly wanted to pay his respects to Trinh.

6

He will do it many more years!

The words echoed in Patsy's ears and once again he began counting the millions he'd make off the old gook. God, it was going to be so great! And so easy! Uncle Tony's contacts would help get the guy into the states where Patsy would set him up in a "clinic." Then he would begin to cure the incurable.

And oh God the prices he'd charge.

How much to cure someone of cancer? Who could say what price was too high? He could ask anything – *anything*!

But Patsy wasn't going to be greedy. He'd be fair. He wouldn't strip the patients bare. He'd just ask for half – half of everything they owned.

He almost laughed out loud. This was going to be *so* sweet! All he had to do was –

Just ahead of him, Tram shouted something in Vietnamese. Patsy didn't recognize the word, but he knew a curse when he heard one. Tram started running. They had broken free of the suffocating jungle atop a small sandy rise. Out ahead, the sun rippled off a calm sea. A breeze off the water brought blessed relief from the heat. Below lay a miserable ville – a jumble of huts made of odd bits of wood, sheet metal, palm fronds, and mud.,

One of the huts was burning. Frantic villagers were hurling sand and water at it.

Patsy followed Tram's headlong downhill run at a cautious walk. He didn't like this. He was far from town and doubted he could find his way back; he was surrounded by gooks and something bad was going down.

He didn't like this at all.

As he approached, the burning hut collapsed in a shower of sparks. To the side, a cluster of black pajama-clad women stood around a supine figure. Tram had pushed his way through to the center of the babbling group and now knelt beside the figure.

Patsy followed him in.

"Aw, shit!"

He recognized the guy on the ground. Wasn't easy. He'd been burned bad and somebody had busted caps all over him, but his face was fairly undamaged and the scarred eye left no doubt that it was the same old gook who'd healed him up last night. His good eye was closed and he looked dead, but his chest still moved with shallow respirations. Patsy's stomach lurched at the sight of all the blood and charred flesh. What was keeping him alive?

Suddenly weak and dizzy, Patsy dropped to his knees beside Tram. His millions... all those sweet dreams of millions and millions of easy dollars were fading away.

Nothing ever goes right for me!

"I share your grief," Tram said, looking at him with sorrowful dark eyes.

"Yeah. What happened?"

Tram glanced around at the frightened, grieving villagers. "They say the Cong bring one of their sick officers here and demand that Trinh heal him. Trinh couldn't. He try to explain that the time not right yet but they grow angry and tie him up and shoot him and set his hut on fire."

"Can't he heal himself?"

Tram shook his head slowly, sadly. "No. *Dat-tay-vao* does not help the one who has it. Only others."

Patsy wanted to cry. All his plans... it wasn't *fair*!

"Those shitbums!"

"Worse than shitbums," Tram said. "These Charlie say they come back soon and destroy whole village."

Patsy's anger and self-pity vanished in a cold blast of fear. He peered at the trees and bushes, feeling naked with a thousand eyes watching him.

...they come back soon...

His knees suddenly felt stronger.

"Let's get back to town." He began to rise to his feet, but Tram held him back.

"Wait. He looking at you."

Sure enough, the old gook's good eye was open and staring directly into his. Slowly, with obvious effort, he raised his charred right hand toward Patsy. His voice rasped something.

Tram translated: "He say, 'You the one.'"

"What's that supposed to mean?"

Patsy didn't have time for this dramatic bullshit. He wanted out of here. But he also wanted to stay tight with Tram because Tram was the only one who could lead him back to Quang Ngai.

"I don't know. Maybe he mean that you the one he fix last night."

Patsy was aware of Tram and the villagers watching him, as if they expected something of him. Then he realized what it was: He was supposed to be grateful, show respect to the old gook. Fine. If it was what Tram wanted him to do, he'd do it. Anything to get them on their way out of here. He took a deep breath and gripped the hand, wincing at the feel of the fire-crisped skin –

Electricity shot up his arm.

His whole body spasmed with the searing bolt. He felt himself flopping around like a fish on a hook, and then he was falling. The air went out of him in a rush as his back slammed against the ground. It was a moment before he could open his eyes, and when he did he saw Tram and the villagers staring down at him with gaping mouths and wide, astonished eyes. He glanced at the old gook.

"What the hell did he do to me?"

The old gook was staring back, but it was a glassy, unfocused, sightless stare. He was dead.

The villagers must have noticed this too because some of the women began to weep.

Patsy staggered to his feet.

"What happened?"

"Don't know," Tram said with a puzzled shake of his head. "Why you fall? He not strong enough push you down."

Patsy opened his mouth to explain, then closed it. Nothing he could say would make sense.

He shrugged. "Let's go."

He felt like hell and just wanted to be gone. It wasn't only the threat of Charlie returning; he was tired and discouraged and so bitterly disappointed he could have sat down on the ground right then and there and cried like a wimp.

"Okay. But first I help bury Trinh. You help, too."

"What? You kidding me? Forget it!"

Tram said nothing, but the look he gave Patsy said it all: It called him fat, lazy, and ungrateful.

Screw you! Patsy thought.

Who cared what Tram or anybody else in this stinking sewer of a country thought? It held nothing for him anymore. All his money was gone, and his one chance for the brass ring lay dead and fried on the ground before him.

7

As he helped dig a grave for Trinh, Tram glanced over at Fatman where he sat in the elephant grass staring morosely out to sea. Tram could sense that he was not grief-stricken over Trinh's fate. He was unhappy for himself.

So...he had been right about Fatman from the first: The American had come here with something in mind other than paying his respects to Trinh. Tram didn't know what it was, but he was sure Fatman had not had the best interests of Trinh or the village at heart.

He sighed. He was sick of foreigners. When would the wars end? Wars could be measured in languages here. He knew numerous Vietnamese dialects, Pidgin, French, and now English. If the North won, would he then have to learn Russian? Perhaps he would have been better off if the booby trap had taken his life instead of just his leg. Then, like Trinh, the endless wars would be over for him.

He looked down into the empty hole where Trinh's body soon would lie. Were they burying the *Dat-tay-vao* with him? Or would it rise and find its way to another? So strange and mysterious, the *Dat-tay-vao*... so many conflicting tales. Some said it came here with the Buddha himself, some said it had always been here. Some said it was as capricious as the wind in the choice of its instruments, while others said it followed a definite plan.

Who was to say truly? The *Dat-tay-vao* was a rule unto itself, full of mysteries not meant to be plumbed.

As he turned back to his digging, Tram's attention was caught by a dark blot in the water's glare. He squinted to make it out, then heard the chatter of one machine gun, then others, saw villagers begin to run and fall, felt sand kick up around him.

A Cong gunboat!

He ran for the tree where Fatman half sat, half crouched with a slack, terrified expression. He was almost there when something hit him in the chest and right shoulder with the force of a sledgehammer, and then he was flying through the air, spinning, screaming with pain.

He landed with his face in the sand and rolled. He couldn't breathe! Panic swept over him. Every time he tried to take a breath, he heard a sucking sound from the wound in his chest wall, but no air reached his lungs. His chest felt ready to explode. Black clouds encroached on his dimming vision.

Suddenly, Fatman was leaning over him, shouting through the typhoon roaring in his ears.

"Tram! Tram! Jesus God get up! You gotta get me outa here! Stop bleeding f'Christsake and get me out of here!"

Tram's vision clouded to total darkness and the roaring grew until it drowned out the voice.

8

Patsy dug his fingers into his scalp.

How was he going to get back to town? Tram was dying, turning blue right here in front of him, and he didn't know enough Vietnamese to use with anyone else and didn't know the way back to Quang Ngai and the whole area was lousy with

Charlie.

What am I gonna do?

As suddenly as they started, the AKs stopped. The cries of the wounded and the terrified filled the air in their place.

Now was the time to get out.

Patsy looked at Tram's mottled, dusky face. If he could stopper up that sucking chest wound, maybe Tram could hang on, and maybe tell him the way back to town. He slapped the heel of his hand over it and pressed.

Tram's body arched in seeming agony. Patsy felt something too – electric ecstasy shot up his arm and spread through his body like subliminal fire. He fell back, confused, weak, dizzy.

What the hell–?

He heard raspy breathing and looked up. Air was gushing in and out of Tram's wide-open mouth in hungry gasps; his eyes opened and his color began to lighten.

Tram's chest wasn't sucking anymore. As Patsy leaned forward to check the wound, he felt something in his hand and looked. A bloody lead slug sat in his palm. He looked at the chest where he'd laid that hand and what he saw made the walls of his stomach ripple and compress as if looking for something to throw up.

Tram's wound wasn't *there* anymore! Only a purplish blotch remained.

Tram raised his head and looked down at where the bullet had torn into him.

"The *Dat-tay-vao!* You have it now! Trinh passed it on to you! You have the *Dat-tay-vao!*"

I do? he thought, staring at the bullet rolling in his palm. Holy shit, I do!

He wouldn't have to get some gook back to the States to make his mint – all he had to do was get himself home in one piece.

Which made it all the more important to get the hell out of this village. Now.

"Let's go!"

"Fatman, you can't go. Not now. You must help. They–"

Patsy threw himself flat as something exploded in the jungle a hundred yards behind them, hurling a brown and green geyser of dirt and underbrush high into the air.

Mortar!

Another explosion followed close on the heels of the first, but this one was down by the waterline south of the village.

Tram was pointing out to sea.

"Look! They firing from boat." He laughed. "Can't aim mortar from boat!"

Patsy stayed hunkered down with his arms wrapped tight around his head, quaking with terror as the ground jittered with each of the next three explosions. Then they stopped.

"See?" Tram said, sitting boldly in the clearing and looking out to sea. "Even *they* know it foolish! They leaving. They only use for terror. Cong very good at terror."

No argument there, Patsy thought as he climbed once more to his feet.

"Get me out of here now, Tram. You owe me!"

Tram's eyes caught Patsy's and pinned him to the spot like an insect on a board. "Look at them, Fatman."

Patsy tore his gaze away and looked at the ville. He saw the villagers – the maimed and bleeding ones and their friends and families – looking back at him. Waiting. They said nothing, but their eyes...

He ripped his gaze loose. "Those Cong'll be back!"

"They need you, Fatman," Tram said. "You are only one who can help them now."

Patsy looked again, unwillingly. Their eyes... calling him. He could almost feel their hurt, their need.

"No way!"

He turned and began walking toward the brush. He'd find his own way back if Tram wouldn't lead him. Better than waiting around here to get caught and tortured by Charlie. It might take him all day, but –

"Fatman!" Tram shouted. "For once in your life!"

That stung. Patsy turned and looked at the villagers once more, feeling their need like a taut rope around his chest, pulling him toward them. He ground his teeth. It was idiotic to stay, but…

One more. Just one, to see if I still have it.

He could spare a couple of minutes for that, then be on his way. At least that way he'd be sure what had happened with Tram wasn't some sort of crazy freak accident.

Just one.

As he stepped toward the villagers, he heard their voices begin to murmur excitedly. He didn't know what they were saying but felt their grateful welcome like a warm current through the draw of their need.

He stopped at the nearest wounded villager, a woman holding a bloody, unconscious child in her arms. His stomach lurched as he saw the wound – a slug had nearly torn the kid's arm off at the shoulder. Blood oozed steadily between the fingers of the hand the woman kept clenched over the wound. Swallowing the revulsion that welled up in him, he slipped his hands under the mother's to touch the wound–

–and his knees almost buckled with the ecstasy that shot through him.

The child whimpered and opened his eyes. The mother removed her hand from the wound.

Make that *former* wound. It was gone, just like Tram's.

She cried out with joy and fell to her knees beside Patsy, clutching his leg as she wept.

Patsy swayed. He had it! No doubt about it – he had the goddamn *Dat-tay-vao!* And it felt so good! Not just the pleasure it caused, but how that little gook kid was looking up at him now with his bottomless black eyes and flashing him a shy smile. He felt high, like he'd been smoking some of his best merchandise.

One more. Just one more.

He disengaged his leg from the mother and moved over to where an old woman writhed in agony on the ground, clutching her abdomen.

Belly wound...I know the feeling, mama-san.

He knelt and wormed his hand under hers. That burst of pleasure surged again as she stiffened and two slugs popped into his hand. Her breathing eased and she looked up at him with gratitude beaming from her eyes.

Another!

On it went. Patsy could have stopped at any time, but found he didn't want to. The villagers seemed to have no doubt that he would stay and heal them all. They knew he could do it and *expected* him to do it. It was so new, such a unique feeling, he didn't want it to end. Ever. He felt a sense of belonging he'd never known before. He felt protective of the villagers. But it went beyond them, beyond this little ville, seemed to take in the whole world.

Finally, it was over.

Patsy stood in the clearing before the huts, looking for another wounded body. He checked his watch – he'd been at it only thirty minutes and there were no more villagers left to heal. They all clustered around him at a respectful distance, watching silently. He gave himself up to the euphoria enveloping him, blending with the sound of the waves, the wind in the trees, the cries of the gulls. He hadn't realized what a beautiful place this was. If only–

A new sound intruded – the drone of a boat engine. Patsy looked out at the water and saw the Cong gunboat returning. Fear knifed through the pleasurable haze as the villagers scattered for the trees. Were the Cong going to land?

No. Patsy saw a couple of the crew crouched on the deck, heard the familiar *choonk!* of a mortar shell shooting out of its tube. An explosion quickly followed somewhere back in the jungle. Tram had been right. No way could they get any accuracy with a mortar on the rocking deck of a gunboat. Just terror tactics.

Damn those bastards! Why'd they have to come back and wreck his mood? Just when he'd been feeling good for the first time since leaving home. Matter of fact, he'd been feeling better than he could ever remember, home or anywhere else. For once, everything seemed *right.*

For once, something was going Patsy's way, and the Cong had to ruin it.

Two more wild mortar shots, then he heard gunfire start from the south and saw three new gunboats roaring up toward the first. But these were flying the old red, white, and blue. Patsy laughed and raised his fist.

"Get 'em!"

The Cong let one more shell go *choonk*! before pouring on the gas and slewing away.

Safe!

Then he heard a whine from above and the world exploded under him.

9

...a voice from far away...Tram's...

"*...chopper coming, Fatman...get you away soon... hear it?... almost here...*"

Patsy opened his eyes and saw the sky, then saw Tram's face poke into view. He looked sick.

"Fatman!' You hear me?"

"How bad?" Patsy asked.

"You be okay."

Patsy turned his head and saw a ring of weeping villagers who were looking everywhere and anywhere but at him. He realized he couldn't feel anything below his neck. He tried to lift his head for a look at himself but didn't have the strength.

"I wanna see."

"You rest," Tram said.

"Get my head up, dammit!"

With obvious reluctance, Tram gently lifted his head. As Patsy looked down at what was left of him, he heard a high, keening wail. His vision swam, mercifully blotting out sight of the bloody ruin that had once been the lower half of his body. He realized that the wail was his own voice.

Tram lowered his head and the wail stopped.

I shouldn't even be alive!

Then he knew. He was waiting for someone. Not just anyone would do. A certain someone.

A hazy peace came. He drifted into it and stayed there until the chopping thrum of a slick brought him out; then he heard an American voice.

"I thought you said he was alive!"

Tram's voice: "He is."

Patsy opened his eyes and saw the shocked face of an American soldier.

"Who are you?" Patsy asked.

"Walt Erskine. Medic. I'm gonna–"

"You're the one," Patsy said. Somehow, he bent his arm at the elbow and lifted his hand. "Shake."

The medic looked confused. "Yeah. Okay. Sure."

He grabbed Patsy's hand and Patsy felt the searing electric charge.

Erskine jerked back and fell on his ass, clutching his hand. "What the *hell*?"

The peace closed in on Patsy again. He'd held on as long as he could. Now he could embrace it. One final thought arced through his mind like a lone meteorite in a starless sky. The *Dattay-vao* was going to America after all.

FACES

I'd been perking a story about a serial killer (this was 1987, before THE SILENCE OF THE LAMBS and the subsequent serial-killer glut) but one with a difference. This one would be female (they're almost always male), hideously deformed, and sympathetic. I felt if I could tell you about the forces driving Carly to these murderous acts – her childhood, her needs, her emotional hungers – you might understand her. You might even find some sort of love for her.

Where does this fit in the Secret History? Carly is part of what became known as the "Monroe Cluster," further explored in *Conspiracies*.

Toward the end of 1968, over a period of ten days, half a dozen deformed children were born in Monroe. Melanie Rubin and Frayne Canfield, from *Conspiracies*, were two. Carly Baker and Susan Harrison of "Faces" were two more. An investigative team from Mount Sinai Medical Center investigated but came up empty as to the cause. Melanie Rubin claimed it was due to "a burst of Otherness" which, in turn, meant that the members of the Monroe Cluster were what she called "Children of the Otherness."

And where might that "burst of Otherness" have originated? Well, all the children of the cluster were conceived right about the same time Rasalom became flesh again by co-opting the newly conceived child of another resident of Monroe – Carol Stevens – in *Reborn*.

Faces

Bite her face off.

No pain. Her dead already. Kill her quick like others. Not want make pain. Not her fault.

The boyfriend groan but not move. Face way on ground now. Got from behind. Got quick. Never see. He can live.

Girl look me after the boyfriend go down. Gasp first. When see face start scream. Two claws not cut short rip her throat before sound get loud.

Her sick-scared look just like all others. Hate that look. Hate it terrible.

Sorry, girl. Not your fault.

Chew her face skin. Chew all. Chew hard and swallow. Warm wet redness make sickish but chew and chew. Must eat face. Must get all down. Keep down.

Leave the eyes.

The boyfriend groan again. Move arm. Must leave quick. Take last look blood and teeth and stare-eyes that once pretty girlface.

Sorry, girl. Not your fault.

Got go. Get way hurry. First take money. Girl money. Take the boyfriend wallet, also too. Always take money. Need money.

Go now. Not too far. Climb wall of near building. Find dark spot where can see and not be seen. Where can wait. Soon the Detective Harrison arrive.

In downbelow can see the boyfriend roll over. Get to knees. Sway. See him look the girlfriend.

The boyfriend scream terrible. Bad to hear. Make so sad. Make cry.

*

Kevin Harrison heard Jacobi's voice on the other end of the line and wanted to be sick.

"Don't say it," he groaned.

"Sorry," said Jacobi. "It's another one."

"Where?"

"West Forty-ninth, right near–"

"I'll find it." All he had to do was look for the flashing red lights. "I'm on my way. Shouldn't take me too long to get in from Monroe at this hour."

"We've got all night, lieutenant." Unsaid, but well understood, was an admonishing, *You're the one who wants to live on Long Island.*

Beside him in the bed, Martha spoke from deep in her pillow as he hung up.

"Not another one?"

"Yeah."

"Oh, God! When is it going to stop?"

"When I catch the guy."

Her hand touched his arm, gently. "I know all this responsibility's not easy. I'm here when you need me."

"I know." He leaned over and kissed her. "Thanks."

He left the warm bed and skipped the shower. No time for that. A fresh shirt, yesterday's rumpled suit, a tie shoved into his pocket, and he was off into the winter night.

With his secure little ranch house falling away behind him, Harrison felt naked and vulnerable out here in the dark. As he headed south on Glen Cove Road toward the LIE, he realized that Martha and the kids were all that were holding him together these days. His family had become an island of sanity and stability in a world gone mad.

Everything else was in flux. For reasons he still could not comprehend, he had volunteered to head up the search for this killer. Now his whole future in the department had come to hinge on his success in finding him.

The papers had named the maniac "the Facelift Killer." As

apt a name as the tabloids could want, but Harrison resented it. The moniker was callous, trivializing the mutilations perpetrated on the victims. But it had caught on with the public and they were stuck with it, especially with all the ink the story was getting.

Six killings, one a week for six weeks in a row, and eight million people in a panic. Then, for almost two weeks, the city had gone without a new slaying.

Until tonight.

Harrison's stomach pitched and rolled at the thought of having to look at one of those faceless corpses again.

*

"That's enough," Harrison said, averting his eyes from the faceless corpse.

The raw, gouged, bloody flesh, the exposed muscle and bone were bad enough, but it was the eyes – those naked, lidless, staring eyes were the worst.

"This makes seven," Jacobi said at his side. Squat, dark, jowly, the sergeant was chewing a big wad of gum, noisily, aggressively, as if he had a grudge against it.

"I can count. Anything new?"

"Nah. Same M.O. as ever – throat slashed, money stolen, face gnawed off."

Harrison shuddered. He had come in as Special Investigator after the third Facelift killing. He had inspected the first three via coroner's photos. Those had been awful. But nothing could match the effect of the real thing up close and still warm and oozing. This was the fourth fresh victim he had seen. There was no getting used to this kind of mutilation, no matter how many he saw. Jacobi put on a good show, but Harrison sensed the revulsion under the sergeant's armor.

And yet...

Beneath all the horror, Harrison sensed something. There was anger here, sick anger and hatred of spectacular proportions. But beyond that, something else, an indefinable something that had drawn him to this case. Whatever it was, that something called to him, and still held him captive.

If he could identify it, maybe he could solve this case and wrap it up. And save his ass.

If he did solve it, it would be all on his own. Because he wasn't getting much help from Jacobi, and even less from his assigned staff. He knew what they all thought – that he had taken the job as a glory grab, a shortcut to the top. Sure, they wanted to see this thing wrapped up, too, but they weren't shedding any tears over the shit he was taking in the press and on TV and from City Hall.

Their attitude was clear: *If you want the spotlight, Harrison, you gotta take the heat that goes with it.*

They were right, of course. He could have been working on a quieter case, like where all the winos were disappearing to. He'd chosen this instead. But he wasn't after the spotlight, dam mit! It was this case – something about this case!

He suddenly realized that there was no one around him. The body had been carted off, Jacobi had wandered back to his car. He had been left standing alone at the far end of the alley.

And yet not alone.

Someone was watching him. He could feel it. The realization sent a little chill – one completely unrelated to the cold February wind – trickling down his back. A quick glance around showed no one paying him the slightest bit of attention. He looked up.

There!

Somewhere in the darkness above, someone was watching him. Probably from the roof. He could sense the piercing scrutiny and it made him a little weak. That was no ghoulish neighborhood voyeur, up there. That was the Facelift Killer.

He had to get to Jacobi, have him seal off the building. But he couldn't act spooked. He had to act calm, casual.

*

See the Detective Harrison's eyes. See from way up in dark. Tall-thin. Hair brown. Nice eyes. Soft brown eyes. Not hard like many-many eyes. Look here. Even from here see eyes make wide. Him know it me.

Watch the Detective Harrison turn slow. Walk slow. Tell inside him want to run. Must leave here. Leave quick.

Bend low. Run cross roof. Jump to next. And next. Again till most block away. Then down wall. Wrap scarf round head. Hide bad-face. Hunch inside big-big coat. Walk through lighted spots.

Hate light. Hate crowds. Theatres here. Movies and plays. Like them. Some night sneak in and see. See one with man in mask. Hang from wall behind big drapes. Make cry.

Wish there mask for me.

Follow street long way to river. See many light across river. Far past there is place where grew. Never want go back to there. Never.

Catch back of truck. Ride home.

Home. Bright bulb hang ceiling. Not care. The Old Jessi waiting. The Jessi friend. Only friend. The Jessi's eyes not see. Ever. When the Jessi look me, her face not wear sick-scared look. Hate that look.

Come in kitchen window. The Jessi's face wrinkle-black. Smile when hear me come. TV on. Always on. The Jessi cannot watch. Say it company for her.

"You're so late tonight."

"Hard work. Get moneys tonight."

Feel sick. Want cry. Hate kill. Wish stop.

"That's nice. Are you going to put it in the drawer?"

"Doing now."

Empty wallets. Put moneys in slots. Ones first slot. Fives next slot. Then tens and twenties. So the Jessi can pay when boy bring foods. Sometimes eat stealed foods. Mostly the Jessi call for foods.

The Old Jessi hardly walk. Good. Do not want her go out. Bad peoples round here. Many. Hurt one who not see. One bad man try hurt Jessi once. Push through door. Thought only the blind Old Jessi live here.

Lucky the Jessi not along that day.

Not lucky bad man. Hit the Jessi. Laugh hard. Then look me. Get sick-scared look. Hate that look. Kill him quick. Put in tub. Bleed there. Bad man friend come soon after. Kill him also too. Late at night take both dead bad men out. Go through window. Carry down wall. Throw in river.

No bad men come again. Ever.

"I've been waiting all night for my bath. Do you think you can help me a little?"

Always help. But the Old Jessi always ask. The Jessi very polite.

Sponge the Old Jessi back in tub. Rinse her hair. Think of the Detective Harrison. His kind eyes. Must talk him. Want stop this. Stop now. Maybe will understand. Will. Can feel

*

Seven grisly murders in eight weeks.

Kevin Harrison studied a photo of the latest victim, taken before she was mutilated. A nice eight by ten glossy furnished by her agent. A real beauty. A dancer with Broadway dreams.

He tossed the photo aside and pulled the stack of files toward him. The remnants of six lives in this pile. Somewhere within had to be an answer, the thread that linked each of them to the Facelift Killer.

But what if there was no common link? What if were all the killings were at random, linked only by the fact that they were beautiful? Seven deaths, all over the city. All with their faces gnawed off. *Gnawed.*

He flipped through the victims one by one and studied their photos. He had begun to feel he knew each one of them personally:

Mary Detrick, 20, a junior at N.Y.U., killed in Washington Square Park on January 5. She was the first.

Mia Chandler, 25, a secretary at Merrill Lynch, killed January 13 in Battery Park.

Ellen Beasley, 22, a photographer's assistant, killed in an alley in Chelsea on January 22.

Hazel Hauge, 30, artist agent, killed in her Soho loft on Jan-

F. Paul Wilson

uary 27.

Elisabeth Paine, 28, housewife, killed on February 2 while jogging late in Central Park.

Joan Perrin, 25, a model from Brooklyn, pulled from her car while stopped at a light on the Upper East Side on February 8.

He picked up the eight by ten again. And the last: Liza Lee, 21. Dancer. Lived across the river in Jersey City. Ducked into an alley for a toot with her boyfriend tonight and never came out.

Three blondes, three brunettes, one redhead. Some stacked, some on the flat side. All caucs except for Perrin. All lookers. But besides that, how in the world could these women be linked? They came from all over town, and they met their respective ends all over town. What could–

"Well, you sure hit the bullseye about that roof!" Jacobi said as he burst into the office.

Harrison straightened in his chair. "What you find?"

"Blood."

"Whose?"

"The victim's."

"No prints? No hairs? No fibers?"

"We're working on it. But how'd you figure to check the roof top?"

"Lucky guess."

Harrison didn't want to provide Jacobi with more grist for the departmental gossip mill by mentioning his feeling of being watched from up there.

But the killer *had* been watching, hadn't he?

"Any prelims from pathology?"

Jacobi shrugged and stuffed three sticks of gum into his mouth. Then he tried to talk.

"Same as ever. Money gone, throat ripped open by a pair of sharp pointed instruments, not knives, the bite marks on the face are the usual: the teeth that made them aren't human, but the saliva is."

The "non-human" teeth part – more teeth, bigger and sharper teeth that found in any human mouth – had baffled

100

them all from the start. Early on someone remembered a horror novel or movie where the killer used some weird sort of false teeth to bite his victims. That had sent them off on a wild goose chase to all the dental labs looking for records of bizarre bite prostheses. No dice. No one had seen or even heard of teeth that could gnaw off a person's face.

Harrison shuddered. What could explain wounds like that? What were they dealing with here?

The irritating pops, snaps, and cracks of Jacobi's gum filled the office.

"I liked you better when you smoked."

Jacobi's reply was cut off by the phone. The sergeant picked it up.

"Detective Harrison's office!" he said, listened a moment, then, with his hand over the mouthpiece, passed the receiver to Harrison. "Some fairy to shpeak to you," he said with an evil grin.

"Fairy?"

"Hey," he said, getting up and walking toward the door. "I don't mind. I'm a liberal kinda guy, y'know?"

Harrison shook his head with disgust. Jacobi was getting less likable every day.

"Hello. Harrison here."

"Shorry dishturb you, Detective Harrishon."

The voice was soft, pitched somewhere between a man's and a woman's, and sounded as if the speaker had half a mouthful of saliva. Harrison had never heard anything like it. Who could be–?

And then it struck him: It was three a.m. Only a handful of people knew he was here.

"Do I know you?"

"No. Watch you tonight. You almosht shee me in dark."

That same chill from earlier tonight ran down Harrison's back again.

"Are...are you who I think you are?"

There was a pause, then one soft word, more sobbed than

spoken:

"Yesh."

If the reply had been cocky – something along the line of *And just who do you think I am?* – Harrison would have looked for much more in the way of corroboration. But that single word, and the soul deep heartbreak that propelled it, banished all doubt.

My God! He looked around frantically. No one in sight. Where the fuck was Jacobi now when he needed him? This was the Facelift Killer! He needed a trace!

Got to keep him on the line!

"I have to ask you something to be sure you are who you say you are."

"Yesh?"

"Do you take anything from the victims – I mean, besides their faces?"

"Money. Take money."

This is him! The department had withheld the money part from the papers. Only the real Facelift Killer could know!

"Can I ask you something else?"

"Yesh."

Harrison was asking this one for himself.

"What do you do with the faces?"

He had to know. The question drove him crazy at night. He dreamed about those faces. Did the killer tack them on the wall, or press them in a book, or freeze them, or did he wear them around the house like that Leatherface character from that chainsaw movie?

On the other end of the line he sensed sudden agitation and panic: *"No! Can not shay! Can not!"*

"Okay, okay. Take it easy."

"You will help shtop?"

"Oh, yes! Oh, God, yes, I'll help you stop!" He prayed his genuine heartfelt desire to end this was coming through. "I'll help you any way I can!"

A long pause, then:

"You hate? Hate me?"

Harrison didn't trust himself to answer that right away. He searched his feelings quickly, but carefully.

"No," he said finally. "I think you have done some awful, horrible things but, strangely enough, I don't hate you."

And that was true. Why didn't he hate this murdering maniac? Oh, he wanted to stop him more than anything in the world, and wouldn't hesitate to shoot him dead if the situation required it, but there was no personal hatred for the Facelift Killer.

What is it in you that speaks to me? he wondered.

"Shank you," said the voice, couched once more in a sob.

And then the killer hung up.

Harrison shouted into the dead phone, banged it on his desk, but the line was dead.

"What the hell's the matter with you?" Jacobi said from the office door.

"That so-called 'fairy' on the phone was the Facelift Killer, you idiot! We could have had a trace if you'd stuck around!"

"Bullshit!"

"He knew about taking the money!"

"So why'd he talk like that? That's a dumb-ass way to try to disguise your voice."

And then it suddenly hit Harrison like a sucker punch to the gut. He swallowed hard and said:

"Jacobi, how do you think your voice would sound if you had a mouth crammed full of teeth much larger and sharper than the kind found in the typical human mouth?"

Harrison took genuine pleasure in the way Jacobi's face blanched slowly to yellow-white.

*

He didn't get home again until after seven the following night. The whole department had been in an uproar all day. This was the first break they had had in the case. It wasn't much, but contact had been made. That was the important part. And although Harrison had done nothing he could think of to de-

F. Paul Wilson

serve any credit, he had accepted the commissioner's compliments and encouragement on the phone shortly before he had left the office tonight.

But what was most important to Harrison was the evidence from the call – Damn! He wished it had been taped – that the killer wanted to stop. They didn't have one more goddam clue tonight than they'd had yesterday, but the call offered hope that soon there might be an end to this horror.

Martha had dinner waiting. The kids were scrubbed and pajamaed and waiting for their goodnight kiss. He gave them each a hug and poured himself a stiff scotch while Martha put them in the sack.

"Do you feel as tired as you look?" she said as she returned from the bedroom wing.

She was a big woman with bright blue eyes and natural dark blond hair. Harrison toasted her with his glass.

"The expression 'dead on his feet' has taken on a whole new meaning for me."

She kissed him, then they sat down to eat.

He had spoken to Martha a couple of times since he had left the house twenty hours ago. She knew about the phone call from the Facelift Killer, about the new hope in the department about the case, but he was glad she didn't bring it up now. He was sick of talking about it. Instead, he sat in front of his cooling meatloaf and wrestled with the images that had been nibbling at the edges of his consciousness all day.

"What are you daydreaming about?" Martha said.

Without thinking, Harrison said, "Annie."

"Annie who?"

"My sister."

Martha put her fork down. "Your sister? Kevin, you don't have a sister."

"Not any more. But I did."

Her expression was alarmed now. "Kevin, are you all right? I've known your family for ten years. You mother has never once mentioned–"

"We don't talk about Annie, Mar. We try not to even think about her. She died when she was five."

"Oh. I'm sorry."

"Don't be. Annie was...deformed. Terribly deformed. She never really had a chance."

*

Open trunk from inside. Get out. The Detective Harrison's house here. Cold night. Cold feel good. Trunk air make sick, dizzy.

Light here. Hurry round side of house.

Darker here. No one see. Look in window. Dark but see good. Two little ones there. Sleeping. Move away. Not want them cry.

Go more round. The Detective Harrison with lady. Sit table near window. Must be wife. Pretty but not oh-so-beauty. Not have mom-face. Not like ones who die.

Watch behind tree. Hungry. They not eat food. Talk-talk-talk. Can not hear.

The Detective Harrison do most talk. Kind face. Kind eyes. Some terrible sad there. Hides. Him understands. Heard in phone voice. Understands. Him one can stop kills.

Spent day watch the Detective Harrison car. All day watch at police house. Saw him come-go many times. Soon dark, open trunk with claw. Ride with him. Ride long. Wonder what town this?

The Detective Harrison look this way. Stare like last night. Must not see me! Must *not!*

*

Harrison stopped in mid-sentence and stared out the window as his skin prickled.

That *watched* feeling again.

It was the same as last night. Something was out in the backyard watching them. He strained to see through the wooded darkness outside the window but saw only shadows within shadows.

But something was there! He could feel it!

He got up and turned on the outside spotlights, hoping, praying that the backyard would be empty.

It was.

He smiled to hide his relief and glanced at Martha.

"Thought that raccoon was back."

He left the spots on and settled back into his place at the table. But the thoughts racing through his mind made eating unthinkable.

What if that maniac had followed him out here? What if the call had been a ploy to get him off-guard so the Facelift Killer could do to Martha what he had done to the other women?

My God...

First thing tomorrow morning he was going to call the local alarm boys and put in a security system. Cost be damned, he had to have it. Immediately!

As for tonight...

Tonight he'd keep the .38 under the pillow.

*

Run way. Run low and fast. Get bushes before light come. Must stay way now. Not come back.

The Detective Harrison *feel* me. Know when watched. Him the one, sure.

Walk in dark, in woods. See back many houses. Come park. Feel strange. See this park before. Can not be –

Then know.

Monroe! This Monroe! Born here! Live here! Hate Monroe! Monroe bad place, bad people! House, home, old home near here! There! Cross park! Old home! New color but same house.

Hate house!

Sit on froze park grass. Cry. Why Monroe? Do not want be in Monroe. The Mom gone. The Sissy gone. The Jimmy very gone. House here.

Dry tears. Watch old home long time till light go out. Wait more. Go to windows. See new folks inside. The Mom must took the Sissy and go. Where? How long?

Go to back. Push cellar window. Crawl in. See good in dark.

New folks make nice cellar. Wood on walls. Rug on floor. No chain.

Sit floor. Remember...

Remember hanging on wall. Look little window near ceiling. Watch kids play in park cross street. Want go with kids. Want play there with kids. Want have friends.

But the Mom won't let. Never leave basement. Too strong. Break everything. Have TV. Broke it. Have toys. Broke them. Stay in basement. Chain round waist hold to center pole. Can not leave.

Remember terrible bad things happen.

Run. Run way Monroe. Never come back.

Till now.

Now back. Still hate house! Want hurt house. See cigarettes. With matches. Light all. Burn now!

Watch rug burn. Chair burn. So hot. Run back to cold park. Watch house burn. See new folks run out. Trucks come throw water. House burn and burn.

Glad but tears come anyway.

Hate house. Now house gone. Hate Monroe.

Wonder where the Mom and the Sissy live now.

Leave Monroe for new home and the Old Jessi.

*

The second call came the next day. And this time they were ready for it. The tape recorders were set, the computers were waiting to begin the tracing protocol. As soon as Harrison recognized the voice, he gave the signal. On the other side of the desk, Jacobi put on a headset and people started running in all directions. Off to the races.

"I'm glad you called," Harrison said. "I've been thinking about you."

"You undershtand?" said the soft voice.

"I'm not sure."

"Musht help shtop."

"I will! I will! Tell me how!"

"Not know."

Harrison paused, not sure what to say next. He didn't want to push, but he had to keep him on the line.

"Did you...hurt anyone last night."

"No. Shaw houshes. Your houshe. Your wife."

Harrison's blood froze. Last night – in the back yard. That had been the Facelift Killer in the dark. He looked up and saw genuine concern in Jacobi's eyes. He forced himself to speak.

"You were at my house? Why didn't you talk to me?"

"No-no! Can not let shee! Run way your house. Go mine!"

"Yours? You live in Monroe?"

"No! Hate Monroe! Once lived. Gone long! Burn old houshe. Never go back!"

This could be important. Harrison phrased the next question carefully.

"You burned your old house? When was that?"

If he could just get a date, a year...

"Lasht night."

"Last night?" Harrison remembered hearing the sirens and fire horns in the early morning darkness.

"Yesh! Hate houshe!"

And then the line went dead.

*

He looked at Jacobi who had picked up another line.

"Did we get the trace?"

"Waiting to hear. Christ, he sounds retarded, doesn't he?"

Retarded. The word sent ripples across the surface of his brain. Non-human teeth...Monroe...retarded...a picture was forming in the settling sediment, a picture he felt he should avoid.

"Maybe he is."

"You'd think that would make him easy to–"

Jacobi stopped, listened to the receiver, then shook his head disgustedly.

"What?"

"Got as far as the Lower East Side. He was probably calling from somewhere in one of the projects. If we'd had another thirty seconds–"

"We've got something better than a trace to some lousy pay phone," Harrison said. "We've got his old address!" He picked up his suit coat and headed for the door.

"Where we goin'?"

"Not 'we.' Me. I'm going out to Monroe."

*

Once he reached the town, it took Harrison less than an hour to find the Facelift Killer's last name.

He first checked with the Monroe Fire Department to find the address of last night's house fire. Then he went down to the brick fronted Town Hall and found the lot and block number. After that it was easy to look up its history of ownership. Mr. and Mrs. Elwood Scott were the current owners of the land and the charred shell of a three-bedroom ranch that sat upon it.

There had only been one other set of owners: Mr. and Mrs. Thomas Baker. He had lived most of his life in Monroe but knew nothing about the Baker family. But he knew where to find out: Captain Jeremy Hall, Chief of Police in the Incorporated Village of Monroe.

Captain Hall hadn't changed much over the years. Still had a big belly, long sideburns, and hair cut bristly short on the sides. That was the "in" look these days, but Hall had been wearing his hair like that for at least thirty years. If not for his Bronx accent, he could have played a redneck sheriff in any one of those southern chain gang movies.

After pleasantries and local-boy-leaves-home-to-become-big-city-cop-and-now-comes-to-question-small-town-cop banter, they got down to business.

"The Bakers from North Park Drive?" Hall said after he had noisily sucked the top layer off his steaming coffee. "Who could forget them? There was the mother, divorced, I believe, and the three kids – two girls and the boy."

Harrison pulled out his note pad. "The boy's name – what was it?"

"Tommy, I believe. Yeah – Tommy. I'm sure of it."

"He's the one I want."

Hall's eyes narrowed. "He is, is he? You're working on that Facelift case aren't you?"

"Right."

"And you think Tommy Baker might be your man?"

"It's a possibility. What do you know about him?"

"I know he's dead."

Harrison froze. "Dead? That can't be!"

"It sure as hell *can* be!" Without rising from his seat, he shouted through his office door. "Murph! Pull out that old file on the Baker case! Nineteen eighty-four, I believe!"

"Eighty-four?" Harrison said. He and Martha had been living in Queens then. They hadn't moved back to Monroe yet.

"Right. A real messy affair. Tommy Baker was thirteen years old when he bought it. And he bought it. Believe me, he bought it!"

Harrison sat in glum silence, watching his whole theory go up in smoke.

*

The Old Jessi sleeps. Stand by mirror near tub. Only mirror have. No like them. The Jessi not need one.

Stare face. Bad face. Teeth, teeth, teeth. And hair. Arms too thin, too long. Claws. None have claws like my. None have face like my.

Face not better. Ate pretty faces but face still same. Still cause sick-scared look. Just like at home.

Remember home. Do not want but thoughts will not go.

Faces.

The Sissy get the Mom-face. Beauty face. The Tommy get the Dad-face. Not see the Dad. Never come home anymore. Who my face? Never see where come. Where my face come? My hands come?

Remember home cellar. Hate home! Hate cellar more! Pull on chain round waist. Pull and pull. Want out. Want play. Please. No one let.

One day when the Mom and the Sissy go, the Tommy bring

friends. Come down cellar. Bunch on stairs. Stare. First time see sick-scared look. Not understand.

Friends! Play! Throw ball them. They run. Come back with rocks and sticks. Still sick-scared look. Throw me, hit me.

Make cry. Make the Tommy laugh.

Whenever the Mom and the Sissy go, the Tommy come with boys and sticks. Poke and hit. Hurt. Little hurt on skin. Big hurt inside. Sick-scared look hurt most of all. Hate look. Hate hurt. Hate them.

Most hate the Tommy.

One night chain breaks. Wait on wall for the Tommy. Hurt him. Hurt the Tommy outside. Hurt the Tommy inside. Know because pull inside outside. The Tommy quiet. Quiet, wet, red. The Mom and the Sissy get sick-scared look and scream.

Hate that look. Run way. Hide. Never come back. Till last night.

Cry more now. Cry quiet. In tub. So the Jessi not hear.

*

Harrison flipped through the slim file on the Tommy Baker murder.

"This is it?"

"We didn't need to collect much paper," Captain Hall said. "I mean, the mother and sister were witnesses. There's some photos in that manila envelope at the back."

Harrison pulled it free and slipped out some large black and whites. His stomach lurched immediately.

"My God!"

"Yeah, he was a mess. Gutted by his older sister."

"His sister?"

"Yeah. Apparently she was some sort of freak of nature."

Harrison felt the floor tilt under him, felt as if he were going to slide off the chair.

"Freak?" he said, hoping Hall wouldn't notice the tremor in his voice. "What did she look like?"

"Never saw her. She took off after she killed the brother. No one's seen hide nor hair of her since. But there's a picture of the rest of the family in there."

Harrison shuffled through the file until he came to a large color family portrait. He held it up. Four people: two adults seated in chairs, a boy and a girl, about ten and eight, kneeling on the floor in front of them. A perfectly normal American family. Four smiling faces.

But where's your oldest child. Where's your big sister? Where did you hide that fifth face while posing for this?

"What was her name? The one who's not here?"

"Not sure. Carla, maybe? Look at the front sheet under Suspect."

Harrison did: "Carla Baker – called 'Carly.'"

Hall grinned. "Right. Carly. Not bad for a guy getting ready for retirement."

Harrison didn't answer. An ineluctable sadness filled him as he stared at the incomplete family portrait.

Carly Baker...poor Carly... where did they hide you away? In the cellar? Locked in the attic? How did your brother treat you? Bad enough to deserve killing?

Probably.

"No pictures of Carly, I suppose."

"Not a one."

That figured.

"How about a description?"

"The mother gave us one but it sounded so weird, we threw it out. I mean, the girl sounded like she was half spider or something!" He drained his cup. "Then later on I got into a discussion with Doc Alberts about it. He told me he was doing deliveries back about the time this kid was born. Said they had a whole rash of monsters, all delivered within a few weeks of each other."

The room started to tilt under Harrison again.

"Early December, 1968, by chance?"

"Yeah! How'd you know?"

He felt queasy. "Lucky guess."

"Huh. Anyway, Doc Alberts said they kept it quiet while

they looked into a cause, but that little group of freaks – 'cluster,' he called them – was all there was. They figured that a bunch of mothers had been exposed to something nine months before, but whatever it had been was long gone. No monsters since. I understand most of them died shortly after birth, anyway."

"Not all of them."

"Not that it matters," Hall said, getting up and pouring himself a refill from the coffee pot. "Someday someone will find her skeleton, probably somewhere out in Haskins' marshes."

"Maybe." But I wouldn't count on it. He held up the file. "Can I get a Xerox of this?"

*

"You mean the Facelift Killer is a twenty-year old girl?"

Martha's face clearly registered her disbelief.

"Not just any girl. A freak. Someone so deformed she really doesn't look human. Completely uneducated and probably mentally retarded to boot."

Harrison hadn't returned to Manhattan. Instead, he'd headed straight for home, less than a mile from Town Hall. He knew the kids were at school and that Martha would be there alone. That was what he had wanted. He needed to talk this out with someone a lot more sensitive than Jacobi.

Besides, what he had learned from Captain Hall and the Baker file had dredged up the most painful memories of his entire life.

"A monster," Martha said.

"Yeah. Born one on the outside, made one on the inside. But there's another child monster I want to talk about. Not Carly Baker. Annie... Ann Harrison."

Martha gasped. "That sister you told me about last night?"

Harrison nodded. He knew this was going to hurt, but he had to do it, had to get it out. He was going to explode into a thousand twitching bloody pieces if he didn't.

"I was nine when she was born. December 2, 1968 – a week after Carly Baker. Seven pounds, four ounces of horror. She looked more fish than human."

His sister's image was imprinted on the rear wall of his brain. And it should have been after all those hours he had spent studying her in loathsome face. Only her eyes looked human. The rest of her was awful. A lipless mouth, flattened nose, sloping forehead, fingers and toes fused so that they looked more like flippers than hands and feet, a bloated body covered with shiny skin that was a dusky gray-blue. The doctors said she was that color because her heart was bad, had a defect that caused mixing of blue blood and red blood.

A repulsed nine-year old Kevin Harrison had dubbed her The Tuna – but never within earshot of his parents.

"She wasn't supposed to live long. A few months, they said, and she'd be dead. But she didn't die. Annie lived on and on. One year. Two. My father and the doctors tried to get my mother to put her into some sort of institution, but Mom wouldn't hear of it. She kept Annie in the third bedroom and talked to her and cooed over her and cleaned up her shit and just hung over her all the time. All the time, Martha!"

Martha gripped his hand and nodded for him to go on.

"After a while, it got so there was nothing else in Mom's life. She wouldn't leave Annie. Family trips became a thing of the past. Christ, if she and Dad went out to a movie, *I* had to stay with Annie. No babysitter was trustworthy enough. Our whole lives seemed to center around that freak in the back bedroom. And me? I was forgotten.

"After a while I began to hate my sister."

"Kevin, you don't have to–"

"Yes, I do! I've got to tell you how it was! By the time I was fourteen – just about Tommy Baker's age when he bought it – I thought I was going to go crazy. I was getting all B's in school but did that matter? Hell, no! 'Annie rolled halfway over today. Isn't that wonderful?' Big deal! She was five years old, for Christ sake! I was starting point guard on the high school junior varsity basketball team as a goddam freshman, but did anyone come to my games? Hell no!

"I tell you, Martha, after five years of caring for Annie, our house was a powder keg. Looking back now I can see it was my mother's fault for becoming so obsessed. But back then, at age fourteen, I blamed it all on Annie. I really hated her for being born a freak."

He paused before going on. This was the really hard part.

"One night, when my dad had managed to drag my mother out to some company banquet that he had to attend, I was left alone to babysit Annie. On those rare occasions, my mother would always tell me to keep Annie company – you know, read her stories and such. But I never did. I'd let her lie back there alone with our old black and white TV while I sat in the living room watching the family set. This time, however, I went into her room."

He remembered the sight of her, lying there with the covers half way up her fat little tuna body that couldn't have been much more than a yard in length. It was winter, like now, and his mother had dressed her in a flannel nightshirt. The coarse hair that grew off the back of her head had been wound into two braids and fastened with pink bows.

"Annie's eyes brightened as I came into the room. She had never spoken. Couldn't, it seemed. Her face could do virtually nothing in the way of expression, and her flipper-like arms weren't good for much, either. You had to read her eyes, and that wasn't easy. None of us knew how much of a brain Annie had, or how much she understood of what was going on around her. My mother said she was bright, but I think Mom was a little whacko on the subject of Annie.

"Anyway, I stood over her crib and started shouting at her. She quivered at the sound. I called her every dirty name in the book. And as I said each one, I poked her with my fingers – not enough to leave a bruise, but enough to let out some of the violence in me. I called her a lousy goddam tuna fish with feet. I told her how much I hated her and how I wished she had never been born. I told her everybody hated her and the only thing she was good for was a freak show. Then I said, 'I wish you were

115

dead! Why don't you die? You were supposed to die years ago! Why don't you do everyone a favor and do it now!'

"When I ran out of breath, she looked at me with those big eyes of hers and I could see the tears in them and I knew she had understood me. She rolled over and faced the wall. I ran from the room.

"I cried myself to sleep that night. I'd thought I'd feel good telling her off, but all I kept seeing in my mind's eye was this fourteen-year old bully shouting at a helpless five-year old. I felt awful. I promised myself that the first opportunity I had to be alone with her the next day I'd apologize, tell her I really didn't mean the hateful things I'd said, promise to read to her and be her best friend, anything to make it up to her.

"I awoke next morning to the sound of my mother screaming. Annie was dead."

"Oh, my God!" Martha said, her fingers digging into his arm.

"Naturally, I blamed myself."

"But you said she had a heart defect!"

"Yeah. I know. And the autopsy showed that's what killed her – her heart finally gave out. But I've never been able to get it out of my head that my words where what made her heart give up. Sounds sappy and melodramatic, I know, but I've always felt that she was just hanging on to life by the slimmest margin and that I pushed her over the edge."

"Kevin, you shouldn't have to carry that around with you! Nobody should!"

The old grief and guilt were like a slowly expanding balloon in his chest. It was getting hard to breathe.

"In my coolest, calmest, most dispassionate moments I convince myself that it was all a terrible coincidence, that she would have died that night anyway and that I had nothing to do with it."

"That's probably true, so–"

"But that doesn't change that fact that the last memory of her life was of her big brother – the guy she probably thought was the neatest kid on earth, who could run and play basketball, one of the three human beings who made up her whole world, who should have been her champion, her defender against a world that could only greet her with revulsion and rejection – standing over her crib telling her how much he hated her and how he wished she was dead!"

He felt the sobs begin to quake in his chest. He hadn't cried in over a dozen years and he had no intention of allowing himself to start now, but there didn't seem to be any stopping it. It was like running downhill at top speed – if he tried to stop before he reached bottom, he'd go head over heels and break his neck.

"Kevin, you were only fourteen," Martha said soothingly.

"Yeah, I know. But if I could go back in time for just a few seconds, I'd go back to that night and rap that rotten hateful fourteen-year old in the mouth before he got a chance to say a single word. But I can't. I can't even say I'm sorry to Annie! I never got a chance to take it back, Martha! I never got a chance to make it up to her!"

And then he was blubbering like a goddam wimp, letting loose half a lifetime's worth of grief and guilt, and Martha's arms were around him and she was telling him everything would be all right, all right, all right...

*

The Detective Harrison understand. Can tell. Want to go kill another face now. Must not. The Detective Harrison not like. Must stop. The Detective Harrison help stop.

Stop for good.

Best way. Only one way stop for good. Not jail. No chain, no little window. Not ever again. Never!

Only one way stop for good. The Detective Harrison will know. Will understand. Will do.

Must call. Call now. Before dark. Before pretty faces come out in night.

*

Harrison had pulled himself together by the time the kids came home from school. He felt strangely buoyant inside, like he'd been purged in some way. Maybe all those shrinks were right after all: sharing old hurts did help.

He played with the kids for a while, then went into the kitchen to see if Martha needed any help with slicing and dicing. He felt as close to her now as he ever had.

"You okay?" she said with a smile.

"Fine."

She had just started slicing a red pepper for the salad. He took over for her.

"Have you decided what to do?" she asked.

He had been thinking about it a lot, and had come to a decision.

"Well, I've got to inform the department about Carly Baker, but I'm going to keep her out of the papers for a while."

"Why? I'd think if she's that freakish looking, the publicity might turn up someone who's seen her."

"Possibly it will come to that. But this case is sensational enough without tabloids like the *Post* and *The Light* turning it into a circus. Besides, I'm afraid of panic leading to some poor deformed innocent getting lynched. I think I can bring her in. She wants to come in."

"You're sure of that?"

"She so much as told me so. Besides, I can sense it in her." He saw Martha giving him a dubious look. "I'm serious. We're somehow connected, like there's an invisible wire between us. Maybe it's because the same thing that deformed her and those other kids deformed Annie, too. And Annie was my sister. Maybe that link is why I volunteered for this case in the first place."

He finished slicing the pepper, then moved on to the mushrooms.

"And after I bring her in, I'm going to track down her mother and start prying into what went on in Monroe in February and March of sixty-eight to cause that so-called 'cluster' of freaks nine months later."

He would do that for Annie. It would be his way of saying

good-bye and I'm sorry to his sister.

"But why does she take their faces?" Martha said.

"I don't know. Maybe because theirs were beautiful and hers is no doubt hideous."

"But what does she do with them?"

"Who knows? I'm not all that sure I want to know. But right now–"

The phone rang. Even before he picked it up, he had an inkling of who it was. The first sibilant syllable left no doubt.

"Ish thish the Detective Harrishon?"

"Yes."

Harrison stretched the coiled cord around the corner from the kitchen into the dining room, out of Martha's hearing.

"Will you shtop me tonight?"

"You want to give yourself up?"

"Yesh. Pleashe, yesh."

"Can you meet me at the precinct house?"

"No!"

"Okay! Okay!" God, he didn't want to spook her now. "Where? Anywhere you say."

"Jusht you."

"All right."

"Midnight. Plashe where lasht fashe took. Bring gun but not more cop."

"All right."

He was automatically agreeing to everything. He'd work out the details later.

"You undershtand, Detective Harrishon?"

"Oh, Carly, Carly, I understand more than you know!"

A sharp intake of breath and then silence at the other end of the line. Finally:

"You know Carly?"

"Yes, Carly. I know you." The sadness welled up in him again and it was all he could do to keep his voice from breaking. "I had a sister like you once. And you... you had a brother like me."

"Yesh," said that soft, breathy voice. *"You undershtand. Come*

tonight, Detective Harrishon."

The line went dead.

*

Wait in shadows. The Detective Harrison will come. Will bring lots cop. Always see on TV show. Always bring lots. Protect him. Many guns.

No need. Only one gun. The Detective Harrison's gun. Him's will shoot. Stop kills. Stop forever.

The Detective Harrison must do. No one else. The Carly can not. Must be the Detective Harrison. Smart. Know the Carly. Understand.

After stop, no more ugly Carly. No more sick-scared look. Bad face will go way. Forever and ever.

*

Harrison had decided to go it alone.

Not completely alone. He had a van waiting a block and a half away on Seventh Avenue and a walkie-talkie clipped to his belt, but he hadn't told anyone who he was meeting or why. He knew if he did, they'd swarm all over the area and scare Carly off completely. So he had told Jacobi he was meeting an informant and that the van was just a safety measure.

He was on his own here and wanted it that way. Carly Baker wanted to surrender to him and him alone. He understood that. It was part of that strange tenuous bond between them. No one else would do. After he had cuffed her, he would call in the wagon.

After that he would be a hero for a while. He didn't want to be a hero. All he wanted was to end this thing, end the nightmare for the city and for poor Carly Baker. She'd get help, the kind she needed, and he'd use the publicity to springboard an investigation into what had made Annie and Carly and the others in their 'cluster' what they were.

It's all going to work out fine, he told himself as he entered the alley.

He walked half its length and stood in the darkness. The brick walls of the buildings on either side soared up into the night. The ceaseless roar of the city echoed dimly behind him. The alley itself was quiet – no sound, no movement. He took out his flashlight and flicked it on.

"Carly?"

No answer.

"Carly Baker – are you here?"

More silence, then, ahead to his left, the sound of a garbage can scraping along the stony floor of the alley. He swung the light that way, and gasped.

A looming figure stood a dozen feet in front of him. It could only be Carly Baker. She stood easily as tall as he – a good six foot two – and looked like a homeless street person, one of those animated rag-piles that live on subway grates in the winter. Her head was wrapped in a dirty scarf, leaving only her glittery dark eyes showing. The rest of her was muffled in a huge, shapeless overcoat, baggy old polyester slacks with dragging cuffs, and torn sneakers.

"Where the Detective Harrishon's gun?" said the voice.

Harrison's mouth was dry but he managed to get his tongue working.

"In its holster."

"Take out. Pleashe."

Harrison didn't argue with her. The grip of his heavy Chief Special felt damn good in his hand.

The figure spread its arms; within the folds of her coat those arms seem to bend the wrong way. And were those black hooked claws protruding from the cuffs of the sleeves?

She said, "Shoot."

Harrison gaped in shock.

*

The Detective Harrison not shoot. Eyes wide. Hands with gun and light shake.

Say again: "Shoot!"

"Carly, no! I'm not here to kill you. I'm here to take you in, just as we agreed."

"No!"

Wrong! The Detective Harrison not understand! Must shoot the Carly! Kill the Carly!

"Not jail! Shoot! Shtop the kills! Shtop the Carly!"

"No! I can get you help, Carly. Really, I can! You'll go to a place where no one will hurt you. You'll get medicine to make you feel better!"

Thought him understand! Not understand! Move closer. Put claw out. Him back way. Back to wall.

"Shoot! Kill! Now!"

"No, Annie, please!"

"Not Annie! Carly! Carly!"

"Right. Carly! Don't make me do this!"

Only inches way now. Still not shoot. Other cops hiding not shoot. Why not protect?

"Shoot!" Pull scarf off face. Point claw at face. "End! End! *Pleashe!*"

The Detective Harrison face go white. Mouth hang open. Say, "Oh, my *God!*"

Get sick-scared look. Hate that look! Thought him understand! Say he know the Carly! Not! Stop look! *Stop!*

Not think. Claw go out. Rip throat of the Detective Harrison. Blood fly just like others.

No - No - No! Not want hurt!

The Detective Harrison gurgle. Drop gun and light. Fall. Stare.

Wait other cops shoot. Please kill the Carly. Wait.

No shoot. Then know. No cops. Only the poor Detective Harrison. Cry for the Detective Harrison. Then run. Run and climb. Up and down. Back to new home with the Old Jessi.

The Jessi glad hear Carly come. The Jessi try talk. Carly go sit tub. Close door. Cry for the Detective Harrison. Cry long time. Break mirror million piece. Not see face again. Not ever. Never.

The Jessi say, "Carly, I want my bath. Will you scrub my back?"

Stop cry. Do the Old Jessi's black back. Comb the Jessi's hair.

Feel very sad. None ever comb the Carly's hair. Ever.

THE CLEANING MACHINE

The Compendium of Srem lists seven Infernals, strange devices of unknown origin left over from the First Age.

The Phedro – Jacob Prather's Mystery Machine – it divides the veil to the Otherness (first seen in *Jack: Secret Circles*, eventually reconstructed as Oz's Device in *The Peabody-Ozymandias Traveling Circus & Oddity Emporium*)

The Kaiilu Éntgab – a mini Tesla tower that opens a passage to the Otherness (see *Conspiracies*)

The Cidsev Nelesso – it looks like a bracelet and allows the wearer to hear the thoughts of others (see "Infernal Night")

The Bagaq – "the sponge" – is reputed to absorb pain and injury

The Lilitongue of Gefreda – it *brings* someone...somewhere (see *Infernal*)

The Kislival – "the Cleaner" – it *sends* things...somewhere

And one more...to be revealed sometime in the future

This was my first published story. At the time I didn't know I was writing about one of the Infernals – the *Kislival* – but I do now.

The Cleaning Machine

Dr. Edward Parker reached across his desk and flipped the power

switch on his recorder to the "on" position.

"Listen if you like, Burke," he said. "But remember: She has classic paranoid symptoms; I wouldn't put much faith in anything she says."

Detective Ronald Burke, an old acquaintance on the city police force, sat across from the doctor.

"She's all we've got," he replied with ill-concealed exasperation. "Over a hundred people disappear from an apartment house and the only person who might be able to tell us anything is a nut."

Parker glanced at the recorder and noticed the glowing warm-up light. He pressed the start button.

"Listen."

⁜

...and I guess I'm the one who's responsible for it but it was really the people who lived there in my apartment who drove me to it—they were jealous of me.

The children were the worst. Every day as I'd walk to the store they'd spit at me behind my back and call me names. They even recruited other little brats from all over town and would wait for me on corners and doorsteps. They called me terrible names and said that I carried awful diseases. Their parents put them up to it, I know it! All those people in my apartment building laughed at me. They thought they could hide it but I heard it. They hated me because they were jealous of my poetry. They knew I was famous and they couldn't stand it.

Why, just the other night I almost caught three of them rummaging through my desk. They thought I was asleep and so they sneaked in and tried to steal some of my latest works, figuring they could palm them off as their own. But I was awake. I could hear them laughing at me as they searched. I grabbed the butcher knife that I always keep under my pillow and ran out into the study. I must have made some noise when I got out of bed because they ran out into the hall and closed the door just before I got there. I heard one of them on the other side say, "Boy, you sure can't fool that old lady!"

They were fiends, all of them! But the very worst was that

John Hendricks fellow next door who was trying to kill me with an ultra-frequency sonicator. He used to turn it on me and try to boil my brains while I was writing. But I was too smart for him. I kept an ice pack on my head at all hours of the day. But even that didn't keep me from getting those awful headaches that plague me constantly. He was to blame.

But the thing I want to tell you about is the machine in the cellar. I found it when I went downstairs to the boiler room to see who was calling me filthy names through the ventilator system. I met the janitor on my way down and told him about it. He just laughed and said that there hadn't been anyone down in the boiler room for two years, not since we started getting our heat piped in from the building next door. But I *knew* someone was down there—hadn't I heard those voices through the vent? I simply turned and went my way.

Everything in the cellar was covered with at least half an inch of dust—everything, that is, except the machine. I didn't know it was a machine at that time because it hadn't done anything yet. It didn't have any lights or dials and it didn't make any noise. Just a metal box with sides that ran at all sorts of odd angles, some of which didn't seem to meet properly.

It just sat there being clean.

I also noticed that the floor around it was immaculately clean for about five foot in all directions. Everywhere else was filth. It looked so strange, being clean. I ran and got George, the janitor.

He was angry at having to go downstairs but I kept pestering him until he did. He was mighty surprised.

"What is that thing?" he said, walking toward the machine.

Then he was gone! One moment he had been there, and then he was gone. No blinding flash or puff of smoke . . . just gone! And it happened just as he crossed into that circle of clean floor around the machine.

I immediately knew who was responsible: John Hendricks! So I went right upstairs and brought him down. I didn't bother to tell him what the machine had done to George since I was sure he knew all about it. But he surprised me by walking right into the circle and disappearing, just like George.

Well, at least I wouldn't be bothered by that ultra-frequency sonicator of his anymore. It was a good thing I had been too careful to go anywhere near that thing.

I began to get an idea about that machine—it was a *cleaning* machine! That's why the floor around it was so clean. Any dust or *anything* that came within the circle was either stored away somewhere or destroyed.

A thought struck me: Why not "clean out" all of my jealous neighbors this way? A wonderful idea!

I started with the children.

I went outside and, as usual, they started in with their name-calling. (They always made sure to do it very softly but I could read their lips.) About twenty of them were playing in the street. I called them together and told them I was forming a club in the cellar and they all followed me down in a group. I pointed to the machine and told them that there was a gallon of chocolate ice cream behind it and that the first one to reach it could have it all. Their greedy little faces lighted up and they scrambled away in a mob.

Three seconds later I was alone in the cellar.

I then went around to all the other apartments in the building and told all those hateful people that their sweet little darlings were playing in the old boiler room and that I thought it was dangerous. I waited for one to go downstairs before I went to the next door. Then I met the husbands as they came home from work and told them the same thing. And if anyone came looking for someone, I sent him down to the cellar. So simple: In searching the cellar they had to cross into the circle sooner or later.

That night I was alone in the building. It was wonderful—no laughing, no name-calling, and no one sneaking into my study. Wonderful!

A policeman came the next day. He knocked on my door and looked very surprised when I opened it. He said he was investigating a number of missing-persons reports. I told him that everyone was down in the cellar. He gave me a strange look but went to check. I followed him.

The machine was gone! Nothing left but the circle of clean floor. I told the officer all about it, about what horrible people they were and how they deserved to disappear. He just smiled and brought me down to the station where I had to tell my story again. Then they sent me here to see you.

They're still looking for my neighbors, aren't they? Won't listen when I tell them that they'll never find them. They don't believe there ever *was* a machine. But they can't find my neighbors, can they? Well, it serves them right! I told them I'm the one responsible for "cleaning out" my apartment building but they don't believe me. Serves them *all* right!

*

"See what I mean?" said Dr. Parker with the slightest trace of a smile as he turned off the recorder. "She's no help at all."

"Yeah, I know," Burke sighed. "As looney as they come. But how can you explain that circle of clean floor in the boiler room with all those footprints around it?"

"Well, I can't be sure, but the 'infernal machine' is not uncommon in the paranoid's delusional system. You found no trace of this 'ultra-frequency sonicator' in the Hendricks apartment, I trust?"

Burke shook his head. "No. From what we can gather, Hendricks knew nothing about electronics. He was a short-order cook in a greasy spoon downtown."

"I figured as much. She probably found everybody gone and went looking for them. She went down to the boiler room as a last resort and, finding it deserted, concluded that everybody had been 'cleaned out' of the building. She was glad but wanted to give herself the credit. She saw the circle of clean floor—probably left there by a round table top that had been recently moved—and started fabricating. By now she believes every word of her fantastic story. We'll never really know what happened until we find those missing tenants."

"I guess not," Burke said as he rose to go, "but I'd still like to know why we can find over a hundred sets of footprints approaching the

circle but none leaving it."

Dr. Parker didn't have an answer for that one.

THE BARRENS

A subgenre of fiction known as "cosmic horror" informs the entire Secret History. It's generally associated with H. P. Lovecraft and the Cthulhu Mythos he created. But during the writing of "The Barrens" I discovered I could write cosmic horror without referencing Lovecraft's mythos.

Let's back up to 1989 when John Betancourt asked me if I'd be interested in participating in a "Special F. Paul Wilson Issue" of *Weird Tales* magazine. Like I could say no? An entire issue of the world's first and greatest horror fiction magazine – where the classics of Lovecraft and Howard and Bloch and Bradbury first saw print – devoted to me? How could I *not* be interested? I was working on *Reprisal* then but promised I'd send the requested 20,000 words of new fiction just as soon as I got free.

I intended "The Barrens" to be those 20,000 words. Since *Weird Tales* was the target market, I designed it to be Lovecraftian, but not slavishly so, not without my own little twists. The Jersey Pine Barrens setting is real, a truly Lovecraftian locale; all the Piney history and lore in the story are true, every locale except Razorback Hill is real. (In fact, I liked Razorback Hill so much I returned there for the backstory of *Freak Show*.) The style is mine, but the cosmic horror is influenced by Lovecraft.

For various reasons explained elsewhere, the novella wound up in an anthology called *Lovecraft's Legacy* instead of *Weird Tales*. The following year it became a finalist for the World Fantasy Award for best novella, which it lost (of course).

I wrote "The Barrens" as I was closing in on the finale of the Adversary Cycle, and coming to the realization that I was developing a secret history of the world. I was also seeing how HPL's mythos and the cosmic horror of my Secret History parted ways. Lovecraft's "gods" have tongue-twisting names like Cthulhu and Yog-Sothoth and Nyarlathotep. The Intrusive Cosmic Entities of the Secret History are so few and so unimaginably vast that they're *nameless*. The designations attributed to them – "the Ally," "the Otherness," etc. – are all of human origin. If we humans can tack a name onto something, we feel we've grasped and pigeonholed it – made it safe (or at least safer) in some vague way.

The entities behind the Secret History aren't gods, they aren't supernatural, they are simply *there*. And whatever agendas they have will remain forever beyond our ken. They are in no way benign, and some are decidedly inimical. The very best we can expect from them is indifference. But indifferent or malign, they all like to toy with us. The Secret History is the result of their interference in human affairs throughout time.

We will never be free of them.

The Barrens

1. *In Search of a Devil*

I shot my answering machine today. Took out the old twelve gauge my father left me, and blew it to pieces. A silly, futile gesture, I know, but it illustrates my present state of mind, I think.

And it felt good. If not for an answering machine, my life would be completely different now. I would have missed Jonathan Creighton's call. I'd be less wise but far, far happier. And I'd still have some semblance of order and meaning in my life.

He left an innocent enough message:

"'The office of Kathleen McKelston and Associates!' Sounds like Big Business! How's it going, Mac? This is Jon Creighton calling. I'm going to be in the area later this week and I'd like to see you. Lunch or dinner – whatever's better. Give me a buzz." And he left a number with a 212 area code.

So simple, so forthright, giving no hint of where it would lead.

You work your way through life day by day, learning how to play the game, carving out your niche, making a place for yourself. You have some good luck, some bad luck, sometimes you make your own luck, and along the way you begin to think that you've figured out some of the answers – not all of them, of course, but enough to make you feel that you've learned something, that you've got a handle on life and just might be able to get a decent ride out of it. You start to think you're in control. Then along comes someone like Jonathan Creighton and he smashes everything. Not just your plans, your hopes, your dreams, but *everything*, up to and including your sense of what is real and what is not.

I'd heard nothing from or about him since college, and had thought of him only occasionally until that day in early August when he called my office. Intrigued, I returned his call and set a date for lunch.

That was my first mistake. If I'd had the slightest inkling of where that simple lunch with an old college lover would lead, I'd have slammed down the phone and fled to Europe, or the Orient, anywhere where Jonathan Creighton wasn't.

We'd met at a freshmen mixer at Rutgers University. Maybe we each picked up subliminal cues – we called them "vibes" in those days – that told us we shared a rural upbringing. We didn't dress like it, act like it, or feel like it, but we were a couple of Jersey hicks. I came from the Pemberton area, Jon came from another rural zone, but in North Jersey, near a place called Gilead. Despite that link, we were polar opposites in most other ways. I'm still amazed we hit it off. I was career oriented while Jon was...well, he was a flake. He earned the name Crazy Creighton and he lived up to it every day. He never stayed with one thing long enough to allow anyone to pin him down. Always on to the Next New Thing before the crowd had tuned into it, *always* into the exotic and esoteric. Looking for the Truth, he'd say.

And as so often happens with people who are incompatible in so many ways, we found each other irresistible and fell madly in love.

Sophomore year we found an apartment off campus and moved in together. It was my first affair, and not at all a tranquil one. I read the strange books he'd find and I kept up with his strange hours, but I put my foot down when it came to the Bruegel prints. There was something deeply disturbing about those paintings that went beyond their gruesome subject matter. Jon didn't fight me on it. He just smiled sadly in his condescending way, as if disappointed that I had missed the point, and rolled them up and put them away.

The thing that kept us together – at least for the year we were together – was our devotion to personal autonomy. We spent weeks of nights talking about how we had to take complete control of our own lives, and brainstorming how we were going to go about it. It seems so silly now, but that was the Sixties, and we really discussed those sorts of things back then.

We lasted sophomore year and then we fell apart. It might

F. Paul Wilson

have gone on longer if Creighton hadn't got in with the druggies. That was the path toward loss of *all* autonomy as far as I was concerned, but Creighton said you can't be free until you know what's real. And if drugs might reveal the Truth, he had to try them. Which was hippie bullshit as far as I was concerned. After that, we rarely ran into each other. He wound up living alone off campus in his senior year. Somehow he managed to graduate, with a degree in anthropology, and that was the last I'd heard of him.

But that doesn't mean he hadn't left his mark.

I suppose I'm what you might call a feminist. I don't belong to NOW and I don't march in the streets, but I don't let anyone leave footprints on my back simply because I'm a woman. I believe in myself and I guess I owe some of that to Jonathan Creighton. He always treated me as an equal. He never made an issue of it – it was simply implicit in his attitude that I was intelligent, competent, worthy of respect, able to stand on my own. It helped shape me. And I'll always revere him for that.

Lunch. I chose Rosario's on the Point Pleasant Beach side of the Manasquan Inlet, not so much for its food as for the view. Creighton was late and that didn't terribly surprise me. I didn't mind. I sipped a Chablis spritzer and watched the party boats roll in from their half-day runs of bottom fishing. Then a voice with echoes of familiarity broke through my thoughts.

"Well, Mac, I see you haven't changed much."

I turned and was shocked at what I saw. I barely recognized Creighton. He'd always been thin to the point of emaciation. Could the plump, bearded, almost cherubic figure standing before me now be–?

"Jon? Is that you?"

"The one and only," he said and spread his arms.

We embraced briefly, then took our seats in a booth by the window. As he squeezed into the far side of the table, he called the waitress over and pointed to my glass.

"Two Lites for me and another of those for her."

At first glance I'd thought that Creighton's extra poundage

made him look healthy for the first time in his life. His hair was still thick and dark brown, but despite his round, rosy cheeks, his eyes were sunken and too bright. He seemed jovial but I sensed a grim undertone. I wondered if he was still into drugs.

"Almost a quarter century since we were together," he said. "Hard to believe it's been that long. The years look as if they've been kind to you."

As far as looks go, I suppose that's true. I don't dye my hair, so there's a little gray tucked in with the red. But I've always had a young face. I don't wear make-p – with my high coloring and freckles, I don't need it.

"And you."

Which wasn't actually true. His open shirt collar was frayed and looked as if this might be the third time he'd worn it since it was last washed. His tweed sport coat was worn at the elbows and a good two sizes too small for him.

We spent the drinks, appetizers, and most of the entrees catching up on each other's lives. I told him about my small accounting firm, my marriage, my recent divorce.

"No children?"

I shook my head. The marriage had gone sour, the divorce had been a nightmare. I wanted off the subject.

"But enough about me," I said. "What have you been up to?"

"Would you believe clinical psychology?"

"No," I said, too shocked to lie. "I wouldn't"

The Jonathan Creighton I'd known had been so eccentric, so out of step, so self-absorbed, I couldn't imagine him as a psychotherapist. Jonathan Creighton helping other people get their lives together – it was almost laughable.

He was the one laughing, however – good-naturedly, too.

"Yeah. It *is* hard to believe, but I went on to get a masters, and then a Ph.D. Actually went into practice."

His voice trailed off.

"You're using the past tense," I said.

"Right. It didn't work out. The practice never got off the ground. But the problem was really within myself. I was using a form of reality therapy but it never worked as it should. And finally I realized why: I don't know – really *know* – what reality is. Nobody does."

This had an all-too-familiar ring to it. I tried to lighten things up before they got too heavy.

"Didn't someone once say that reality is what trips you up whenever you walk around with your eyes closed?"

Creighton's smile showed a touch of the old condescension that so infuriated some people.

"Yes, I suppose someone would say something like that. Anyway, I decided to go off and see if I could find out what reality really was. Did a lot of traveling. Wound up in a small New England university where I hooked up with the anthropology department – that was my undergraduate major, after all. But now I've left academe to write a book."

"A book?"

This was beginning to sound like a pretty disjointed life. But that shouldn't have surprised me.

"What a deal!" he said, his eyes sparkling. "I've got grants from Rutgers, Princeton, the American Folklore Society, the New Jersey Historical Society, and half a dozen others, just to write a book!"

"What's it about?"

"The origins of folk tales. I'm going to select a few and trace them back to their roots. That's where you come in."

"Oh?"

"I'm going to devote a significant chapter to the Jersey Devil."

"There've been whole books written about the Jersey Devil. Why don't you–"

"I want real sources for this, Mac. Primary all the way. Nothing second-hand. This is going to be definitive."

"What can I do for you?"

"You're a Piney, aren't you?"

Resentment flashed through me. Even though people nowadays described themselves as "Piney" with a certain amount of pride, and I'd even seen bumper stickers touting "Piney Power," some of us still couldn't help bristling when an outsider said it. When I was a kid it was always used as a pejorative. Like "clam-digger" here on the coast. Fighting words. Officially it referred to the multigenerational natives of the great Pine Barrens that ran south from Route 70 all the way down to the lower end of the state. I've always hated the term. To me it was the equivalent of calling someone a redneck.

Which, to be honest, wasn't so far from the truth. The true Pineys are poor rural folk, often working truck farms and doing menial labor in the berry fields and cranberry bogs – a lot of them do indeed have red necks. Many are uneducated, or at best undereducated. Those who can afford wheels drive the prototypical battered pick-up with the gun rack in the rear window. They even speak with an accent that sounds southern. They're Jersey hillbillies. Country bumpkins in the very heart of the industrial Northeast. Anachronisms.

Pineys.

"Who told you that?" I said as levelly as I could.

"You did. Back in school."

"Did I?"

It shook me to see how far I'd traveled from my roots. As a scared, naive, self-deprecating frosh at Rutgers I probably had indeed referred to myself as a Piney. Now I never mentioned the word, not in reference to myself or anyone else. I was a college educated woman; I was a respected professional who spoke with a colorless northeast accent. No one in his right mind would consider me a Piney.

"Well, that was just a gag," I said. "My family roots are back in the Pine Barrens, but I am by no stretch of the imagination a Piney. So I doubt I can help you."

"Oh, but you can! The McKelston name is big in the Barrens. Everybody knows it. You've got plenty of relatives there."

"Really? How do you know?"

Suddenly he looked sheepish.

"Because I've been into the Barrens a few times now. No

one will open up to me. I'm an outsider. They don't trust me. Instead of answering my questions, they play games with me. They say they don't know what I'm talking about but they know someone who might, then they send me driving in circles. I was lost out there for two solid days last month. And believe me, I was getting scared. I thought I'd never find my way out."

"You wouldn't be the first. Plenty of people, many of them experienced hunters, have gone into the Barrens and never been seen again. You'd better stay out."

His hand darted across the table and clutched mine.

"You've got to help me, Kathy. My whole future hinges on this."

I was shocked. He'd always called me "Mac." Even in bed back in our college days he'd never called me "Kathy." Gently, I pulled my hand free, saying.

"Come on, Jon–"

He leaned back and stared out the window at the circling gulls.

"If I do this right, do something really definitive, it may get me back into the anthropology department where I can finish my doctoral thesis."

I was immediately suspicious.

"I thought you said you 'left' the university, Jon. Why can't you get back in without it?"

"'Irregularities,'" he said, still not looking at me. "The old farts in the antiquities department didn't like where my research was leading me."

"This 'reality' business?"

"Yes."

"They told you that?"

Now he looked at me.

"Not in so many words, but I could tell." He leaned forward. His eyes were brighter than ever. "They've got books and manuscripts locked in huge safes there, one-of-a-kind volumes from times most scholars think of as pre-history. I managed to get a pass, a forgery that got me into the vaults. It's incredible what they have there, Mac. *Incredible!* I've got to get back there. Will you help me?"

His intensity was startling. And tantalizing.

"What would I have to do?"

"Just accompany me into the Pine Barrens. Just for a few trips. If I can use you as a reference, I know they'll talk to me about the Jersey Devil. After that, I can take it on my own. All I need is some straight answers from these people and I'll have my primary sources. I may be able to track a folk myth to its very roots! I'll give you credit in the book, I'll pay you, anything, Mac, just don't leave we twisting in the wind!"

He was positively frantic by the time he finished speaking.

"Easy, Jon. Easy. Let me think."

Tax season was over and I had a loose schedule for the summer. And even if I was looking ahead to a tight schedule, so what? Frankly, the job wasn't anywhere near as satisfying as it once had been. The challenge of overcoming the business community's prejudice and doubts about a woman accountant, the thrill of building a string of clients, that was all over. Everything was mostly routine now. Plus, I no longer had a husband. No children to usher toward adulthood. I had to admit that my life was pretty empty at that moment. And so was I. Why not take a little time to inspect my roots and help Crazy Creighton put his life on track, if such a thing was possible? In the bargain maybe I could gain a little perspective on my own life.

"All right, Jon," I said. "I'll do it."

Creighton's eyes lit with true pleasure, a glow distinct from the feverish intensity since he'd sat down. He thrust both his hands toward me.

"I could kiss you, Mac! I can't tell you how much this means to me! You have no idea how important this is!"

He was right about that. No idea at all.

2. *The Pine Barrens*

Two days later we were ready to make our first foray into the woods.

Creighton was wearing a safari jacket when he picked me up in a slightly battered four-wheel drive Jeep Wrangler.

"This isn't Africa we're headed for," I told him.

"I know. I like the pockets. They hold all sorts of things."

I glanced in the rear compartment. He was surprisingly well equipped. I noticed a water cooler, a food chest, back packs, and what looked like sleeping bags. I hoped he wasn't harboring any romantic ideas. I'd just split from one man and I wasn't looking for another, especially not Jonathan Creighton.

"I promised to help you look around. I didn't say anything about camping out."

He laughed. "I'm with you. Holiday Inn is my idea of roughing it. I was never a Boy Scout, but I do believe in being prepared. I've already been lost once in there."

"And we can do without that happening again. Got a compass?"

He nodded. "And maps. Even have a sextant."

"You actually know how to use one?"

"I learned."

I dimly remember being bothered then by his having a sextant, and not being quite sure why. Before I could say anything else, he tossed me the keys.

"You're the Piney. You drive."

"Still Mr. Macho, I see."

He laughed. I drove.

It's easy to get into the Pine Barrens from northern Ocean County. You just get on Route 70 and head west. About half way between the Atlantic Ocean and Philadelphia, say, near a place known as Ongs Hat, you turn left. And wave bye-bye to the Twentieth Century, and civilization as you know it.

How do I describe the Pine Barrens to someone who's never been through them? First of all, it's big. You have to fly over it in a small plane to appreciate just how big. It runs through seven counties, takes up one fourth of the state, but since Jersey's not a big state, that doesn't tell the story. How does 2,000 square miles sound? Or a million acres? Almost the size of Yosemite

National Park. Does that give you an idea of its vastness?

How do I describe what a wilderness this is? Maps will give you a clue. Look at a road map of New Jersey. If you don't happen to have one handy, imagine an oblong platter of spaghetti; now imagine what it looks like after someone's devoured most of the spaghetti out of the middle of the lower half, leaving only a few strands crossing the exposed plate. Same thing with a population density map – a big gaping hole in the southern half where the Pine Barrens sits. New Jersey is the most densely populated state in the U.S., averaging a thousand bodies per square mile. But the New York City suburbs in north Jersey teem with forty thousand per square mile. After you account for the crowds along the coast and in the cities and towns along the western interstate corridor, there aren't too many people left over when you get to the Pine Barrens. I've heard of an area of over a hundred thousand acres – that's in the neighborhood of 160 square miles – in the south-central Barrens with twenty-one known inhabitants. *Twenty-one.* One human being per eight square miles in an area that lies on the route between Boston, New York, Philadelphia, Baltimore, and D.C.

Even when you take a turn off one of the state or federal roads that cut through the Barrens, you feel the isolation almost immediately. The forty-foot scrub pines close in behind you and quietly but oh so effectively cut you off from the rest of the world. I'll bet there are people who've lived to ripe old ages in the Barrens who have never seen a paved road. Conversely, there are no complete topographical maps of the Barrens because there are vast areas that no human eyes have ever seen.

Are you getting the picture?

"Where do we start?" Creighton asked as we crawled past the retirement villages along Route 70. This had been an empty stretch of road when I was a kid. Now it was Wrinkle City.

"We start at the capitol."

"Trenton? I don't want to go to Trenton."

"Not the state capital. The capital of the pines. Used to be called Shamong Station. Now it's known as Chatsworth."

He pulled out his map and squinted through the index.

"Oh, right. I see it. Right smack in the middle of the Barrens. How big is it?"

"A veritable Piney megalopolis, my friend. Three hundred souls."

Creighton smiled, and for a second or two he seemed almost...innocent.

"Think we can get there before rush hour?"

3. Jasper Mulliner

I stuck to the main roads, taking 70 to 72 to 563, and we were there in no time.

"You'll see something here you won't see in any place else in the Barrens," I said as I drove down Chatsworth's main street.

"Electricity?" Creighton said.

He didn't look up from the clutter of maps on his lap. He'd been following our progress on paper, mile by mile.

"No. Lawns. Years ago a number of families decided they wanted grass in their front yards. There's no topsoil to speak of out here; the ground's mostly sand. So they trucked in loads of topsoil and seeded themselves some lawns. Now they've got to cut them."

I drove past the general store and its three gas pumps out on the sidewalk.

"*Esso*," Creighton said, staring at the sign over the pumps. "That says it all, doesn't it."

"That it do."

We continued on until we came to a sandy lot occupied by a single trailer. No lawn here.

"Who's this?" Creighton said, folding up his maps as I hopped out of the wrangler.

"An old friend of the family."

This was Jasper Mulliner's place. He was some sort of an uncle – on my mother's side, I think. But distant blood relationships are nothing special in the Barrens. An awful lot of people are related in one way or another. Some said he was a descendant of the notorious bandit of the pines, Joseph Mulliner. Jasper had never confirmed that, but he'd never denied it, either.

I knocked on the door, wondering who would answer. I wasn't even sure Jasper was still alive. But when the door opened, I immediately recognized the grizzled old head that poked through the opening.

"You're not sellin' anything, are you?" he said.

"Nothing, Mr. Mulliner," I said. "I'm Kathleen McKelston. I don't know if you remember me, but–"

His eyes lit as his face broke into a toothless grin.

"Danny's girl? The one who got the college scholarship? Sure I remember you! Come on in!"

Jasper was wearing khaki shorts, a sleeveless orange tee shirt, and duck boots – no socks. His white hair was neatly combed and he was freshly shaved. He'd been a salt hay farmer in his younger days and his hands were still callused from it. He'd moved on to overseeing a cranberry bog in his later years. His skin was a weathered brown and looked tougher than saddle leather. The inside of the trailer reminded me more of a low ceilinged freight car than a home, but it was clean. The presence of the television set told me he had electricity but I saw no phone sign or running water.

I introduced him to Creighton and we settled onto a three-legged stool and a pair of ladderback chairs as I spent the better part of half an hour telling him about my life since leaving the Barrens and answering questions about my mother and how she was doing since my father died. Then he went into a soliloquy about what a great man my father was. I let him run on, pretending to be listening, but turning my mind to other things. Not because I disagreed with him, but because it had been barely a year since Dad had dropped dead and I was still hurting.

Dad had not been your typical Piney. Although he loved the Barrens as much as anyone else who grew up here, he'd known there was a bigger though not necessarily better life beyond them. That bigger world didn't interest him in the least, but just because he was content with where he was didn't mean that I'd be. He wanted to allow his only child a choice. He knew I'd need a decent education if that choice was to be meaningful. And to provide that education for me, he did what few Pineys like to do: he took a steady job.

That's not to say that Pineys are afraid of hard work. Far from it. They'll break their backs at any job they're doing. It's simply that they don't like to be tied down to the same job day after day, month after month. Most of them have grown up flowing with the cycle of the Barrens. Spring is for gathering sphagnum moss to sell to the florists and nurseries. In June and July they work the blueberry and huckleberry fields. In the fall they move into the bogs for the cranberry harvest. And in the cold of winter they cut cordwood, or cut holly and mistletoe, or go "pineballing"–collecting pine cones to sell. None of this is easy work. But it's not the same work. And that's what matters.

The Piney attitude toward jobs is the most laid back you'll ever encounter. That's because they're in such close harmony with their surroundings. They know that with all the pure water all around them and flowing beneath their feet, they'll never go thirsty. With all the wild vegetation around them, they'll never lack for fruit and vegetables. And whenever the meat supply gets low, they pick up a rifle and head into the brush for squirrel, rabbit, or venison, whatever the season.

When I neared fourteen, my father bit the bullet and moved us close to Pemberton where he took a job with a well-drilling crew. It was steady work, with benefits, and I got to go to Pemberton High. He pushed me to take my school work seriously, and I did. My high grades coupled with my gender and low socioeconomic status earned me a full ride – room, board, and tuition – at Rutgers. As soon as that was settled, he was ready to move back into the Barrens. But my mother had become used to the conveniences and amenities of town living. She wanted to stay in Pemberton. So they stayed.

I still can't help but wonder whether Dad might have lived longer if he'd moved back into the woods. I've never mentioned that to my mother, of course.

When Jasper paused, I jumped in: "My friend Jon's doing a book and he's devoting a chapter to the Jersey Devil."

"Is that so?" Jasper said. "And you brought him to me, did you?"

"Well, Dad always told me there weren't many folks in the Pines you didn't know, and not much that went on that you didn't know about."

The old man beamed and did what many Pineys do: he repeated a phrase three times.

"Did he now? Did he now? Did he really now? Ain't that somethin'! I do believe that calls for a little jack."

As Jasper turned and reached into his cupboard, Creighton threw me a questioning look.

"Applejack," I told him.

He smiled. "Ah. Jersey lightning."

Jasper turned back with three glasses and a brown quart jug. With a practiced hand he poured two fingers' worth into each and handed them to us. The tumblers were smudged and maybe a little crusty, but I wasn't worried about germs. There's never been a germ that could stand up to straight jack from Jasper Mulliner's still. I remember siphoning some off from my father's jug and sneaking off into the brush at night to meet a couple of my girlfriends from high school, and we'd sit around and sing and get plastered.

I could tell by the way the vapor singed my nasal membranes that this was from a potent batch. I neglected to tell Creighton to go slow. As I took a respectful sip, he tossed his off. I watched him wince as he swallowed, saw his face grow red and his eyes begin to water.

"Whoa!" he said hoarsely. "You could etch glass with that stuff!" He caught Jasper looking at him sideways and held out his glass. "But delicious! Could I have just a drop more?"

"Help yourself," Jasper said, pouring him another couple of fingers. "Plenty more where this came from. But down it slow. This here's sippin' whiskey. You go puttin' too much of it down like that and you'll get apple palsy. Slow and leisurely does it when you're drinking Gus Sooy's best."

"This isn't yours?" I said.

"Naw! I stopped that long time ago. Too much trouble and gettin' too civilized 'round here. Besides, Gus's jack is as good as mine ever was. Maybe better."

He set the jug on the floor between us.

"About that Jersey Devil," I said, prompting him before he got off on another tangent.

"Right. The ol' Devil. He used to be known as the Leeds' Devil. I'm sure you've heard various versions of the story, but I'll tell you the real one. That ol' devil's been around a spell, better'n two and a half centuries. All started back around seventeen-thirty or so. That was when Mrs. Leeds of Estellville found herself in the family way for the thirteenth time. Now she was so fed up and angry about this that she cried out, 'I hope this time it's the Devil!' Well now, Someone must've been listenin' that night, because she got her wish. When that thirteenth baby was born, it was an ugly-faced thing, born with teeth like no one'd ever seen before, and it had a curly, sharp-pointed tail, and leathery wings like a bat. It bit its mother and flew out through the window. It grew up out in the pine wilds, stealing and eating chickens and small piglets at first, then graduating to cows, children, even growed men. All they ever found of its victims was their bones, and they was chipped and nicked by powerful sharp teeth. Some say it's dead now, some say it'll never die. Every so often someone says he shot and killed it, but most folks think it can't be killed. It gets blamed for every missing chicken and every pig or cow that wanders off, and so after a while you think it's just an ol' Piney folk tale. But it's out there. It's out there. It's surely out there."

"Have you ever seen it?" Creighton asked. He was sipping his jack with respect this time around.

"Saw its shadow. It was up on Apple Pie Hill, up at the top, in the days before they put up the fire tower. Before you was born, Kathleen. I'd been out doing some summer hunting, tracking a big ol' stag. You know what a climb Apple Pie is, dontcha?"

I nodded. "Sure do."

It didn't look like much of a hill. No cliffs or precipices, just a slow incline that seemed to go on forever. You didn't have to do much more than walk to get to the top, but you were bushed when you finally reached it.

"Anyways, I was about three-quarters the way up when it got too dark to do any more tracking. Well, I was tired and it was a warm summer night so's I just settled down on the pine needles and decided I'd spend the night. I had some jerky and some pone and my jug." He pointed to the floor. "Just like that one. You two be sure to help yourselves, hear me?"

"I'm fine," I said.

I saw Creighton reach for the jug. He always could handle a lot. I was already feeling my two sips. It was getting warmer in here by the minute.

"Anyways," Jasper went on, "I was sitting there chewing and sipping when I saw some pine lights."

Creighton started in mid-pour and spilled some applejack over his hand. He was suddenly very alert, almost tense.

"Pine lights?" he said. "You saw pine lights? Where were they?"

"So you've heard of the pine lights, have you?"

"I sure have. I've been doing my homework. Where did you see them? Were they moving?"

"They were streaming across the crest of Apple Pie Hill, just skirting the tops of the trees."

Creighton put his tumbler down and began fumbling with his map.

"Apple Pie Hill...I remember seeing that somewhere. Here it is." He jabbed his finger down on the map as if he were driving a spike into the hill. "Okay. So you were on Apple Pie Hill when you saw the pine lights. How many were there?"

"A whole town's worth of them, maybe a hunnert, more than I've ever seen before or since."

"How fast were they going?"

"Different speeds. Different sizes. Some gliding peacefully, some zipping along, moving past the slower ones. Looked like the Turnpike on a summer weekend."

Creighton leaned forward, his eyes brighter than ever.

"Tell me about it."

Something about Creighton's intensity disturbed me. All of a sudden he'd become an avid listener. He'd been listening politely to Jasper's retelling of the Jersey Devil story, but he'd seemed more interested in the applejack than in the tale. He hadn't bothered to check the location of Apple Pie Hill when Jasper had said he'd seen the Jersey Devil there, but he'd been in a rush to find it at the first mention of the pine lights.

The pine lights. I'd heard of them but I'd never seen one. People tended to catch sight of them on summer nights, mostly toward the end of the season. Some said it was ball lightning or some form of St. Elmo's fire, some called it swamp gas, and some said it was the souls of dead Pineys coming back for periodic visits. Why was Creighton so interested?

"Well," Jasper said, "I spotted one or two moving along the crest of the hill and didn't think too much of it. I spot a couple just about every summer. Then I saw a few more. And then a few more. I got a little excited and decided to get up to the top of Apple Pie and see what was going on. I was breathing hard by the time I got there. I stopped and looked up and there they was, flowing along the tree tops forty feet above me, pale yellow, some ping-pong sized and some big as beach balls, all moving in the same direction."

"What direction?" Creighton said. If he leaned forward any farther, he was going to fall off his stool. "Which way were they going?"

"I'm getting to that, son," Jasper said. "Just hold your horses. So as I was saying, I was standing there watching them flow against the clear night sky, and I was feeling this strange tightness in my chest, like I was witnessing something I shouldn't. But I couldn't tear my eyes away. And then they thinned out and was gone. They'd all passed. So I did something crazy. I climbed a tree to see where they was going. Something in my gut told me not to, but I was filled with this wonder, almost like holy rapture. So I climbed as far as I could, until the tree started to bend with my weight and the branches got too thin to hold me. And I watched them go. They was strung out in long trail, dipping down when the land dipped down, and moving up when the land rose, moving just above the tops of the pines, like they was being pulled along strings." He looked at Creighton. "And they was heading southwest."

"You're sure of that?"

Jasper looked insulted. "Course I'm sure of that. Bear Swamp Hill was behind my left shoulder, and everybody knows Bear Swamp is east of Apple Pie. Those lights was on their way southwest."

"And this was the summer?"

"Nigh on to Labor Day, if I 'member correct."

"And you were on the crest of Apple Pie Hill?"

"The tippy top."

"Great!" He began folding his map.

"I thought you wanted to hear about the Jersey Devil."

"I do, I do."

"Then how come you're asking me all these questions about the lights and not asking me about my meeting with the Devil?"

I hid a smile. Jasper was as sharp as ever.

Creighton looked confused for a moment. An expression darted across his face. It was only there for a second, but I caught it. Furtiveness. Then he leaned forward and spoke to Jasper is a confidential tone.

"Don't tell anybody this, but I think they're connected. The pine lights and the Jersey Devil. Connected."

Jasper leaned back. "You know, you might have something there. Cause it was while I was up that tree that I spotted the ol' Devil himself. Or at least his shadow. I was watching the lights flow out of sight when I heard this noise in the brush. It had a slithery sound to it. I looked down and there was this dark shape moving below. And you know what? It was heading in the same direction as the lights. What do you think of that?"

F. Paul Wilson

Creighton's voice oozed sincerity.

"I think that's damn interesting, Jasper."

I thought they both were shoveling it, but I couldn't decide who was carrying the bigger load.

"But don't you go getting too interested in those pine lights, son. Gus Sooy says they're bad medicine."

"The guy who made this jack?" I said, holding up my empty tumbler.

"The very same. Gus says there's lots of pine light activity in his neighborhood every summer. Told me I was a fool for climbing that tree. Says he wouldn't get near one of those lights for all the tea in China."

I noticed that Creighton was tense again.

"Where's this Gus Sooy's neighborhood?" he said. "Does he live in Chatsworth?"

Jasper burst out laughing.

"Gus live in Chatsworth? That's a good un! Gus Sooy's an old Hessian who lives way out in the wildest part of the pines. Never catch him *near* a city like this!"

City? I didn't challenge him on that.

"Where do we find him then?" Creighton said, his expression like a kid who's been told there's a cache of M&M's hidden somewhere nearby.

"Not easy," Jasper said. "Gus done a good job of getting himself well away from everybody. He's well away. Yes, he's well away. But if you go down to Apple Pie Hill and head along the road there that runs along its south flank, and you follow that about two mile and turn south onto the sand road by Applegate's cranberry bog, then follow that for about ten-twelve mile till you come to the fork where you bear left, then go right again at the cripple beyond it, then it's a good ten mile down that road till you get to the big red cedar–"

Creighton was scribbling furiously.

"I'm not sure I know what a red cedar looks like," I said.

"You'll know it," Jasper said. "Its kind don't grow naturally around here. Gus planted it there a good many year ago so people could find their way to him. The *right* people," he said, eyeing Creighton. "People who want to buy his wares, if you get my meaning."

I nodded. I got his meaning: Gus made his living off his still.

"Anyways, you turn right at the red cedar and go to the end of the road. Then you've got to get out and walk about a third of the way up the hill. That's where you'll find Gus Sooy."

I tried to drive the route across a mental map in my head. I couldn't get there. My map was blank where he was sending us. But I was amazed at how far I did get. As a Piney, even a girl, you've got to develop a good sense of where you are, got to have a store of maps in your head that you can picture by reflex, otherwise you'll spend most of your time being lost. Even with a good library of mental maps, you'll still get lost occasionally. I could still travel my old maps. The skill must be like the proverbial bicycle – once you've learned, you never forget.

I had a sense that Gus Sooy's place was somewhere far down in Burlington County, near Atlantic County. But county lines don't mean much in the Pinelands.

"That's *really* in the middle of nowhere!" I said.

"That it is, Kathy, that it is. That it surely is. It's on the slope of Razorback Hill."

Creighton shuffled through his maps again.

"Razorback...Razorback...there's no Razorback Hill here."

"That's because it ain't much of a hill. But it's there all right. Just 'cause it ain't on your diddly map don't mean it ain't there. Lots of things ain't on that map."

Creighton rose to his feet.

"Maybe we can run out there now and buy some of this applejack from him. What do you say, Mac?"

"We've got time."

I had a feeling he truly did want to buy some of Sooy's jack, but I was sure some questions about the pine lights would come up during the transaction.

"Better bring your own jugs if you're goin'," Jasper said. "Gus don't carry no spares. You can buy some from the Buzbys at the general store."

"Will do," I said.

I thanked him and promised I'd say hello to my mom for him, then I joined Creighton out at the Wrangler. He had one of his maps unfolded on the hood and was drawing a line southwest from Apple Pie Hill through the emptiest part of the Barrens.

"What's that for?" I asked.

"I don't know just yet. We'll see if it comes to mean anything."

It would. Sooner than either of us realized.

4. *The Hessian*

I bought a gallon-sized brown jug at the Chatsworth general store; Creighton bought two.

"I want this Sooy fellow to be *real* glad to see me!"

I drove us down 563, then off to Apple Pie Hill. We got south of it and began following Jasper's directions. Creighton read while I drove.

"What the hell's a cripple?" he said.

"That's a spong with no cedars."

"Ah! That clears up everything!"

"A spong is a low wet spot; if it's got cedars growing around it, it's a cripple. What could be clearer?"

"I'm not sure, but I know I'll think of something. By the way, why's this Sooy fellow called a Hessian? Mulliner doesn't really think he's–?"

"Of course not. Sooy's an old German name around the Pine Barrens. Comes from the Hessians who deserted the British army and fled into the woods after the battle of Trenton."

"The Revolution?"

"Sure. This sand road we're riding on now was here three hundred-odd years ago as a wagon trail. It probably hasn't changed any since. Might even have been used by the smugglers who used to unload freight in the marshes and move it overland through the Pines to avoid port taxes in New York and Philly.

A lot of them settled in here. So did a good number of Tories and Loyalists who were chased from their land after the Revolution. Some of them probably arrived dressed in tar and feathers and little else. The Lenape Indians settled in here, too, so did Quakers who were kicked out of their churches for taking up arms during the Revolution."

Creighton laughed. "Sounds like Australia! Didn't anyone besides outcasts settle here?"

"Sure. Bog iron was a major industry. This was the center of the colonial iron production. Most of the cannon balls fired against the British in the Revolution and the War of 1812 were forged right here in the Pine Barrens."

"Where'd everybody go?"

"A place called Pittsburgh. There was more iron there and it was cheaper to produce. The furnaces here tried to shift over to glass production but they were running out of wood to keep them going. Each furnace consumed something like a thousand acres of pine a year. With the charcoal industry, the lumber industry, even the cedar shake industry all adding to the daily toll on the tree population, the Barrens couldn't keep up with the demand. The whole economy collapsed after the Civil War. Which probably saved the area from becoming a desert."

I noticed the underbrush between the ruts getting higher, slapping against the front bumper as we passed, a sure sign that not many people came this way. Then I spotted the red cedar. Jasper had been right – it didn't look like it belonged here. We turned right and drove until we came to a cul-de-sac at the base of a hill. Three rusting cars hugged the bushes along the perimeter.

"This must be the place," I said.

"This is not a place. This is *no*where."

We grabbed our jugs and walked up the path. About a third of the way up the slope we broke into a clearing with a slant-roofed shack in the far left corner. It looked maybe twenty feet on a side, and was covered with tar paper that was peeling away in spots, exposing the plywood beneath. Somewhere behind the shack a dog had begun to bark.

Creighton said, "Finally!" and started forward.

I laid a hand on his arm.

"Call out first," I told him. "Otherwise we may be ducking buckshot."

He thought I was joking at first, then saw that I meant it.

"You're serious?"

"We're dressed like city folk. We could be revenuers. He'll shoot first and ask questions later."

"Hello in the house!" Creighton cried. "Jasper Mulliner sent us! Can we come up?"

A wizened figure appeared on the front step, a twelve gauge cradled in his arms.

"How'd he send you?"

"By way of the red cedar, Mr. Sooy!" I replied.

"C'mon up then!"

Where Jasper had been neat, Gus Sooy was slovenly. His white hair looked like a deranged bird had tried to nest in it; for a shirt he wore the stained top from a set of long johns and had canvas pants secured around his waist with coarse rope. His lower face was obscured by a huge white beard, stained around the mouth. An Appalachian Santa Claus, going to seed in the off-season.

We followed him into the single room of his home. The floor was covered with a mismatched assortment of throw rugs and carpet remnants. A bed sat in the far left corner, a kerosene stove was immediately to our right. Set about the room were a number of Aladdin lamps with the tall flues. Dominating the scene was a heavy legged kitchen table with an enamel top.

We introduced ourselves and Gus said he'd met my father years ago.

"So what brings you two kids out here to see Gus Sooy?"

I had to smile, not just at the way he managed to ignore the jugs we were carrying, but at being referred to as a "kid." A long time since anyone had called me that. I wouldn't let anyone call me a "girl" these days, but somehow I didn't mind "kid."

"Today we tasted some of the best applejack in the world," Creighton said with convincing sincerity, "and Jasper told us you were the source." He slammed his two jugs on the table. "Fill 'em up!"

I placed my own jug next to Creighton's.

"I gotta warn you," Gus said. "It's five dollars a quart."

"Five dollars!" Creighton said.

"Yeah," Gus added quickly, "but seein' as you're buying so much at once–"

"Don't get me wrong, Mr. Sooy. I wasn't saying the price is too high. I was just shocked that you'd be selling such high grade sipping whiskey for such a low price."

"You were?" The old man beamed with delight. "It is awful good, isn't it?"

"That it is, sir. That it is. That it surely is."

I almost burst out laughing. I don't know how Creighton managed to keep a straight face.

Gus held up a finger. "You kids stay right here. I'll dip into my stock and be back in a jiffy."

We both broke down into helpless laughter as soon as he was gone.

"You're laying it on awful thick," I said when I caught my breath.

"I know, but he's lapping up every bit."

Gus returned in a few minutes with two gallon jugs of his own.

"Hadn't we ought to test this first before you begin filling our jugs?" Creighton said.

"Not a bad idea. No, sir, not a bad idea. Not a bad idea at all."

Creighton produced some paper cups from one of the pockets in his safari jacket and placed them on the table. Gus poured. We all sipped.

"This is even smoother than what Jasper served us. How do you do it, Mr. Sooy?"

"That's a secret," he said with a wink as he brought out a funnel and began decanting from his jugs into ours.

I brought up Jon's book and Gus launched into a slightly different version of the Jersey Devil story, saying it was born in Leeds, which is at the opposite end of the Pine Barrens from Estellville. Otherwise the tales were almost identical.

"Jasper says he saw the devil once," Creighton said as Gus topped off the last of our jugs.

"If he says he did, then he did. That'll be sixty dollar."

Creighton gave him three twenties.

"And now I'd like to buy you a drink, Mr. Sooy."

"Call me Gus. And I don't mind if I do."

Creighton was overly generous, I thought, with the way he filled the three paper cups. I didn't want any more, but I felt I had to keep up appearances. I sipped while the men quaffed.

"Jasper told us about the time he saw the Jersey Devil. He mentioned seeing pine lights at the same time."

I sensed rather than saw Gus stiffen.

"Is that so?"

"Yeah. He said you see pine lights around here all the time. Is that true?"

"You interested in pine lights or the Jersey Devil, boy?"

"Both. I'm interested in all the folk tales of the pines."

"Well, don't get too interested in the pine lights.

"Why not?"

"Just don't."

I watched Creighton tip his jug and refill Gus's cup.

"A toast!" Creighton said, lifting his cup. "To the Pine Barrens!"

"I'll drink to that!" Gus said, and drained his cup.

Creighton followed suit, causing his eyes to fill with tears. I sipped while he poured another round.

"To the Jersey Devil!" Creighton cried, hoisting his cup again.

And again they both tossed off their drinks. And then another round.

"To the pine lights!"

Gus wouldn't drink to that one. I was glad. I don't think either of them would have remained standing if he had.

"Have you seen any pine lights lately, Gus," Creighton said.

"You don't give up, do you, boy," the old man said.

"It's an affliction."

"So it is. All right. Sure. I see 'em all the time. Saw some last night."

"Really? Where?"

"None of your business."

"Why not?"

"Because you'll probably try to do something stupid like catch one, and then I'll be responsible for what happens to you and this young lady here. Not on my conscience, no thank you."

"I wouldn't dream of trying to catch one of those things!" Creighton said.

"Well, if you did you wouldn't be the first. Peggy Clevenger was the first." Gus lifted his head and looked at me. "You heard of Peggy Clevenger, ain't you, Miss McKelston?"

I nodded. "Sure. The Witch of the Pines. In the old days people used to put salt over their doors to keep her away."

Creighton began scribbling.

"No kidding? This is great! What about her and the pine lights?"

"Peggy was a Hessian, like me. Lived over in Pasadena. Not the California Pasadena, the Pines Pasadena. A few mile east of Mount Misery. The town's gone now, like it never been. But she lived thereabouts by herself in a small cabin, and people said she had all sorts of strange powers, like she could change her shape and become a rabbit or a snake. I don't know about that stuff, but I heard from someone who should know that she was powerful interested in the pine lights. She told this fella one day that she had caught one of the pine lights, put a spell on it and brought it down."

Creighton had stopped writing. He was staring at Gus.

"How could she...?"

"Don't know," Gus said, draining his cup and shaking his head. "But that very night her cabin burned to the ground. They found her blackened and burned body among the ashes the next morning. So I tell you, kids, it ain't a good idea to get too interested in the pine lights."

"I don't want to capture one," Creighton said. "I don't even want to see one. I just want to know where other people have seen them. How can that be dangerous?"

Gus thought about that. And while he was thinking, Creighton poured him another cupful.

"Don't s'pose it would do any harm to show you where they was," he said after a long slow sip.

"Then it's settled. Let's go."

We gathered up the jugs and headed out into the late afternoon sunshine. The fresh air was like a tonic. It perked me up but didn't dissipate the effects of all the jack I'd consumed.

When we reached the Wrangler, Creighton pulled out his sextant and compass.

"Before we go, there's something I've got to do."

Gus and I watched in silence as he took his sightings and scribbled in his notebook. Then he spread his map out on the hood again.

"What's up?" I said.

"I'm putting Razorback Hill on the map," he said.

He jotted his readings on the map and drew a circle. Before he folded everything up, I glanced over his shoulder and noticed that the line he had drawn from Apple Pie Hill ran right by the circle that was Razorback Hill.

"You through dawdlin'?" Gus said.

"Sure am. You want to ride in front?"

"No thanks," Gus said, heading for the rusty DeSoto. "I'll drive myself and you kids follow."

I said, "Won't it be easier if we all go together?"

"Hell no! You kids have been drinkin'!"

When we stopped laughing, we pulled ourselves into the Wrangler and followed the old Hessian back up his private sand road.

5. *The Firing Place.*

"I used to make charcoal here when I was young," Gus said.

We were standing in a small clearing surrounded by young pines. Before us was a shallow sandy depression, choked with weeds.

"This used to be my firing place. It was deeper then. I made some fine charcoal here before the big companies started selling their bags of 'brick-*etts*.'" He fairly spat the word. "Ain't no way any one of those smelly little things was ever part of a tree, I'll tell you that."

"Is this where you saw the lights, Gus?" Creighton said. "Were they moving?"

Gus said, "You got a one track mind, don't you, boy?" He glanced around. "Yeah, this is where I saw them. Saw them here last night and I saw them here fifty years ago, and I seen them near about every summer in between. Lots of memories here. I remember how while I was letting my charcoal burn I'd use the time to hunt up box turtles."

"And sell them as snail hunters?" I said.

I'd heard of box turtle hunting – another Pinelands mini-industry – but I'd never met anyone who'd actually done it.

"Sure. Folks in Philadelphia'd buy all I could find. They liked to let them loose in their cellars to keep the snails and slugs under control."

"The lights, Gus," Creighton said. "Which way were they going?"

"They was goin' the same way they always went when I seen them here. That way."

He was pointing southeast.

"Are you sure?"

"Sure as shit, boy." Gus's tone was getting testy, but he quickly turned to me. "'Scuse me, miss," then back to Creighton. "I was standing back there right where my car is when about a half dozen of them swooped in low right overhead – not a hunting swoop, but a floaty sort of swoop – and traveled away over that pitch pine there with the split top."

"Good!" said Creighton, eying the sky.

A thick sheet of cloud was pulling up from the west, encroaching on the sinking sun. Out came the sextant and compass. Creighton took his readings, wrote his numbers, then took a bearing on the tree Gus had pointed out. A slow, satisfied smile crept over his face as he drew the latest line on his map. He folded it up before I had a chance to see where that line went. I didn't have to see. His next question told me.

"Say, Gus," he said offhandedly. "What's on the far side of Razorback Hill?"

Gus turned on Creighton like an angry bear.

"Nothing! There's nothing there! So don't you even think about going over there!"

Creighton's smile was amused. "I was only asking. No harm in a little question, is there?"

"There is. There is. Yes, there surely is! Especially when those questions is the wrong ones. And you've been asking a whole lot of wrong questions, boy. Questions that's gonna get you in a whole mess of bad trouble if you don't get smart and learn that certain things is best left alone. You hear me?"

He sounded like a character from one of those old Frankenstein movies.

"I hear you," Creighton said, "and I appreciate your concern. But can you tell me the best way to get to the other side of that hill?"

Gus threw up his hands with an angry growl.

"That's it! I'm havin' no more to do with the two of you! I've already told you too much as it is." He turned to me, his eyes blazing. "And you, Miss McKelston, you get yourself away from this boy. He's headed straight to hell!"

With that he turned and headed for his car. He jumped in, slammed the door, and roared away with a spray of sand.

"I don't think he likes me," Creighton said.

"He seemed genuinely frightened," I told him.

Creighton shrugged and began packing away his sextant.

"Maybe he really believes in the Jersey Devil," he said. "Maybe he thinks it lives on the other side of Razorback Hill."

"I don't know about that. I got the impression he thinks the Jersey Devil is something to tell tall tales about while sitting around the stove and sipping jack. But those pine lights... he's scared of them."

"Just swamp gas, I'm sure," Creighton said.

Suddenly I was furious. Maybe it was all the jack I'd consumed, or maybe it was his attitude, but I think at that particular moment it was mostly his line of bull.

"Cut it, Jon!" I said. "If you really believe they're swamp gas, why are you tracking them on your map? You got me to guide you out here, so let's have it straight. What's going on?"

"I don't know what's going on, Mac. If I did, I wouldn't be here. Isn't that obvious? These pine lights mean something. Whether or not they're connected to the Jersey Devil, I don't know. Maybe they have a hallucinatory effect on people – after they pass overhead, people think they see things. I'm trying to establish a pattern."

"And after you've established this pattern, what do you think you'll find?"

"Maybe Truth," he said. "Reality. Who knows? Maybe the meaning – or meaninglessness – of life."

He looked at me with eyes so intense, so full of longing that my anger evaporated.

"Jon...?"

His expression abruptly shifted back to neutral and he laughed.

"Don't worry, Mac. It's only me, Crazy Creighton, putting you on again. Let's have another snort of Gus Sooy's best and head for civilization. Okay?"

"I've had enough for the day. The *week!*"

"You don't mind if I partake, do you?"

"Help yourself."

I didn't know how he could hold so much.

While Creighton uncorked his jug, I strolled about the firing place to clear my fuzzy head. The sky was fully overcast now and the temperature was dropping to a more comfortable level.

He had everything packed away by the time I completed the circle.

"Want me to drive?" he said, tossing his paper cup onto the sand.

Normally I would have picked it up – the was something sacrilegious about leaving a Dixie cup among the pines – but I was afraid to bend over that far, afraid I'd keep on going head first into the sand and become litter myself.

"I'm okay. You'll get us lost."

We had traveled no more than a hundred feet or so when I realized that I didn't know this road. But I kept driving. I hadn't been paying close attention while following Gus here, but I was pretty sure it wouldn't be long before I'd come to a fork or a cripple or a bog that I recognized, and then we'd be home free.

It didn't quite work out that way. I drove for maybe five miles or so, winding this way and that with the roads, making my best guess when we came to a fork – and we came to plenty of those – and generally trying to keep us heading in the same general direction. I thought I was doing a pretty good job until we drove through an area of young pines that looked familiar. I stopped the Wrangler.

"Jon," I said. "Isn't this–?"

"Damn right it is!" he said, pointing to the sand beside the road. "We're back at Gus's firing place! There's my Dixie cup!"

I turned the Jeep around and headed back the way I came.

"What are you doing?" Creighton said.

"Making sure I don't make the same mistake twice!" I told him.

I didn't know how I could have driven in a circle. I usually had an excellent sense of direction. I blamed it on too much Jersey lightning and on the thickly overcast sky. Without the sun as a marker, I'd been unable to keep us on course. But that would change here and now. I'd get us out of here this time around.

Wrong.

After a good forty-five minutes of driving, I was so embar-rassed when I recognized the firing place again that I actually accelerated as we passed through, hoping Creighton wouldn't recognize the spot in the thickening dusk. But I wasn't quick enough.

"Hold it!" he cried. "Hold it just a damn minute! There's my cup again! We're right back where we started!"

"Jon," I said, "I don't understand it. Something's wrong."

"You're stewed, that's what's wrong!"

"I'm not!"

I truly believed I wasn't. I'd been feeling the effects of the jack before, true, but my head was clear now. I was sure I'd been heading due east, or at least pretty close to it. How I'd come full circle again was beyond me.

Creighton jumped out of his seat and came around the front of the Wrangler.

"Over you go, Mac. It's my turn."

I started to protest, then thought better of it. I'd blown it twice already. Maybe my sense of direction had fallen prey to the "apple palsy," as it was known. I lifted myself over the stick shift and dropped into the passenger seat.

"Be my guest."

Creighton drove like a maniac, seemingly choosing forks at random.

"Do you know where you're going?" I said.

"Yeah, Mac," he said. "I'm going whichever way you *didn't!* I think."

As darkness closed in and he turned on the headlights, I noticed that the trees were thinning out and the underbrush was closing in, rising to eight feet or better on either side of us. Creighton pulled off to the side at a widening of the road.

"You should stay on the road," I told him.

"I'm lost," he said. "We've got to think."

"Fine. But it's not as if somebody's going to be coming along and want to get by."

He laughed. "That's a fact!" He got out and looked up at

the sky. "Damn! If it weren't for the clouds we could figure out where we are. Or least know where north is."

I looked around. We were surrounded by bushes. It was the Pine Barrens' equivalent of an English hedge maze. There wasn't a tree in sight. A tree can be almost as good as a compass – its moss faces north and its longest branches face south. Bushes are worse than useless for that, and the high ones only add to your confusion.

And we were confused.

"I thought Pineys never get lost," Creighton said.

"Everybody gets lost sooner or later out here."

"Well, what do Pineys do when they get lost?"

"They don't exhaust themselves or waste their gas by running around in circles. They hunker down and wait for morning."

"To hell with that!" Creighton said.

He threw the Wrangler into first and gunned it toward the road. But the vehicle didn't reach the road. It lurched forward and rocked back. He tried again and I heard the wheels spinning.

"Sugar!" I said.

Creighton looked at me and grinned.

"Stronger language is allowed and even encouraged in this sort of situation."

"I was referring to the sand."

"Don't worry. I've got four-wheel drive."

"Right. And all four wheels are spinning. We're in a patch of what's known as 'sugar sand.'"

He got out and pushed and rocked while I worked the gears and throttle, but I knew it was no use. We weren't going to get out of this superfine sand until we found some wood and piled it under the tires to give them some traction.

And we weren't going to be able to hunt up that kind of wood until morning.

I told Creighton that we'd only waste what gas we had left and that our best bet was to call it a night and pull out the sleeping bags. He seemed reluctant at first, worrying about deer ticks and catching Lyme disease, but he finally agreed.

He had no choice.

6. *The Pine Lights*

"I owe you one, Jon," I said.

"How was I to know we'd get lost?" he said defensively. "I don't like this any more than you!"

"No. You don't understand. I meant that in the good sense. I'm glad you talked me into coming with you."

I'd found us a small clearing not too far from the Jeep. It surrounded the gnarled trunk of an old lone pine that towered above the dominant brush. We'd eaten the last of the sandwiches and now we sat on our respective bedrolls facing each other across the Coleman lamp sitting between us on the sand. Creighton was back to sipping his applejack. I would have killed, or at least maimed, for a cup of coffee.

I watched his face in the lamp light. His expression was puzzled.

"You must still be feeling the effects of that Jersey lightning you had this afternoon," he said.

"No. I'm perfectly sober. I've been sitting here realizing that I'm glad to be back. I've had a feeling for years that something's been missing from my life. Never had an inkling as to what it was until now. But this is it. I'm..." My throat constricted around the word. "I'm home."

It wasn't the jack talking, it was my heart. I'd learned something today. I'd learned that I loved the Pine Barrens. And I loved its people. So rich in history, so steeped in its own lore, somehow surviving untainted in the heart of Twentieth Century urban madness. I'd turned my back on it. Why? Too proud? Too good for it now? Maybe I'd thought I'd pulled myself up by my bootstraps and gone on to bigger and better things. I could see that I hadn't. I'd taken the girl out of the Pinelands but I hadn't taken the Pinelands out of the girl.

I promised myself to come back here again. Often. I was going to look up my many relatives, renew old ties. I wasn't ready to move back here, and perhaps I never would, but I'd never turn my back on the Pinelands again.

Creighton raised his cup to me.

"I envy anyone who's found the missing piece. I'm still looking for mine."

"You'll find it," I said, crawling into my bedroll. "You've just got to keep your eyes open. Sometimes it's right under your nose."

"Go to sleep, Mac. You're starting to sound like Dorothy from *The Wizard of Oz*."

I smiled at that. For a moment there he was very much like the Jonathan Creighton I'd fallen in love with. As I closed my eyes, I saw him pull out a pair of binoculars and begin scanning the cloud-choked sky. I knew what he was looking for, and I was fairly confident he'd never find them.

It must have been a while later when I awoke, because the sky had cleared and the stars were out when Creighton's shouts yanked me to a sitting position.

"They're coming! Look at them, Mac! My God, they're coming!"

Creighton was standing on the far side of the lamp, pointing off to my left. I followed the line of his arm and saw nothing.

"What are you talking about?"

"Stand up, damn it! They're coming! There must be a dozen of them!"

I struggled to my feet and froze.

The starlit underbrush stretched away in a gentle rise for maybe a mile or two in the direction he was pointing, broken only occasionally by the angular shadows of the few scattered trees. And coming our way over that broad expanse, skimming along at treetop level, was an oblong cluster of faintly glowing lights. *Lights*. That's what they were. Not glowing spheres. Not UFOs or any of that nonsense. They had no discernible substance. They were just light. Globules of light.

I felt my hackles rise at the sight of them. Perhaps because I'd never seen light behave that way before – it didn't seem right or natural for light to concentrate itself in a ball. Or perhaps it was the way they moved, gliding through the night with such purpose, cutting through the dark, weaving from tree to tree, floating by the topmost branches, and then forging a path toward the next. Almost as if the trees were sign posts. Or perhaps it was the silence. The awful silence. The Pine Barrens are quiet as far as civilized sounds are concerned, but there's always the noise of the living things, the hoots and cries and rustlings of the animals, the incessant insect susurration. That was all gone now. There wasn't even a breeze to rustle the bushes. Silence. More than a mere absence of noise. A holding of breath.

"Do you see them, Mac? Tell me I'm not hallucinating! Do you see them?"

"I see them, Jon."

My voice sounded funny. I realized my mouth was dry. And not just from sleep.

Creighton turned around in a quick circle, his arms spread.

"I don't have a camera! I need a picture of this!"

"You didn't bring a camera?" I said. "My God, you brought everything else!"

"I know, but I never dreamed–"

Suddenly he was running for the tree at the center of our clearing.

"Jon! You're not really–?"

"They're coming this way! If I can get close to them–!"

I was suddenly afraid for him. Something about those lights was warning me away. Why wasn't it warning Creighton? Or was he simply not listening?

I followed him at a reluctant lope.

"Don't be an idiot, Jon! You don't know what they are!"

"Exactly! It's about time somebody found out!"

He started climbing. It was a big old pitch pine with no branches to speak of for the first dozen feet or so of its trunk, but its bark was knobby and rough enough for Creighton's rubber soled boots to find purchase. He slipped off twice, but he was determined. Finally he made it to the lowest branch, and from there on it looked easy.

I can't explain the crawling sensation in my gut as I watched Jonathan Creighton climbing toward a rendezvous with the approaching pine lights. He was three-quarters of the way to the top when the trunk began to shake and sway with his weight. Then a branch broke under his foot and he almost fell. When I saw that he'd regained safe footing, I sighed with relief. The branches above him were too frail to hold him. He couldn't go any higher. He'd be safe from the lights.

And the lights were here, a good dozen of them, from baseball to basketball size, gliding across our clearing in an irregular cylindrical cluster perhaps ten feet across and twenty feet long, heading straight for Creighton's tree.

And the closer they got, the faster my insides crawled. They may have been made up of light but it was not a clean light, not the golden healthy light of day. This was a wan, sickly, anemic glow, tainted with the vaguest hint of green. But thankfully it was a glow out of Creighton's reach as the lights brushed the tree's topmost needles.

I watched their glow limn Creighton's upturned face as his body strained upward, and I wondered at his recklessness, at this obsession with finding "reality." Was he flailing and floundering about in his search, or was he actually on the trail of something? And were the pine lights part of it?

As the first light passed directly above him, not five feet beyond his outstretched hand, I heard him cry out.

"They're humming, Mac! High pitched! Can you hear it? It's almost musical! And the air up here tingles, almost as if it's charged! This is fantastic!"

I didn't hear any music or feel any tingling. All I could hear was my heart thudding in my chest, all I could feel was the cold sweat that had broken out all over my body.

Creighton spoke again, he was practically shouting now, but in a language that was not English and not like any other language I'd ever heard. He made clicks and wheezes, and the few noises that sounded like words did not seem to fit comfortably on the human tongue.

"Jon, what are you doing up there?" I cried.

He ignored me and kept up the alien gibberish, but the lights, in turn, ignored him and sailed by above him as if he didn't exist.

The cluster was almost past now, yet still I couldn't shake the dread, the dark feeling that something awful was going to happen.

And then it did.

The last light in the cluster was basketball-sized. It seemed as if it was going to trail away above Creighton just like the others, but as it approached the tree, it slowed and began to drop toward Creighton's perch.

I was panicked now.

"Jon, look out! It's coming right for you!"

"I see it!"

As the other lights flowed off toward the next treetop, this last one hung back and circled Creighton's tree at a height level with his waist.

"Get down from there!" I called.

"Are you kidding? This is more than I'd ever hoped for!"

The light suddenly stopped moving and hovered a foot or so in front of Creighton's chest.

"It's cold," he said in a more subdued tone. "Cold light."

He reached his hand toward it and I wanted to shout for him not to but my throat was locked. The tip of his index finger touched the outer edge of the glow.

"*Really* cold."

I saw his finger sink into the light to perhaps the depth of the fingernail, and then suddenly the light moved. It more than moved, it *leapt* onto Creighton's hand, engulfing it.

That's when Creighton began to scream. His words were barely intelligible but I picked out the words "cold" and "burning" again and again. I ran to the base of the tree, expecting him to lose his balance, hoping I could do something to break his fall. I saw the ball of light stretch out and slide up the length of his arm, engulfing it.

Then it disappeared.

For an instant I thought it might be over. But when Creighton clutched his chest and cried out in greater agony, I realized to my horror that the light wasn't gone – it was inside him!

And then I saw the back of his shirt begin to glow. I watched the light ooze out of him and reform itself into a globe. Then it rose and glided off to follow the other lights into the night, leaving Creighton alone in the tree, sobbing and retching.

I called up to him. "Jon! Are you all right? Do you need help?"

When he didn't answer, I grabbed hold of the tree trunk. But before I could attempt to climb, he stopped me.

"Stay there, Mac." His voice was weak, shaky. "I'm coming down."

It took him twice as long to climb down as it had to go up. His movements were slow, unsteady, and three times he had to stop to rest. Finally, he reached the lowest branch, hung from it by one hand, and made the final drop. I grabbed him immediately to keep him from collapsing into a heap, and helped him back toward the lamp and the bedrolls.

"My God, Jon! Your arm!"

In the light from the lamp his flesh seemed to be smoking. The skin on his left hand and forearm was red, almost scalded looking. Tiny blisters were already starting to form.

"It looks worse than it feels."

"We've got to get you to a doctor."

He dropped to his knees on his bedroll and hugged his injured arm against his chest with his good one.

"I'm all right. It only hurts a little now."

"It's going to get infected. Come on. I'll see if I can get us to civilization."

"Forget it," he said, and I sensed some of the strength returning to his voice. "Even if we get the Jeep free, we're still lost. We couldn't find our way out of here when it was daylight. What makes you think we'll do any better in the dark?"

He was right. But I felt I had to do something.

"Where's your first aid kit?"

"I don't have one."

I blew up then.

"Jesus Christ, Jon! You're crazy, you know that? You could have fallen out of that tree and been killed! And if you don't wind up with gangrene in that arm it'll be a miracle! What on God's earth made you do something so stupid?"

He grinned. "I knew it! You still love me!"

I was not amused.

"This is serious, Jon. You risked your life up there! For what?"

"I have to know, Mac."

"'Know?' What do you have to 'know?' Will you stop giving me this bullshit?"

"I can't. I can't stop because it's true. I have to know what's real and what's not."

"Spare me—"

"I mean it. You're sure you know what's real and so you're content and complacent with that. You can't imagine what it's like not to know. To sense there's a veil across everything, a barrier that keeps you from seeing what's really there. You don't know what it's like to spend your life searching for the edge of that veil so you can lift it and peek – just peek – at what's behind it. I know it's out there, and I can't reach it. You don't know what that's like, Mac. It makes you crazy."

"Well, that's one thing we can agree on."

He laughed – it sounded strained – and reached for his jug of applejack with his good hand.

"Haven't you had enough of that tonight?"

I hated myself for sounding like an old biddy, but what I just seen had shaken me to the core. I was still trembling.

"No. Mac. The problem is I haven't had enough. Not nearly enough."

Feeling helpless and angry, I sat down on my own bedroll and watched him take a long pull from the jug.

"What happened up there, Jon?"

"I don't know. But I don't ever want it to happen again."

"And what were you saying? It almost sounded as if you were calling to them."

He looked up sharply and stared at me.

"Did you hear what I said?"

"Not exactly. It didn't even sound like speech."

"That's because it wasn't," he said, and I was sure I detected relief in his voice. "I was trying to attract their attention."

"Well, you sure did that."

Across the top of the Coleman lamp, I thought I saw him smile.

"Yeah. I did, didn't I?"

In the night around us, I noticed that the insects were becoming vocal again.

7. The Shunned Place

I'd planned to stay awake the rest of the night, but somewhere along the way I must have faded into sleep. The next thing I knew there was sunlight in my eyes. I leaped up, disoriented for a moment, then I remembered where I was.

But where was Creighton? His bedroll lay stretched out on the sand, his compass, sextant, and maps upon it, but he was nowhere in sight. I called his name a couple of times. He called back from somewhere off to my left. I followed the sound of his voice through the brush and emerged on the edge of a small pond rimmed with white cedars.

Creighton was kneeling at the edge, cupping some water in his right hand.

"How'd you find this?" I said.

"Simple." He pointed out toward a group of drakes and mallards floating on the still surface. "I followed the quacking."

"You're becoming a regular Mark Trail. How's the water?"

"Polluted." He pointed to a brownish blue slick on the surface of the pond, then held up a palmful of clear, brownish water. "Look at that color. Looks like tea."

"That's not polluted," I told him. "That's the start of some bog iron floating over there. And this is cedar water. It gets brown from the iron deposits and from the cedars but it's as pure as it comes."

I scooped up double handful and took a long swallow.

"Almost sweet," I said. "Sea captains used to come into these parts to fill their water casks with cedar water before long voyages. They said it stayed fresher longer."

"Then I guess it's okay to bathe this in it," he said, twisting and showing me his left arm.

I gasped. I couldn't help it. I'd almost half-convinced myself that last night's incident with the pine light had been a nightmare. But the reddened, crusted, blistered skin on Creighton's arm said otherwise.

"We've got to get you to a doctor," I said.

"It's all right, Mac. Doesn't really hurt. Just feels hot."

He sank it past his elbow into the cool cedar water.

"Now *that* feels good!"

I looked around. The sun shone from a cloudless sky. We'd have no trouble finding our way out of here this morning. I stared out over the pond. Water. The sandy floor of the Pine Barrens was like a giant sponge that absorbed a high percentage of the rain that fell on it. It was the largest, untapped aquifer in the northeast. No rivers flowed into the Pinelands, only out. The water here was glacial in its purity. I'd read somewhere that the Barrens held an amount of water equivalent to a lake with a surface area of a thousand square miles and an average depth of 75 feet.

This little piece of wetness here was less than fifty yards across. I watched the ducks. They were quacking peacefully, tooling around, dipping their heads. Then one of them made a different sound, more like a squawk. It flapped its wings once and was gone. It happened in the blink of an eye. One second a floating duck, next second some floating bubbles.

"Did you see that?" Creighton said.

"Yeah, I did."

"What happened to that duck?" I could see the excitement starting to glow in his eyes. "What's it mean?"

"It means a snapping turtle. A big one. Fifty pounds or better, I'm sure."

Creighton pulled his arm from the pond.

"I do believe I've soaked this enough for now."

He dipped a towel in the water and wrapped it around his scorched arm.

We walked back to the bedrolls, packed up our gear, and made our way through the brush to the Wrangler.

The Jeep was occupied.

There were people inside, and people sitting on the hood and standing on the bumpers as well. A good half dozen in all.

Only they weren't like any people I'd ever seen.

They were dressed like typical Pineys, but dirty, raggedy. The four men in jeans or canvas pants, collared shirts of various fabrics and colors or plain white tee-shirts; the two women wore cotton jumpers. But they were all deformed. Their heads were odd shapes and sizes, some way too small, others large and lopsided with bulbous protrusions. The eyes on a couple weren't lined up on the level. Everyone seemed to have one arm or leg longer than the other. Their teeth, at least in the ones who still had any, seemed to have come in at random angles.

When they spotted us, they began jabbering and pointing our way. They left the Wrangler and surrounded us. It was an intimidating group.

"Is that your car?" a young man with a lopsided head said to me.

"No." I pointed to Creighton. "It's his."

"Is that your car?" he said to Creighton.

I guessed he didn't believe me.

"It's a Jeep," Creighton said.

"Jeep! Jeep!" He laughed and kept repeating the word. The others around him took it up and chorused along.

I looked at Creighton and shrugged. We'd apparently come upon an enclave of the type of folks who'd helped turn "Piney" into a term of derision shortly before World War I. That was when Elizabeth Kite published a report titled "The Pineys" which was sensationalized by the press and led to the view that the Pinelands was a bed of alcoholism, illiteracy, degeneracy, incest, and resultant "feeblemindedness."

Unfair and untrue. But not entirely false. There has always been illiteracy and alcoholism deep in the Pinelands. Schooling here tended to be rudimentary if at all. And as for drinking? The first "drive-thru" service originated before the Revolution in the Piney jug taverns, allowing customers to ride up to a window, get their jugs topped off with applejack, pay, and move on without ever dismounting. But after the economy of the Pine Barrens faltered, and most of the workers moved on to greener pastures, much of the social structure collapsed. Those who stayed on grew a little lax as to the whys, hows, and to-whoms of marriage. The results were inevitable.

All that had supposedly changed in modern times, except in the most isolated area of the Pines. We had stumbled upon one of those areas. Except that the deformities here were extra-ordinary. I'd seen a few of the inbreds in my youth. There'd been something subtly odd about them, but nothing that terribly startling. These folk would stop you in your tracks.

"Let's head for the Jeep while they're yucking it up," I said out of the corner of my mouth.

"No. Wait. This is fascinating. Besides, we need their help."

He spoke to the group as a whole and asked their aid in freeing the Jeep.

Somebody said, "Sugar sand," and this was repeated all around. But they willingly set their shoulders against the Wrangler and we were on hard ground again in minutes.

"Where do you live?" Creighton said to anyone who was listening.

Someone said, "Town," and as one they all pointed east, toward the sun. It was also the direction the lights had been headed last night.

"Will you show me?"

They nodded and jabbered and tugged on our sleeves, anxious to show us.

"Really, Jon," I said. "We should get you to–"

"My arm can wait. This won't take long."

We followed the group in a generally uphill direction along a circuitous footpath unnavigable by any vehicle other than a motorcycle. The trees thickened and soon we were in shade. And then those trees opened up and we were in their "town."

A haze of blue wood smoke hung over a ramshackle collection of shanties made of scrap lumber and sheet metal. Garbage everywhere, and everyone coming out to look at the strangers. I'd never seen such squalor.

The fellow with the lopsided head who'd asked about the jeep before pulled Creighton toward one of the shacks.

"Hey, mister, you know about machines. How come this don't work?"

He had an old TV set inside his one room hut. He turned the knobs back and forth.

"Don't work. No pictures."

"You need electricity," Creighton told him.

"Got it. Got it. Got it."

He led us around to the back to show us the length of wire he had strung from a tree to the roof of the shack.

Creighton turned to me with stricken eyes.

"This is awful. No one should have to live like this. Can we do anything for them?"

His compassion surprised me. I'd never thought there was room for anyone else's concerns in his self-absorbed life. But then, Jonathan Creighton had always been a motherlode of surprises.

"Not much. They all look pretty content to me. Seem to have their own little community. If you bring them to the government's attention they'll be split up and most of them will probably be placed in institutions or group homes. I guess the best you can do is give them whatever you can think of to make the living easier here."

Creighton nodded, still staring around him.

"Speaking of 'here,'" he said, unshouldering his knapsack, "let's find out where we are."

The misshapen locals stared in frank awe and admiration as he took his readings. Someone asked him, "What is that thing?" a hundred times. At least. Another asked "What happened to your arm?" an equal number of times. Creighton was heroically patient with everyone. He knelt on the ground to transfer his readings to the map, then looked up at me.

"Know where we are?"

"The other side of Razorback Hill, I'd say."

"You got it."

He stood up and gathered the locals around him.

"I'm looking for a special place around here," he said.

Most of them nodded eagerly. Someone said, "We know every place there is around here, I reckon."

"Good. I'm looking for a place where nothing grows. Do you know a place like that?"

It was as if all of these people had a common plug and Creighton had just pulled it. The lights went out, the shades came down, the "Open" signs flipped to "Closed." They began to turn away.

"What'd I say?" he said, turning his anxious, bewildered eyes on me. "What'd I *say?*"

"You're starting to sound like Ray Charles," I told him. "Obviously they want nothing to do with this 'place where nothing grows' you're talking about. What's this all about, Jon?"

He ignored my question and laid his good hand on the shoulder of one of the small-headed men.

"Won't you take me there if you know where it is?"

"We know where it is," the fellow said in a squeaky voice. "But we never go there so we can't take you there. How can we take you there if we never go there?"

"You *never* go there? Why not?"

The others had stopped and were listening to the exchange. The small headed fellow looked around at his neighbors and gave them a look that asked how stupid could anyone be? Then he turned back to Creighton.

"We don't go there 'cause nobody goes there."

"What's your name?" Creighton said.

"Fred."

"Fred, my name is Jon, and I'll give you..." He patted his pockets, then tore the watch off his wrist. "I'll give you this beautiful watch that you don't have to wind – see how the numbers change with every second? – if you'll take me to a place where you *do* go, and point out the place where nothing grows. How's that sound?"

Fred took the watch and held it up close to his right eye, then smiled.

"Come on! I'll show you!"

Creighton took off after Fred, and I took off after Creighton.

Again we were led along a circuitous path, this one even narrower than before, becoming less well defined as we went along. I noticed the trees becoming fewer in number and more stunted and gnarled, and the underbrush thinning out, the leaves fewer and curled on their edges. We followed Fred until he halted as abruptly as if he had run into an invisible wall. I saw why: the footpath we'd been following stopped here. He pointed ahead through what was left of the trees and underbrush.

"The bald spot's over yonder atop that there rise."

He turned and hurried back along the path.

Bald spot?

Creighton looked at me, then shrugged.

"Got your machete handy, Mac?"

"No, Bwana."

"Too bad. I guess we'll just have to bull our way through."

He rewrapped his burned arm and pushed ahead. It wasn't such rough going. The underbrush thinned out quickly and so we had an easier time of it than I'd anticipated. Soon we broke into a small field lined with scrappy weeds and occupied by the scattered, painfully gnarled trunks of dead trees. And in the center of the field was a patch of bare sand.

...a place where nothing grows...

Creighton hurried ahead. I held back, restrained by a sense of foreboding. The same something deep within me that had feared the pine lights feared this place as well. Something was wrong here, as if Nature had been careless, had made a mistake in this place and had never quite been able to rectify it. As if...

What was I thinking? It was an empty field. No eerie lights buzzing through the sky. No birds, either, for that matter. So what? The sun was up, a breeze was blowing – or at least it had been a moment ago.

Overruling my instincts, I followed Creighton. I touched the tortured trunk of one of the dead trees as I passed. It was hard and cold, like stone. A petrified tree. In the Pinelands.

I hurried ahead and caught up to Creighton at the edge of the "bald spot." He was staring at it as if in a trance. The spot was a rough oval, maybe thirty feet across. Nothing grew in that oval. Nothing.

"Look at that pristine sand," he said in a whisper. "Birds don't fly over it, insects and animals don't walk on it. Only the wind touches and shapes it. That's the way sand looked at the beginning of time."

It had always been my impression that sand wasn't yet sand at the beginning of time, but I didn't argue with him. He was on a roll. I remembered from college: You don't stop Crazy Creighton when he's on a roll.

I saw what he meant, though. The sand was rippled like water, like sand must look in areas of the Sahara far off the trade routes. I saw animal tracks leading up to it and then turning aside. Creighton was right: nothing trod this soil.

Except Creighton.

Without warning he stepped across the invisible line and walked to the center of the bald spot. He spread his arms, looked up and the sky, and whirled in dizzying circles. His eyes were aglow, his expression rapturous. He looked stoned out of his mind.

"This is it! I've found it! This is the place!"

"*What* place, Jon?"

I stood at the edge of the spot, unwilling to cross over, talking in the flat tone you might use to coax a druggie back from a bad trip, or a jumper down from a ledge.

"Where it all comes together and all comes apart! Where the Truth is revealed!"

"What the hell are you talking about, Jon?"

I was tired and uneasy and I wanted to go home. I'd had enough, and I guessed my voice showed it. The rapture faded. Abruptly, he was sober.

"Nothing, Mac. Nothing. Just let me take a few readings and we're out of here."

"That's the best news I've heard this morning."

He shot me a quick glance. I didn't know if it conveyed annoyance or disappointment. And I didn't care.

8. *Spreading Infection*

I got us back to a paved road without too much difficulty. We spoke little on the way home. He dropped me off at my house and promised to see a doctor before the day was out.

"What's next for you?" I said as I closed the passenger door and looked at him through the open window.

I hoped he wouldn't ask me to guide him back into the Pines again. I was sure he hadn't been straight with me about his research. I didn't know what he was after, but I knew it wasn't the Jersey Devil. A part of me said it was better not to know, that this man was a juggernaut on a date with disaster.

"I'm not sure. I may go back and see those people, the ones on the far side of Razorback Hill. Maybe bring them some clothing, some food."

Against my will, I was touched.

"That would be nice. Just don't bring them toaster cakes or microwave dinners."

He laughed. "I won't."

"Where are you staying?"

He hesitated, looking uncertain.

"A place called the Laurelton Circle Motor Inn."

"I know it."

A tiny place. Sporting the name of a traffic circle that no longer existed.

"I'm staying in room five if you need to get hold of me but...can you do me a favor? If anybody comes looking for me, don't tell them where I am. Don't tell them you've even seen me."

"Are you in some sort of trouble?"

"A misunderstanding, that's all."

"You wouldn't want to elaborate on that, would you?"

His expression was bleak.

"The less you know, Mac, the better."

"Like everything else these past two days, right?"

He shrugged. "Sorry."

"Me, too. Look. Stop by before you head back to Razorback. I may have a few old things I can donate to those folks."

He waved with his burnt hand, and then he was off.

*

Creighton stopped by a few days later on his way back to Razorback Hill. His left arm was heavily bandaged in gauze.

"You were right," he said. "It got infected."

I gave him some old sweaters and shirts and a couple of pairs of jeans that no longer fit the way they should.

*

The following week I bumped into him in the housewares aisle at Pathmark. He'd picked up some canned goods and was buying a couple of can openers for the Razorback folks. His left arm was bandaged as before, but I was concerned to see that there was gauze on his right hand now.

"The infection spread a little, but the doctor says it's okay. He's got me on this new antibiotic. Sure to kill it off."

Looking more closely now in the supermarket's fluorescent glare, I saw that he was pale and sweaty. He seemed to have lost weight.

"Who's your doctor?"

"Guy up in Neptune. A specialist."

"In pine light burns?"

His laugh was a bit too loud, a tad too long.

"No! Infections."

I wondered. But Jon Creighton was a big boy now. I couldn't be his mother.

I picked out some canned goods myself, checked out behind Creighton, and gave the bagful to him.

"Give them my best," I told him.

He smiled wanly and hurried off.

*

At the very tail end of August I was driving down Brick Boulevard when I spotted his Wrangler idling at the Burger King drive-thru window. I pulled into the lot and walked over.

Jon!" I said through the window and saw him jump.

"Oh, Mac. Don't ever do that!"

He looked relieved, but he didn't look terribly glad to see me. His face seemed thinner, but maybe that was because of the beard he had started to grow. A fugitive's beard.

"Sorry," I said. "I was wondering if you wanted to get together for some *real* lunch."

"Oh. Well. Thanks, but I've got a lot of errands to run. Maybe some other time."

Despite the heat, he was wearing corduroy pants and a long sleeved flannel shirt. I noticed that both his hands were still wrapped in gauze. An alarm went off inside me.

"Isn't that infection cleared up yet?"

"It's coming along slowly, but it's coming."

I glanced down at his feet and noticed that his ankles looked thick. His sneakers were unlaced, their tongues lolling out as the sides stretched to accommodate his swollen feet.

"What happened to your feet?"

"A little edema. Side effect of the medicine. Look, Mac, I've got to run." He threw the Wrangler into gear. "I'll call you soon."

*

Labor Day was a couple of weeks gone and I'd been thinking about Creighton a lot. I was worried about him, and was realizing that I still harbored deeper feelings for him than I cared to admit.

Then the state trooper showed up at my office. He was big and intimidating behind his dark glasses; his haircut came within a millimeter of complete baldness. He held out a grainy photo of Jon Creighton.

"Do you know this man?" he said in a deep voice.

My mouth was dry as I wondered if he was going to ask me if I was involved in whatever Creighton had done; or worse: if I'd care to come down and identify the body.

"Sure. We went to college together."

"Have you seen him in the past month?"

I didn't hesitate. I did the stand-up thing.

"Nope. Not since graduation."

"We have reason to believe he's in the area. If you see him, contact the State Police or your local police immediately."

"What's he done, officer?"

He turned and started toward the door without deigning to answer. That brand of arrogance never failed to set something off in me.

"I asked you a question, *officer*. I expect the courtesy of a reply."

He turned and looked at me, then shrugged. Some of the Dirty Harry facade slipped away with the shrug.

"Why not?" he said. "He's wanted for grand theft."

Oh, great.

"What did he steal?"

"A book."

"A *book*?"

"Yeah. Would you believe it? We've got rapes and murders and armed robberies, but this book is given a priority. I don't care how valuable it is or how much some university in Massachusetts wants it, it's only a book. But the Massachusetts people are really hot to get it back. Their governor got to our governor and... well, you know how it goes. We found his car abandoned out near Lakehurst a while back, so we know he's been through here."

"You think he's on foot?"

"Maybe. Or maybe he rented or stole another car. We're running it down now."

"If he shows up, I'll let you know."

"Do that. I get the impression that if he gives the book back in one piece, all will be forgiven."

"I'll tell him that if I get the chance."

As soon as he was gone, I got on the phone to Creighton's motel. His voice was thick when he said hello.

"Jon! The state cops were just here looking for you!"

He mumbled a few words I didn't understand. Something was wrong. I hung up and headed for my car.

There are only about 20 rooms in that particular motel. I spotted the Wrangler backed into a space at the far end of the tiny parking lot. Number 5 was on a corner of the first floor. A *Do Not Disturb* sign hung from the knob. I knocked on the door twice and got no answer. I tried the knob. It turned.

It was dark inside except for the daylight I'd let in. And that light revealed a disaster area. The room looked like the inside of a dumpster behind a block of fast food stores. Smelled like one, too. There were pizza boxes, hamburger wrappers, submarine sleeves, Chinese food cartons, a sampling from every place in the area that delivered. And it was hot. Either the air conditioner had quit or it hadn't been turned on.

"Jon?" I flipped on the light. "Jon, are you here?"

He was in a chair in a corner on the far side of the bed, huddled under a pile of blankets. Papers and maps were piled on the night table beside him. His face, where visible above his matted beard, was pale and drawn. He looked as if he'd lost thirty pounds. I slammed the door closed and stood there, stunned.

"My God, Jon, what's wrong?"

"Nothing. I'm fine." His hoarse, thick voice said otherwise. "What are you doing here, Mac?"

"I came to tell you that the State Police are cruising around with photos of you, but I can see that's the least of your problems! You're really sick!" I reached for the phone. "I'm calling an ambulance."

"*No!* Mac, please *don't!*"

The terror and soul-wrenching anguish in his voice stopped me. I stared at him but still kept a grip on the receiver.

"Why not?"

"Because I'm begging you not to!"

"But you're sick, you could be dying, you're out of your head!"

"No. That's one thing I'm not. Trust me when I say that no hospital in the world can help me – because I'm not dying. And if you ever loved me, if you ever had any regard for who I am and what I want from my life, then you'll put down that phone and walk out that door."

I stood there in the hot, humid squalor of that tiny room, receiver in hand, smelling the garbage, detecting the hint of another odor, a subtle sour foulness that underlay the others, and felt myself being torn apart by the choice that faced me.

"Please, Mac," he said. "You're the only person in the world who'll understand. Don't hand me over to strangers." He sobbed once. "I can't fight you. I can only beg you. Please. Put down the phone and leave."

It was the sob that did it. I slammed the receiver onto its cradle.

"Damn you!"

"Two days, Mac. In two days I'll be better. You wait and see."

"You're damn right I'll see – I'm staying here with you!"

"No! You can't! You have no right to intrude! This is *my* life! You've got to let me take it where I must! Now leave, Mac. Please."

He was right, of course. This was what we'd been all about when we'd been together. I had to back off. And it was killing me.

"All right," I said around the lump in my throat. "You win.

See you in two days."

Without waiting for a reply, I opened the door and stepped out into the bright September sunlight.

"Thanks, Mac," he said. "I love you."

I didn't want to hear that. I took one last look back as I pulled the door closed. He was still swaddled from his neck to the floor in the blankets, but in the last instant before the door shut him from view, I thought I saw something white and pointed, about the circumference of a garden hose, snake out on the carpet from under the blankets and then quickly pull back under cover.

A rush of nausea slammed me against the outer wall of the motel as the door clicked closed. I leaned there, sick and dizzy, trying to catch my breath.

A trick of the light. That was what I told myself as the vertigo faded. I'd been squinting in the brightness and the light had played a trick.

Of course, I didn't have to settle for merely telling myself. I could simply open the door and check it out. I actually reached for the knob, but couldn't bring myself to turn it.

Two days. Creighton had said two days. I'd find out then.

*

But I didn't last two days. I was unable to concentrate the following morning and wound up canceling all my appointments. I spent the entire day pacing my office or my living room; and when I wasn't pacing, I was on the phone. I called the American Folklore Society and the New Jersey Historical Society. Not only had they not given Creighton the grants he'd told me about, they'd never heard of him.

By nightfall I'd taken all I could. I began calling Creighton's room. I got no answer. I tried few more times, but when he still hadn't picked up by eleven o'clock, I headed for the motel.

I was almost relieved to see the Wrangler gone from the parking lot. Room five was still unlocked and still a garbage dump, which meant he was still renting it – or hadn't been gone too long.

What was he up to?

I began to search the room. I found the book under the bed. It was huge, heavy, wrapped in plastic with a scrawled note taped to the front:

Please return to Department of Anthropology archives

I slipped it out of the plastic. It was leatherbound and hand-written in Latin. I could barely decipher the title – something like *Liben Damnatus.* But inside the front cover were Creighton's maps and a sheaf of notes in his back-slanted scrawl. The notes were in disarray and probably would have been disjointed even if arranged in proper order. But certain words and phrases kept recurring: *nexus point* and *equinox* and *the lumens* and *the veil.*

It took me awhile but eventually I got the drift of the jot-tings. Apparently a section the book Creighton had stolen con-cerned "nexus points" around the globe where twice a year at the vernal and autumnal equinox "the veil" that obscures real-ity becomes detached for a short while, allowing an intrepid soul to peek under the hem and see the true nature of the world around us, the world we are not "allowed" to see. These "nexus points" are few and widely scattered. Of the four known, there's one near each pole, one in Tibet, and one near the east coast of North America.

I sighed. Crazy Creighton had really started living up to his name. It was sad. This was so unlike him. He'd been the ulti-mate cynic, and now he was risking his health and his freedom pursuing this mystical garbage.

And what was even sadder was how he had lied to me. Obvi-ously he hadn't been searching for tales of the Jersey Devil – he'd been searching for one of these 'nexus points." And he was prob-ably convinced he'd found one behind Razorback Hill.

I pitied him. But I read on.

According to the notes, these "nexus points" can be located by following "the lumens" to a place shunned equally by man, beast, and vegetation.

Suddenly I was uneasy. "The lumens." Could that refer to the pine lights? And the "bald spot" that Fred had showed us –

that was certainly a place shunned by man, beast, and vegetation.

I found a whole sheet filled with notes about the Razorback folk. The last paragraph was especially upsetting:

The folks behind Razorback Hill aren't deformed from inbreeding, although I'm sure that's contributed its share. I believe they're misshapen as a result of living near the nexus point for generations. The semi-annual lifting of the veil must have caused genetic damage over the years.

I pulled out Creighton's maps and unfolded them on the bed. I followed the lines he had drawn from Apple Pie Hill, from Gus's firing place, and from our campsite. All three lines represented paths of pine lights, and all three intersected at a spot near the circle he had drawn and labeled as Razorback Hill. And right near the intersection of the pine light paths, almost on top of it, he had drawn another circle, a tiny one, penciled in the latitude and longitude, and labeled it, *Nexus!*

I was worried now. Even my own skepticism was beginning to waver. Everything was fitting too neatly. I looked at my watch. 11:32. The date read "21." September 21. When was the equinox? I grabbed the phone and called an old clamdigger who'd been a client since I'd opened my office. He knew the answer right off:

"The autumnal equinox. That's September twenty-second. 'Bout a half hour from now."

I dropped the phone and ran for my car. I knew exactly where to find Jon Creighton.

9. *The Hem of the Veil*

I raced down the Parkway to the Bass River exit and tried to find my way back to Gus Sooy's place. What had been a difficult trip in the day proved to be several orders of magnitude more difficult in the dark. But I managed to find Gus's red cedar. It was my plan to convince him to show me a short way to the far side of Razorback Hill, figuring the fact that Creighton was already there might make him more tractable. But when I rushed up to Gus Sooy's clearing, I discovered that he wasn't alone.

The Razorback folk were there. All of them, from the looks of the crowd.

I found Gus standing on his front step, a jug dangling from his hand. He was obviously shocked to see me, and was anything but hospitable.

"What do you want?"

Before I could answer, the Razorback folks recognized me and a small horde of them crowded around.

"Why are they all here?" I asked Gus.

"Just visiting,' he said casually, but did not look me in the eye.

"It wouldn't have anything to do with what's happening at the bald spot on the other side of Razorback Hill would it?"

"Damn you! You've been snoopin' around, haven't you? You and your friend. They told me he was coming around, askin' all sorts of questions. Where's he now? Hidin' in the bushes?"

"He's over there," I said, pointing to the top of Razorback Hill. "And if my guess is correct, he's standing right in the middle of the bald spot."

Gus dropped his jug. It shattered on the boards of his front step.

"Do you know what'll happen to him?"

"No," I said. "Do you?" I looked around at the Razorback folk. "Do they?"

"I don't think anyone knows, leastmost them. But they're scared. They come here twice a year, when that bald spot starts acting up."

"Have you ever seen what happens there?"

"Once. Never want to see it again."

"Why haven't you ever told anyone?"

"What? And bring all sorts of pointyheads here to look and gawk and build and ruin the place. We'd all rather put up with the bald spot craziness twice a year than pointyhead craziness every day all year long."

I didn't have time to get into Creighton's theory that the bald spot was genetically damaging the Razorback folks. I had to find Creighton.

"How do I get there? What's the fastest way?"

"You can't–"

"*They* got here!" I pointed to the Razorback folks.

"All right!" he said with open hostility. "Suit yourself. There's a trail behind my cabin here. Follow it over the left flank of the hill."

"And then?"

"And then you won't need any directions. You'll know where to go."

His words had an ominous ring, but I couldn't press him. I was being propelled by a sense of enormous urgency. Time was running out. Quickly. I already had my flashlight, so I hurried to the rear of his shanty and followed the trail.

Gus was right. As I crossed the flank of the hill I saw flashes through the trees ahead, like lightning, as if a very tiny and very violent electrical storm had been brought to ground and anchored there. I increased my pace, running when the terrain would allow. The wind picked up as I neared the storm area, growing from a fitful breeze to a full scale gale by the time I broke through the brush and stumbled into the clearing that surrounded the bald spot.

Chaos. That's the only way I can describe it. A nightmare of cascading lights and roaring wind. The pine lights – or *lumens* – were there, hundreds of them, all sizes, unaffected by the rushing vortex of air as they swirled about in wild arcs, each flaring brilliantly as it looped through the space above the bald spot. And the bald spot itself – it glowed with a faint purplish light that reached thirty or forty feet into the air before fading into the night.

The stolen book, Creighton's notes – they weren't mystical madness. Something cataclysmic was happening here, something that defied all the laws of nature – if indeed those laws had any real meaning. Whether this was one of the nexus points he had described, a fleeting rent in the reality that surrounded us, only Creighton could say for sure right now.

For I could see someone in the bald spot. I couldn't make out his features from where I was, but I knew it was Jonathan Creighton.

I dashed forward until I reached the edge but slewed to a halt in the sand before actually crossing into the glow. Creighton was there, on his knees, his hands and feet buried in the sand. He was staring about him, his expression an uneasy mix of fear and wonder. I shouted his name but he didn't hear me above the roar of the wind. Twice he looked directly at me but despite my frantic shouting and waving, did not see me.

I saw no other choice. I had to step onto the bald spot... the nexus point. It wasn't easy. Every instinct I possessed screamed at me to run in the other direction, but I couldn't leave him there like that. He looked helpless, trapped like an insect on fly-paper. I had to help him.

Taking a deep breath, I closed my eyes and stepped across –

–and began to stumble forward. Up and down seemed to have a slightly different orientation here. I opened my eyes and dropped to my knees, nearly landing on Creighton. I looked around and froze.

The Pine Barrens were gone. *Night* was gone. It seemed to be pre-dawn or dusk here, but the wind still howled about us and the pine lights flashed around us, appearing and disappearing above as though passing through invisible walls. We were someplace... *else*: on a huge misty plain that seemed to stretch on forever, interrupted only by clumps of vegetation and huge fog banks, one of which was nearby on my left and seemed to go on and up forever. Off in the immeasurable distance, mountains the size of the moon reached up and disappeared into the haze of the purple sky. The horizon – or what I imagined to be the horizon – didn't curve as it should. This place seemed so much *bigger* than the world – our world – that waited just a few feet away.

"My God, Jon, where are we!"

He started and turned his head. His hands and feet remained buried in the sand. His eyes went wide with shock at the sight of me.

"No! You shouldn't be here!"

His voice was thicker and more distorted than yesterday. Oddly enough, his pale skin looked almost healthy in the mauve light.

"Neither should you!"

I heard something then. Above the shriek of the wind came another sound. A rumble like an avalanche. It came from somewhere within the fog bank to our left. There was something massive, something immense moving about in there, and the fog seemed to be drifting this way.

"We've got to get out of here, Jon!"

"No! I'm staying!"

"No way! Come on!"

He was wracked with infection and obviously deranged. I didn't care what he said, I wasn't going to let him risk his life in this place. I'd pull him out of here and let him think about it for six months. *Then* if he still wanted to try this, it would be his choice. But he wasn't competent now.

I looped my arms around his chest and tried to pull him to his feet.

"Mac, please! Don't!"

His hands remained fixed in the sand. He must have been holding onto something. I grabbed his right elbow and yanked. He screamed as his hand pulled free of the sand. Then I screamed, too, and let him go and threw myself back on the sand away from him.

Because his hand wasn't a hand anymore.

It was big and white and had these long, ropey, tapered root like projections, something like an eye on a potato when it sprouts after being left under the sink too long, only these things were moving, twisting and writing like a handful of albino snakes.

"Go, Mac!" he said in that distorted voice, and I could tell from his face and eyes that he hadn't wanted me to see him like this. "You don't belong here!"

"And you do?"

"*Now* I do!"

I couldn't bring myself to touch his hand, so I reached forward and grabbed some of his shirt. I pulled.

"We can find doctors! They can fix you! You can–"

"*NO!*"

It was a shout and it was something else. Something long and white and hard as flexed muscle, much like the things protruding from his shirt sleeve, darted out of his mouth and slammed against my chest, bruising my breasts as it thrust me away. Then it whipped back into his mouth.

I snapped then. I scrambled to my feet and blindly lurched away in the direction I'd come. Suddenly I was back in the Pine Barrens, in the cool night with the lights swirling madly above my head. I stumbled for the bushes, away from the nexus point, away from Jonathan Creighton.

At the edge of the clearing, I forced myself to stop and look back. I saw Creighton. His awful transformed hand was raised. I knew he couldn't see me, but it was almost as if he was waving good-bye. Then he lowered his hand and worked the tendrils back into the sand.

The last thing I remember of that night is vomiting.

10. *Aftermath*

I awoke among the Razorback folk who'd found me the next morning and watched over me until I was conscious and lucid again. They offered me food but I couldn't eat. I walked back up to the clearing, to the bald spot.

It looked exactly as it had when Creighton and I had first seen it in August. No lights, no wind, no purple glow. Just bare sand.

And no Jonathan Creighton. I could have convinced myself that last night had never happened if not for the swollen, tender, violet bruise on my chest. Would that I had. But as much as my mind shrank from it, I could not deny the truth. I'd seen the other side of the veil and my life would never be the same.

I looked around and knew that everything I saw was a sham, an elaborate illusion. Why? Why was the veil there? To protect us from harm? Or to shield us from madness? The truth had brought me no peace. Who could find comfort in the knowledge that huge, immeasurable forces beyond our comprehension were out there, moving about us, beyond the reach of our senses?

I wanted to run...but where?

I ran home. I've been home for months now. Housebound. Moving beyond my door only for groceries. My accounting clients have all left me. I'm living on my savings, learning Latin, translating Jon's stolen book. Was what I saw the true reality of our existence, or another dimension, or what? I don't know. Creighton was right: knowing that you don't know is maddening. It consumes you.

So I'm waiting for spring. Waiting for the vernal equinox. Maybe I'll leave the house before then and hunt up some pine lights – or *lumens*, as the book calls them. Maybe I'll touch one, maybe I won't. Maybe when the equinox comes, I'll return to Razorback Hill, to the bald spot. Maybe I'll look for Jon. He may be there, he may not. I may cross into the bald spot, I may not. And if I do, I may not come back. Or I may.

I don't know what I'll do. I don't know anything anymore. I've come to the point now where I'm sure of only one thing: Nothing is sure anymore.

At least on this side of the veil.

TENANTS

"When time is unfurled and we're called by the world."

The idea for "Tenants" had been wandering through the back of my mind for years. A simple little story about an escaped killer who thinks he's found the perfect hideout from the law in a remote house at the end of a road through a salt marsh. The old coot who lives there is crazy: He keeps talking about his "tenants," but he's alone in the shack. Or is he?

I could have set it anywhere, but I chose Monroe because I was writing it while also working on *Reborn*, also set in Monroe, and I saw a connection. George Haskins knows his tenants are decidedly strange, but he doesn't know how strange, doesn't know they're survivors from the First Age who are biding their time until "time is unfurled and we're called by the world."

Like the *Dat-Tay-Vao*, they too wound up in Monroe for a reason and play a crucial role in *Nightworld*.

Tenants

The mail truck was coming.

Gilroy Connors, shoes full of water and shirt still wet from the morning's heavy dew, crouched in the tall grass and punk-topped reeds. He ached all over; his thighs particularly were cramped from holding his present position. But he didn't dare move for fear of giving his presence away.

So he stayed hunkered down across the road from the battered old shack that looked deserted but wasn't – there had been lights on in the place last night. With its single pitched roof and rotting cedar shake siding, it looked more like an overgrown outhouse that a home. A peeling propane tank squatted on the north side; a crumbling brick chimney supported a canted TV antenna. Beyond the shack, glittering in the morning sunlight, lay the northeast end of Monroe Harbor and the Long Island Sound. The place gave new meaning to the word *isolated*. As if a few lifetimes ago someone had brought a couple of tandems of fill out to the end of the hard-packed dirt road, dumped them, and built a shack. Except for a rickety old dock with a sodden rowboat tethered to it, there was not another structure in sight in either direction. Only a slender umbilical cord of insulated wire connected it to the rest of the world via a long column of utility poles marching out from town. All around was empty marsh.

Yeah. Isolated as all hell.

It was perfect.

As Gil watched, the shack's front door opened and a grizzled old man stumbled out, a cigarette in his mouth and a fistful of envelopes in his hand. Tall and lanky with an unruly shock of gray hair standing off his head, he scratched his slightly protruding belly as he squinted in the morning sunlight. He wore a torn undershirt that had probably been white once and a pair of faded green work pants held up by suspenders, He looked as rundown as his home, and as much in need of a shave and a bath as Gil felt. With timing so perfect that it could only be the result of daily practice, the old guy reached the mailbox at exactly the same time as the white jeep-like mail truck.

Must have been watching from the window.

Not an encouraging thought. Had the old guy seen Gil out here? If he had, he gave no sign. Which meant Gil was still safe.

He fingered the handle of the knife inside his shirt.

Lucky for him.

While the old guy and the mailman jawed, Gil studied the shack again. The place was a sign that his recent run of good luck hadn't deserted him yet. He had come out to the marshes to hide until things cooled down in and around Monroe and had been expecting to spend a few real uncomfortable nights out here. The shack would make things a lot easier.

Not much of a place. At most it looked big enough for two rooms and no more. Barely enough space for an ancient couple who didn't move around much – who ate, slept, crapped, watched TV and nothing more. Hopefully, it wasn't a couple. Just the old guy. That would make it simple. A wife, even a real sickly one, could complicate matters.

Gil wanted to know how many were living there before he invited himself in. Not that it would matter much. Either way, he was going in and staying for a while. He just liked to know what he was getting into before he made his move.

One thing was sure: He wasn't going to find any money in there. The old guy had to be next to destitute. But even ten bucks would have made him richer than Gil. He looked at the rusting blue late-sixties Ford Torino with the peeling vinyl roof and hoped it would run. But of course it ran. The old guy had to get into town to cash his Social Security check and buy groceries, didn't he?

Damn well better run.

It had been a long and sloppy trek into these marshes. He intended to drive out.

Finally the mail truck clinked into gear, did a U-turn, and headed back the way it had come. The old guy shoved a couple of envelopes into his back pocket, picked up a rake that had been leaning against the Ford, and began scratching at the dirt on the south side of the house.

Gil decided it was now or never. He straightened up and walked toward the shack. As his feet crunched on the gravel of the yard, the old man wheeled and stared at him with wide, startled eyes.

"Didn't mean to scare you," Gil said in his friendliest voice.

"Well, you sure as hell did, poppin' outta nowhere like that!" the old man said in a deep, gravelly voice. The cigarette between his lips bobbed up and down like a conductor's baton. "We don't exactly get much drop-in company out here. What happen? Boat run outta gas?"

Gil noticed the *we* with annoyance but played along. A stalled boat was as good an excuse as any for being out here in the middle of nowhere.

"Yeah. Had to paddle it into shore way back over there," he said, jerking a thumb over his shoulder.

"Well, I ain't got no phone for you to call anybody–"

No phone! It was all Gil could do to keep from cheering.

"–but I can drive you down to the marina and back so you can get some gas."

No hurry." He moved closer and leaned against the old Torino's fender. "You live out here all by yourself?"

The old man squinted at him, as if trying to recognize him. "I don't believe we've been introduced, son."

"Oh, right." Gil stuck out his hand. "Rick... Rick Summers."

"And I'm George Haskins," he said, giving Gil's hand a firm shake.

"What're you growing there?"

"Carrots. I hear fresh carrots are good for your eyes. Mine are so bad I try to eat as many as I can."

Half blind and no phone. This was sounding better every minute. Now, if he could just find out who the rest of the *we* was, he'd be golden.

He glanced around. Even though he was out in the middle of nowhere at the end of a dirt road that no one but the mailman and this old fart knew existed, he felt exposed. Naked, even. He wanted to get inside.

"Say, I sure could use a cup of coffee, Mr. Haskins. You think you might spare me some?"

*

George hesitated. Making coffee for the stranger would mean bringing him inside. He didn't like that idea at all. He hadn't had anybody into the house since the late sixties when he took in his tenants. And he'd had damn few visitors before that. People didn't like coming this far out, and George was just as glad. Most people pried. They wanted to know what you did way out here all by yourself. Couldn't believe anybody sane would prefer his own company to theirs.

And of course, there was the matter of the tenants.

He studied this young man who had popped out of nowhere. George's eyes weren't getting any better– "Cataracts only get worse," the doctor had told him – but he could plainly see that the stranger wasn't dressed for boating, what with that blue work shirt and gray denims he was wearing. And those leather shoes! Nobody who knew boats ever wore leather shoes on board. But they were selling boats to anybody with cash these days. This landlubber probably didn't know the first thing about boating. That no doubt was why he was standing here on land instead of chugging about the harbor.

He seemed pleasant enough, though. Good-looking, too, with his muscular build and wavy dark hair. Bet he had an easy time with the girls. *Especially* easy, since from what George understood of the world today, *all* the girls were easy.

Maybe he could risk spotting him a cup of coffee before driving him down to the marina. What harm could there be in that? The tenants were late risers and had the good sense to keep quiet if they heard a strange voice overhead.

He smiled. "Coffee? Sure. Come on inside. And call me George. Everybody else does." He dropped his cigarette into the sandy soil and stomped on it, then turned toward the house.

Just a quick cup of coffee and George would send him off. The longer he stayed, the greater the chances of him finding out about the tenants. And George couldn't risk that. He was more than their landlord.

He had sworn to protect them.

*

Gil followed close on the old guy's back up the two steps to the door. Inside was dark and stale, reeking of years of cigarette smoke. He wondered when was the last time George had left a window open.

But being indoors was good. Out of sight and inside – even if it stank, it was better than good. It was super. He felt as if a great weight had been lifted from him.

Now to find out who made up the rest of the *we*.

"Got this place all to yourself, ay?" he said, glancing quickly about. They were standing in a rectangular space that passed for a living room/dining room/kitchen. The furniture consisted of an old card table, a rocker, a tilted easy chair, and a dilapidated couch. Shapeless piles of junk cluttered every corner. An ancient Motorola television set with a huge chassis and a tiny screen stood on the far side of the room diagonally across from the door. The screen was lit and a black chick was reading some news into the camera:

"...*eriously injuring an orderly in a daring escape from the Monroe Neuropsychiatric Institute. He was last reported in Glen Cove–*"

Gil whooped. "Glen Cove! Awright!" That was the wrong direction! He was safe for the moment. "Fan*tas*tic!" he yelled, stomping his foot on the floor.

"Hey! Hold it down!" George said as he filled a greasy, dented aluminum kettle with water and put it on the gas stove.

Gil felt the customary flash of anger at being told what he could or couldn't do, but cooled it. He stepped between George and the TV set as he saw his most recent mug shot appear on the screen. The black chick was saying:

"If you see this man, do not approach him. He might be armed and is considered dangerous."

Gil said, "Sorry. It's just that sometimes I get excited by the news."

"Yeah?" George said, lighting another cigarette. "Don't follow it much myself. But you got to keep quiet. You might disturb the tenants and they–"

"*Tenants?*" Gil said a – lot more loudly than he intended. "You've got *tenants*?"

The old guy was biting his upper lip with what few teeth he had left and saying nothing.

Gil stepped down the short hall, gripping the handle of the knife inside his shirt as he moved. Two doors: The one on the left was open, revealing a tiny bathroom with a toilet, sink, and mildewy shower stall; the one on the right was closed. He gave it a gentle push. Empty: dirty, wrinkled sheets on a narrow bed, dresser, mirror, clothes thrown all around, but nobody there.

"Where are they?" he said, returning to the larger room.

George laughed – a little too loudly, Gil thought – and said, "No tenants. Just a joke. Creepy-crawlies in the crawlspace is all. You know, snapping turtles and frogs and snakes and crickets."

"You keep things like that under your house?" This was turning out to be one weird guy.

"In a manner of speaking, yes. You see, a zillion years ago when I built this place, a big family of crickets took up residence"–he pointed down–"in the crawl space. Drove me crazy at night. So one day I get the bright idea of catching some frogs and throwing them in there to eat the crickets. Worked great. Within two days, there wasn't a chirp to be heard down there."

"Smart."

"Yeah. So I thought. Until the frogs started croaking all night. They were worse than the crickets!"

Gil laughed. "I get it. So you put the snakes down there to catch the frogs!"

"Right. Snakes are quiet. They eat crickets, too. Should've thought of them in the first place. Except I wasn't crazy about living over a nest of snakes."

This was getting to sound like the old lady who swallowed the fly.

Gill said, "And so the next step was to put the turtles down there to eat the snakes."

"Yeah." As George spooned instant coffee into a couple of stained mugs, Gil tried not to think about when they last might have had a good washing. "But I don't think they ate them all, just like I don't think the snakes ate all the frogs, or the frogs ate all the crickets. I still hear an occasional chirp and croak once in a while. Anyway, they've all been down there for years. I ain't for adding anything else to the stew, or even looking down there."

"Don't blame you."

George poured boiling water into the mugs and handed him one.

"So if you hear something moving underfoot, it's just one of my tenants."

"Yeah. Okay. Sure."

This old guy was fruitcake city. As crazy as –

...*Crazy.* That was what that college chick had called him that night when he had tried to pick her up along the road. She was cute. There were a lot of cute girls at Monroe Community College, and he'd always made it a point to drive by every chance he could. She'd said he was crazy to think she'd take a ride from a stranger at that hour of the night. That had made him mad. All these college broads thought they were better and smarter than everybody else. And she'd started to scream when he grabbed her, so he'd hit her to make her stop but she wouldn't stop. She kept on screaming so he kept on hitting her and hitting her and hitting and hitting...

"You're spilling your coffee," George said.

Gil looked down. So he was. It was dripping over the edge of his tilted mug and splashing onto the floor. As he slurped some off the top and sat on the creaking couch, he realized how tired he was. No sleep in the past twenty-four hours. Maybe the coffee would boost him.

"So how come you live out here all by yourself?" Gil asked, hoping to get the conversation on a saner topic than snakes and snapping turtles in the crawlspace.

"I *like* being by myself."

"You must. But whatever rent you pay on this place, it's too much."

"Don't pay no rent at all. I own it."

"Yeah, but the land–"

"My land."

Gil almost dropped his coffee mug. "*Your* land! That's impossible!"

"Nope. All twenty acres been in my family for a zillion and two years."

Gil's brain whirled as he tried to calculate the value of twenty acres of real estate fronting on Monroe Harbor and Long Island Sound.

"You're a fucking millionaire!"

George laughed. "I wish! I'm what you call 'land poor', son. I've got to pay taxes on all this land if I want to keep it, and the damn bastards down at City Hall keep raising my rates and my assessed value so that I've got to come up with more and more money every year just to stay here. Trying to force me out, that's what they're up to."

"So sell, for Christ sake! There must be developers chomping at the bit to get ahold of this land. You could make 'em pay through the nose for a piece of waterfront and all your money worries would be over!"

George shook his head. "Naw. Once you sell one little piece, it's like a leak in a dam. It softens you, weakens you. Soon you're selling another piece, and then another. Pretty soon, I'll be living on this little postage stamp surrounded by big ugly condos, listening to cars and mopeds racing up and down the road with engines roaring and rock and roll blasting. No thanks. I've lived here in peace, and I want to die here in peace."

"Yeah, but–"

"Besides, lots of animals make their homes on my land. They've been pushed out of everywhere else in Monroe. All the trees have been cut down back there, all the hollows and gullies filled in and paved over. There's no place else for them to go. This is their world, too, you know. I'm their last resort. It's my duty to keep this place wild as long as I can. As long as I live... which probably won't be too much longer."

Oh, yes...crazy as a loon. Gil wondered if there might be some way he could get the old guy to will him the property and then cork him off. He stuffed the idea away in the To-Be-Developed file.

"Makes me glad I don't have a phone," George was saying.

Right...no phone and no visitors.

Gil knew this was the perfect hiding place for him. Just a few days was all he needed. But he had to stay here *with* the old guy's cooperation. He couldn't risk anything forceful – not if George met the mailman at the box every day.

And from a few things the old man had said, he thought he knew just what buttons to push to convince George to let him stay.

*

George noted that his guest's coffee mug was empty. Good. Time to get him moving on. He never had company, didn't like it, and wasn't used to it. Made him itchy. Besides, he wanted this guy on his way before another remark about the tenants slipped out. That had been a close call before.

He stood up.

"Well, guess it's about time to be running you down to the marina for that tank of gas."

The stranger didn't move.

"George," he said in a low voice, "I've got a confession to make."

"Don't want to hear it!" George said. "I ain't no priest! Tell it somewhere else. I just want to help get you where you're going!"

"I'm on the run, George."

Oh, hell, George thought. At least that explained why he was acting so skittish. "You mean there's no boat waiting for gas somewhere?"

"I..." His voice faltered. "I lied about the boat."

"Well, ain't that just swell? And who, may I ask" – George wasn't so sure he wanted the answer to this, but he had to ask – "are you on the run from?"

"The Feds."

Double hell. "What for?"

"Income tax evasion."

"No kidding?" George was suddenly interested. "How much you take them for?"

"It's not so much 'how much' as 'how long.'"

"All right: How long?"

"Nine years. I haven't filed a return since I turned eighteen."

"No shit! Is that because you're stupid or because you've got balls?"

"Mr. Haskins," the stranger said, looking at him levelly and speaking with what struck George as bone-deep conviction, "I don't believe any government's got the right to tax what a working man earns with the sweat of his brow."

"Couldn't of said it better myself!" George cried. He thought his heart was going to burst. This boy was talking like he'd have wanted his son to talk, if he'd ever had one. "The sonsabitches'll bleed you dry if you let 'em! Look what they've been doin' to me!"

The young stranger stared at the floor. "I was hoping you'd understand."

"Understand? Of course I understand! I've been fighting the IRS for years but never had the guts to actually *resist*! My hat's off to you!"

"Can I stay the night?"

That brought George up short. He wanted to help this courageous young man, but what was he going to do about the tenants?

F. Paul Wilson

"What's going to happen to you if they catch you? What kind of sentence you facing?"

"Twenty."

George's stomach turned. A young guy like this in the hole for twenty years just for not paying taxes. He felt his blood begin to boil.

"Bastards!"

He'd have to chance it. Tenants or not, he felt obligated to give this guy a place to stay for the night. It would be okay. The tenants could take the day off and just rest up. They'd been working hard lately. He'd just have to watch his mouth so he didn't make another slip about them.

"Well, George? What do you say?"

"I can let you stay one night and one night only," George said. "After that–"

The young fellow leaped forward and shook his hand. "Thanks a million, George!"

"Hear me out now. Only tonight. Come tomorrow morning, I'll drive you down to the train station, get you a ticket, and put you on board for New York with all the commuters. Once in the city, you can get lost real easy."

George thought he saw tears in the young man's eyes. "I don't know how to thank you."

"Never mind that. You just hit the sack in my room. You look bushed. Get some rest. No one'll know you're here."

He nodded, then went to the window and gazed out at the land. "Beautiful here," he said.

George realized it would probably look even more beautiful if the window were cleaner, but his eyes weren't good enough to notice much difference.

"If this were mine," the young fellow said passionately, "I'd sure as hell find a way to keep it out of the hands of the developers *and* the tax men. Maybe make it into a wildlife preserve or bird sanctuary or something. *Anything* to keep it wild and free."

Shaking his head, he turned and headed for the back room. George watched him in wonder. A wildlife preserve! Why hadn't he thought of that? It would be untaxable and unsubdividable! What a perfect solution!

But it was too late to start the wheels turning on something like that now. It would take years to submit all the proposals and wade through all the red tape to get it approved. And he didn't have years. He didn't need a doctor to tell him that his body was breaking down. He couldn't see right, he couldn't breathe right, and Christ Almighty, he couldn't even pee right. The parts were wearing out and there were no replacements available.

And what would happen when he finally cashed in his chips? What would happen to his land? And the tenants? Where would *they* go?

Maybe this young fellow was the answer. Maybe George could find a way to leave the land to him. He'd respect it, preserve it, just as George would if he could go on living. Maybe that was the solution.

But that meant he'd have to tell him the real truth about the tenants. He didn't know if the guy was ready for that.

He sat down in the sun on the front steps and lit another cigarette. He had a lot of thinking to do.

*

The five o'clock news was on.

George had kept himself busy all day, what with tending to the carrot patch outside and cleaning up a bit inside. Having company made him realize how long it had been since he'd given the place a good sweeping.

But before he'd done any of that, he'd waited until the young fellow had fallen asleep, then he'd lifted the trapdoor under the rug in the corner of the main room and told the tenants to lay low for the day. They'd understood and said they'd be quiet.

Now he was sitting in front of the TV watching *Eyewitness News* and going through today's mail: Three small checks from the greeting card companies – not much, but it would help pay this quarter's taxes. He looked up at the screen when he heard "the Long Island town of Monroe" mentioned. Some pretty

F. Paul Wilson

Oriental girl was sitting across from a scholarly looking fellow in a blue suit. She was saying,

"...explain to our viewers just what it is that makes Gilroy Connors so dangerous, Dr. Kline."

"He's a sociopath."

"And just what is that?"

"Simply put, it is a personality disorder in which the individual has no sense of 'mine' and 'not-mine,' no sense of right or wrong in the traditional sense."

"No conscience, so to speak."

"Exactly."

"Are they all murderers like Connors?"

"No. History's most notorious criminals and serial killers are sociopaths, but violence isn't a necessary facet of their make-up. The confidence men who rip off the pensions of widows or steal from a handicapped person are just as sociopathic as the Charles Mansons of the world. The key element in the sociopathic character is his or her complete lack of guilt. They will do whatever is necessary to get what they want and will feel no remorse over anyone they have to harm along the way."

"Gilroy Connors was convicted in the Dorothy Akers murder. Do you think he'll kill again?"

"He has to be considered dangerous. He's a sociopathic personality with a particularly low frustration threshold. But he is also a very glib liar. Since the truth means nothing to him, he can take any side of a question, any moral stance, and speak on it with utter conviction."

A voice – George recognized it as belonging to one of the anchormen – called from off-camera: "Sounds like he'd make a great politician!"

Everyone had a good laugh, and then the Oriental woman said, "But all kidding aside, what should our viewers do if one of them should spot him?"

Dr. Kline's expression was suddenly grim. "Lock the doors and call the police immediately."

208

The camera closed in on the Asian girl. "There you have it. We've been speaking to Dr. Edward Kline, a Long Island psychiatrist who examined Gilroy Connors and testified for the state at the Dorothy Akers murder trial.

"In case you've been asleep or out of the country during the last twenty-four hours, all of Long Island is being combed for Gilroy Connors, convicted killer of nineteen year old college coed Dorothy Akers. Connors escaped custody last night when, due to an error in paperwork, he was accidentally transferred to the Monroe Neuropsychiatric Institute instead of a maximum security facility as ordered by the court. The victim's father, publisher Jeffrey Akers, is offering a fifty thousand dollar reward for information leading to his recapture."

Fifty thousand! George thought. What I could do with that!

"You've heard Dr. Kline," she continued. "If you see this man, call the police immediately."

A blow-up of a mug shot appeared on the screen. George gasped. He knew that man! Even with his rotten vision, he could see that the face on the TV belonged to the man now sleeping in his bed! He turned around to look toward the bedroom and saw his house guest standing behind him, a knife in his hand.

"Don't even think about that reward, old man," Connors said in a chillingly soft voice. "Don't even *dream* about it."

*

"You're hurtin' my hands!" the old fart whined as Gil knotted the cord around his wrists.

"I'm putting you down for the night, old man, and you're staying down!"

He pulled the rope tighter and the old man yelped.

Gil said, "There – that ought to hold you."

George rolled over onto his back and stared up at him. "What are you going to do with me?"

"Haven't figured that out yet."

"You're gonna kill me, aren't you?" There was more concern than fear in his eyes.

"Maybe. Maybe not. Depends on how you behave."

Truthfully, he didn't know what to do. It would be less of a hassle to kill him now and get it over with, but there was the problem of the mailman. If George wasn't waiting curbside at the box tomorrow morning, the USPS might come knocking on the door. So Gil had to figure out a way to pressure George into acting as if everything was nice and normal tomorrow. Maybe he'd have George stand at the door and wave to the mailman. That might work. He'd have to spend some time figuring this out.

"All that stuff you said about dodging the tax man was just lies, wasn't it?"

Gil smiled at the memory. "Yeah. Pretty good, wasn't it? I mean, I made that up right off the top of my head. Sucked you in like smoke, didn't I?"

"Nothing to be proud of."

"Why not?"

"You heard what they called you on the TV: a 'socialpath'. Means you're crazy."

"You watch your mouth, old man!" Gil could feel the rage surging up in him like a giant wave. He hated that word. "I'm not crazy! And I don't ever want to hear that word out of your mouth again!"

"Doesn't matter anyway," George said. "Soon as you're out of here, my tenants will untie me."

Gil laughed. "Now who's crazy?"

"It's true. They'll free me."

"That's enough of that," Gil said. It wasn't funny anymore. He didn't like being called crazy any more than he liked being near crazy people. And this old man was talking crazy now. "No more of that kind of talk out of you!"

"You'll see. I'm their protector. Soon as you're–"

"Stop that!" Gil yanked George off the bed by his shirt front. He was losing it – he could feel it going. "God *damn* that makes me mad!"

He shoved the old man back against the wall with force

enough to rattle the whole house. George's eyes rolled up as he slumped back onto the bed. A small red trickle crawled along his scalp and mixed with the gray of his hair at the back of his head.

"Sleep tight, Pops," Gils said.

He left George on the bed and returned to the other room. He turned the antique TV back on. After what seemed like an inordinately long warm-up time, the picture came in, flipped a few times, then held steady. He hoped there wasn't another psychiatrist on talking about him.

He hated psychiatrists. *Hated* them! Since he'd been picked up for killing that college chick, he'd seen enough of their kind to last a couple of lifetimes. Why'd she have to go and die? It wasn't fair. He hadn't meant to kill her. If only she'd been a little more cooperative. But no – she'd had to go and laugh in his face. He'd just got mad, that was all. He wasn't crazy. He just had a bad temper.

Psychiatrists! What'd they know about him? Labeling him, pigeonholing him, saying he had no conscience and never felt sorry for anything he did. What'd they know? Did they know how he'd cried after Mom had burnt up in that fire in Dad's car? He'd cried for days. Mom wasn't supposed to be anywhere near that car when it caught fire. Only Dad.

He had *loads* of feelings, and nobody had better tell him any different!

He watched the tube for a while, caught a couple of news broadcasts, but there was only passing mention of his escape and the reward the girl's old man had posted for him. Then came a report that he had been sighted on Staten Island and the search was being concentrated there.

He smiled. They were getting further and further away from where he really was.

He shut off the set at eleven-thirty. Time for some more sleep. Before he made himself comfortable on the couch, he checked out the old man's room. He was there, snoring comfortably under the covers. Gil turned away and then spun back again.

How'd he get under the covers?

Two strides took him to the bedside. His foot kicked against something that skittered across the floor. He found what it was: the old guy's shoes. They'd been on his feet when he'd tied him up! He yanked back the covers and stared in open-mouthed shock at the old man.

George's hands and feet were free. The cords were nowhere in sight.

Just then he thought he caught a blur of movement by the doorway. He swung around but there was nothing there. He turned back to George.

"Hey, you old fart!" He shook George's shoulder roughly until his eyes opened. "Wake up!"

George's eyes slowly came into focus. "Wha–?"

"How'd you do it?"

"Go 'way!"

George rolled onto his other side and Gil saw a patch of white gauze where he had been bleeding earlier. He flipped him onto his back again.

"How'd you untie yourself, goddammit?"

"Didn't. My tenants–"

"You stop talking that shit to me, old man!" Gil said, cocking his right arm.

George flinched away but kept his mouth shut. Maybe he was finally learning.

"You stay right there!"

Gil tore through the drawers and piles of junk in the other room until he found some more cord. During the course of the search he came across a check book and some uncashed checks. He returned to the bedroom and began tying up George again.

"Don't know how you did it the first time, but you ain't doing it again!"

He spread-eagled George on the sheet and tied each skinny limb to a separate corner of the bed, looping the cord down and around on the legs of the frame. Each knot was triple-tied.

"There! See if you can get out of that!"

As George opened his mouth to speak, Gil glared at him and the old man shut it with an almost audible snap.

"That's the spirit," Gil said softly.

He pulled the knife out of his shirt and held its six inch blade up before George. The old man's eyes widened.

"Nice, isn't it? I snatched it from the kitchen of that wimpy Monroe Neuropsychiatric Institute. Would've preferred getting myself a gun, but none of the guards there were armed. Still, I can do a whole lot of damage with something like this and still not kill you. Understand what I'm saying to you, old man?"

George nodded vigorously.

"Good. Now what we're going to have here tonight is a nice quiet little house. No noise, no talk. Just a good night's sleep for both of us. Then we'll see what tomorrow brings."

He gave George one last hard look straight in the eye, then turned and headed back to the couch.

*

Before sacking out for the night, Gil went through George's check book. Not a whole lot of money in it. Most of the checks went out to cash or to the township for quarterly taxes. He noticed one good-sized regular monthly deposit that was probably his Social Security check, and lots of smaller sporadic additions.

He looked through the three undeposited checks. They were all made out to George Haskins, each from a different greeting card company. The attached invoices indicated they were in payment for varying numbers of verses.

Verses?

You mean old George back there tied up to the bed was a poet? He wrote greeting card verse?

Gil looked around the room. Where? There was no desk in the shack. Hell, he hadn't seen a piece of paper since he got here! Where did George write this stuff?

He went back to the bedroom. He did his best not to show the relief he felt when he saw that old George was still tied up nice and tight.

"Hey, old man," he said, waving the checks in the air. "How come you never told me you were a poet?"

George glared at him. "Those checks are mine! I need them to pay my taxes!"

"Yeah? Well, right now I need them a lot more than you do. I think tomorrow morning we'll make a little trip down to the bank so you can cash these." He checked the balance in the account. "And I think you just might make a cash withdrawal, too."

"I'll lose my land if I don't pay those taxes on time!"

"Well then, I guess you'll just have to come up with some more romantic 'verses' for these card companies. Like, 'George is a poet / And nobody know it.' See? It's easy!"

Gil laughed as he thought of all the broads who get those flowery, syrupy birthday and anniversary cards and sit mooning over the romantic poems inside, never knowing they were written by this dirty old man in a falling down shack on Long Island!

"I love it!" he said, heading back to the couch. "I just love it!"

He turned out all the lights, shoved the knife between two of the cushions, and bedded down on the dusty old couch for the night. As he drifted off to sleep, he thought he heard rustling movements from under the floorboards. George's 'tenants', no doubt. He shuddered at the thought. The sooner he was out of here, the better.

*

What time is it?

Gil was rubbing the sleep from his eyes and peering around in the mineshaft blackness that surrounded him. Something had awakened him. But what? He sat perfectly still and listened.

A few crickets, maybe a frog – the noises seemed to come from outside instead of from the crawlspace – but nothing more than that.

Still, his senses were tingling with the feeling that something was wrong. He stood up and stepped over toward the light switch. As he moved, his foot caught on something and he fell forward. On the way down his ribs slammed against something else, something hard, like a chair. He hit the floor with his left shoulder. Groaning, he got to his knees and crawled until his fingers found the wall. He fumbled around for the light switch and flipped it.

When his eyes had adjusted to the glare, he glanced at the clock over the kitchen sink – going on 4:00 a.m. He thought he saw something move by the sink but when he squinted for a better look, it was just some junk George had left there. Then he turned back toward the couch to see what had tripped him up.

It was the little hassock that had been over by the rocking chair when he had turned the lights out. At least he was pretty sure it had been there. He *knew* it hadn't been next to the couch where it was now. And the chair he had hit on his way down – that had been over against the wall.

In fact, as he looked around he noticed that not a single piece of furniture in the whole room was where it had been when he had turned out the lights and gone to sleep three or four hours ago. It had all been moved closer to the couch.

Someone was playing games. And Gil only knew of one possible someone.

Retrieving his knife from the couch, he hurried to the bedroom and stopped dead at the door. George was tied hand and foot to the corners of the bed, snoring loudly.

A chill rippled over Gil's skin.

"How the hell...?"

He went back to the main room and checked the door and windows – all were locked from the inside. He looked again at the furniture, clustered around the couch as if the pieces had crept up and watched him as he slept.

Gil didn't believe in ghosts but he was beginning to believe this little shack was haunted.

And he wanted out.

He had seen the keys to the old Torino in one of the drawers. He found them again and hurried outside to the car. He hoped the damn thing started. He wasn't happy about hitting the road so soon, but he preferred taking his chances with the cops out in the open to being cooped up with whatever was haunting that shack.

As he slipped behind the wheel, he noticed a sliver of light shining out from inside the shack's foundation. That was *weird.* Really weird. Nobody kept a light on in a crawlspace. He was about to turn the ignition key but held up. He knew it was going to drive him nuts if he left without seeing what was down there.

Cursing himself for a jerk, he turned on the Ford's headlamps and got out for a closer look.

The light was leaking around a piece of plywood fitted into an opening in the foundation cinder blocks. It was hinged at the bottom and held closed by a short length of one-by-two shoved through the handle at the top. He pulled out the one-by-two and hesitated.

Connors, you are an asshole, he told himself, but he had to see what was in there. If it was snakes and snapping turtles, fine. That would be bad enough. But if it was something worse, he had to know.

Gripping the knife tightly in one hand, he yanked the board toward him with the other and quickly peered in, readying himself to slam it shut in an instant. But what he saw within so shocked him he almost dropped the knife.

There was a furnished apartment inside.

The floor of the crawlspace was carpeted. It was worn, industrial grade carpet, but it was *carpet.* There were chairs, tables, bunk beds, the works. A fully furnished apartment... with a ceiling two feet high.

Everything was doll size except the typewriter. That was a portable electric model that looked huge in contrast to every-thing else.

Maybe George wasn't really crazy after all. One thing was certain: The old fart had been lying to him. There were no snakes and snapping turtles living down here in his crawlspace.

But just what the hell *was* living down here?

Gil headed back inside to ask the only man who really knew.

As he strode through the big room, his foot caught on something and he went down again, landing square on his belly. It took him a moment to catch his breath, then he rolled over and looked to see what had tripped him.

It wasn't the hassock this time. A length of slim cord was stretched between the leg of the couch and an eye-hook that had been screwed into the wall.

"Son of a bitch!"

He got up and continued on his way – carefully now, scanning the path for more trip ropes. There were none. He made it to the bedroom without falling again–

–and found George sitting on the edge of the bed, massaging his wrists.

Dammit! Every time he turned around it was something else! He could feel the anger and frustration begin to bubble up toward the overflow levels.

"Who the hell untied you?"

"I ain't talking to you."

Gil pointed the knife at him. "You'll talk, old man, or I'll skin you alive!"

"Leave him alone and leave our home!"

It was a little voice, high-pitched without being squeaky, and it came from directly behind him. Gil whirled and saw a fully dressed little man – or something squat, hairy, and bull-necked that came pretty close to looking like a little man – no more than a foot and a half high, standing outside the bedroom door. By the time Gil realized what he was looking at, the creature had started to run.

Gil's first thought was, I'm going crazy! But suddenly he had an explanation for that two-foot high furnished apartment in the crawlspace, and for the moving furniture and trip cords.

He bolted after it. Here was what had been tormenting him tonight! He'd get the little sucker and–

He tripped again. A cord that hadn't been there a moment ago was stretched across the narrow hall. Gil went down on one knee and bounded up again. He'd been half ready for that one. They weren't going to–

Something caught him across the chin and his feet went out from under him. He landed flat on his back and felt a sharp, searing pain in his right thigh. He looked down and saw he had jabbed himself in the leg with his own knife during the fall.

Gil leapt to his feet, the pain a distant cry amid the blood rage that hammered though his brain. He roared and slashed at the rope that had damn near taken his head off and charged into the big room. There he saw not one but two of the little bastards. A chant filled the air:

"Leave him alone and leave our home! Leave him alone and leave our home!"

Over and over, from a good deal more than two voices. He couldn't see any others. How many of the little runts were there? No matter. He'd deal with these two first, then hunt down the others and get to the bottom of this.

The pair split, one darting to the left, the other to the right. Gil wasn't going to let them both escape. He took a single step and launched himself through the air at the one fleeing leftward. He landed with a bone-jarring crash on the floor but his outstretched free hand caught the leg of the fleeing creature. It was hairier than he had realized – furry, really – and it struggled in his grasp, screeching and thrashing like a wild animal as he pulled it toward him. He squeezed it harder and it bit his thumb. Hard. He howled with the pain, hauled the thing back, and flung it against the nearest wall.

Its screeching stopped as it landed against the wall with an audible crunch and fell to the floor, but the chant went on:

"...our home! Leave him alone, and leave our home! Leave him..."

"God damn it!" Gil said, sucking on his bleeding thumb. It hurt like hell.

Then he saw the thing start to move. Mewling in pain, it had begun a slow crawl toward one of the piles of junk in the corner.

"No, you don't!" Gil shouted.

The pain, the rage, that goddamn chant, they all came together in a black cloud of fury that engulfed him. No way was he going to let that little shit get away and set more booby traps for him. Through that cloud, he charged across the room, lifted the thing up with his left hand, and raised the knife in his right. Dimly he heard a voice shouting somewhere behind him but he ignored it.

He rammed the knife through the damned thing, pinning it to the wall.

The chant stopped abruptly, cut off in mid verse. All he could hear was George's wail.

*

"Oh, no! Oh, Lord, no!"

George stood in the hall and stared at the tiny figure impaled on the wall, watched it squirm as dark fluid flowed down the peeling wallpaper. Then it went slack. He didn't know the little guy's name – they all looked pretty much the same through his cataracts – but he felt like he'd lost an old friend. His anguish was a knife lodged in his own chest.

"You've killed him! Oh, God!"

Gil glared at him, his eyes wild, his breathing ragged. Saliva dripped from a corner of his mouth. He was far over the edge.

"Right, old man. And I'm gonna get the other one and do the same to him!"

George couldn't let that happen. The little guys were his responsibility. He was their protector. He couldn't just stand here like a useless scarecrow.

He launched himself at Gil, his long, nicotine-stained fingernails extended like claws, raking for the younger man's eyes. But Gil pushed him aside easily, knocking him to the floor with a casual swipe if his arm. Pain blazed through George's left hip as he landed, shooting down his leg like a bolt of white hot lightning.

"You're next, you worthless old shit!" Gil screamed. "Soon as I finish with the other little squirt!"

George sobbed as he lay on the floor. If only he were

younger, stronger. Even ten years ago he probably could have kicked this punk out on his ass. Now all he could do was lie here on the floor like the worthless old half-blind cripple he was. He pounded the floor helplessly. Might as well be dead!

Suddenly he saw another of the little guys dash across the floor toward the couch, saw the punk spot him and leap after him.

"Run!" George screamed. *"Run!"*

*

Gil rammed his shoulder against the back of the couch as he shoved his arm far beneath it, slashing back and forth with the knife, trying to get a piece of the second runt. But the blade cut only air and dust bunnies.

As he began to withdraw his arm, he felt something snake over his hand and tighten on his wrist. He tried to yank away but the cord – he was sure it was a cord like the one he had used to truss George – tightened viciously.

A slip knot!

The other end must have been tied to one of the couch legs. He tried to slash at the cord with the knife but he couldn't get the right angle. He reached under with his free left hand to get the knife and realized too late that they must have been waiting for him to do that very thing. He felt another noose tighten over that wrist–

–and still another over his right ankle.

The first cold trickles of fear ran down Gil's spine.

In desperation he tried to tip the couch over to give him some room to maneuver but it wouldn't budge. Just then something bit deeply into his right hand. He tried to shake it off and in doing so he loosened his grip on the knife. It was immediately snatched from his grasp.

At that moment the fourth noose tightened around his left ankle, and he knew he was in deep shit.

They let him lay there for what must have been an hour. He strained at the ropes, trying to break them, trying to untie the knots. All he accomplished was to sink their coils more deeply into his flesh. He wanted to scream out his rage – and his fear – but he wouldn't give them the satisfaction. He heard George moving around somewhere behind him, groaning with pain, heard little voices – How many of the little fuckers were there, anyway? – talking in high-pitched whispers. There seemed to be an argument going on. Finally, it was resolved.

Then came a tugging on the cords as new ones were tied around his wrists and ankles and old ones released. Suddenly he was flipped over onto his back.

He saw George sitting in the rocker holding an ice pack to his left hip. And on the floor there were ten – *Jesus*, ten of them! – foot-and-a-half tall furry little men standing in a semi-circle, staring at him.

One of them stepped forward. He was dressed in doll clothes: a dark blue pullover – it even had an Izod alligator on the left breast – and tan slacks. He had the face of a sixty-year old man with a barrel chest and furry arms and legs. He pointed at Gil's face and spoke in a high pitched voice:

"C'ham is dead and it's on your head."

Gil started to laugh. It was like landing in Munchkinland, but then he saw the look in the little man's eyes and knew this was not one of the Lollipop Kids. The laugh died in his throat.

He glanced up at the wall where he'd pinned the first little runt like a bug on a board and saw only a dark stain.

The talking runt gestured two others forward and they approached Gil, dragging his knife. He tried the squirm away from them but the ropes didn't allow for much movement.

"Hey, now, wait a minute! What're you–?"

"The decision's made: You'll make the trade."

Gill was beginning to know terror. "Forget the goddamn rhymes! What's going on here?"

"Hold your nose," the talking runt said to the pair with the knife, "and cut off his clothes. Best be cautious lest he make you nauseous."

Gil winced as the blade began to slice along the seams of his shirt, waiting for the sharp edge to cut him. But it never touched him.

*

George watched as the little guys stripped Connors. He had no idea what they were up to and he didn't care. He felt like more of a failure than ever. He'd never done much with his life, but at least since the end of the Sixties he had been able to tell himself that he had provided a safe harbor for the last of the world's Little People.

When had it been – Sixty-nine, maybe – when all eleven of them had first shown up at his door looking for shelter. They'd said they were waiting for "when time is unfurled and we're called by the world." He hadn't the vaguest notion what that meant but he'd experienced an immediate rapport with them. They were Outsiders, just like he was. And when they offered to pay rent, the deal was sealed.

He smiled. That rhymed. If you listened to them enough, you began to sound like them. Since they spoke in rhyme all the time – there was another one – it was nothing for them to crank out verse for the greeting card companies. Some of the stuff was pretty sappy, but it paid the taxes.

But what next? One of the little guys had been murdered by this psycho who now knew their secret. Soon all the world would know about these Little People. George had doubly failed at his job: He hadn't protected them and hadn't kept their secret. He was just what the punk had called him: a worthless old shit.

He heard Connors groan and looked up. He was nude as a jaybird and the little guys had tied him with new ropes looped through rings fastened high on the walls at each end of the room. They were hauling him off the floor, stringing him across the room like laundry hung out to dry.

George suddenly realized that although he wasn't too pleased with being George Haskins, at this particular moment he preferred it by far to being Gilroy Connors.

*

Gil felt as if his arms and legs were going to come out of their sockets as the runts hauled him off the floor and stretched him out in the air. For a moment he feared that might be their plan, but when he got half way between the floor and the ceiling, they stopped pulling on the ropes.

He couldn't ever remember feeling so damn helpless in all his life.

The lights went out and he heard a lot of shuffling below him but he couldn't see what they were doing. Then came the sound, a new chant, high-pitched and staccato in a language he had never heard before, a language that didn't seem at home on the human tongue.

A soft glow began to rise from below him. He wished he could see what they were doing. All he could do was watch their weird shadows on the ceiling. So far they hadn't caused him too much pain, but he was beginning to feel weak and dizzy. His back got warm while his front grew cold and numb, like there was a cool wind coming from the ceiling and passing right through him, carrying his energy with it. All of his juice seemed to be flowing downward and collecting in his back.

So tired...and his back felt so heavy. What were they doing below him?

*

They were glowing.

George had watched them carry C'ham, their dead member, to a spot directly below Connors's suspended body. They had placed one of George's coffee mugs at C'ham's feet, then they stripped off their clothes and gathered in a circle around him. They had started to chant. After a while, a faint yellow light began to shimmer around their furry little bodies.

George found the ceremony fascinating in a weird sort of way – until the glow brightened and flowed up to illuminate the suspended punk. Then even George's lousy eyes could see the horror of what was happening to Gilroy Connors.

His legs, arms, and belly were a cold dead white, but his back was a deep red-purple color, like a gigantic bruise, and it bulged like the belly of a mother-to-be carrying triplets. George could not imagine how the skin was holding together, it was stretched so tight. Looked like it would rupture any minute. George shielded his face, waiting for the splatter. But when it didn't come, he chanced another peek.

It was raining on the Little People.

The skin hadn't ruptured as George had feared. No, a fine red mist was falling from Connors' body. Red microdroplets were slipping from the pores in the purpled swelling on his back and falling through the yellow glow, turning it orange. The scene was as beautiful as it was horrifying.

The bloody dew fell for something like half an hour, then the glow faded and one of the little guys boosted another up to the wall switch and the lights came on. George did not have to strain his eyes to know that Gilroy Connors was dead.

As the circle dissolved, he noticed that the dead little guy was gone. Only the mug remained under Conners.

George found his mouth dry when he tried to speak.

"What happened to... to the one he stabbed?"

"C'ham?" said the leader. George knew this one; his name was Kob. "He's over there."

Sure enough. There were ten little guys standing over by the couch, one of them looking weak and being supported by the others.

"But I thought–"

"Yes. C'ham was dead, but now he's back because of the Crimson Dew."

"And the other one?"

Kob glanced over his shoulder at Connors. "I understand there's a reward for his capture. You should have it. And there's something else you should have."

The little man stepped under Connors' suspended body and returned with the coffee mug.

"This is for you," he said, holding it up.

George took the mug and saw that it was half-filled with a thin reddish liquid.

"What am I supposed to do with this?"

"Drink it."

George's stomach turned. "But it's... from him."

"Of course. From him to you." Kob gave George's calf a gentle slap. "We need you George. You're our shield from the world–"

"Some shield!" George said.

"It's true. You've protected us from prying eyes and we need you to go on doing that for some time to come."

"I don't think I've got much time left."

"That's why you should drain that cup."

"What do you mean?"

"Think of it as extending your lease," Kob said.

George looked over at C'ham who'd surely been dead half an hour ago and now was up and walking about. He looked down into the cup again.

...extending your lease.

Well, after what he'd just seen, he guessed anything might be possible.

Tightening his throat against an incipient gag, George raised the cup to his lips and sipped. The fluid was lukewarm and salty – like a bouillon that had been allowed to cool too long. Not good, but not awful, either. He squeezed his eyes shut and chugged the rest. It went down and stayed down, thank the Lord.

"Good!" Kob shouted, and the ten other Little People applauded.

"Now you can help us cut him down and carry him outside."

*

"So what're you going to do with all that money, George?" Bill said as he handed George the day's mail.

"I ain't got it yet."

George leaned against the roof of the mail truck and dragged on his cigarette. He felt good. His morning backache was pretty much a thing of the past, and he could pee with the best of them – hit a wall from six feet away, he bet. His breathing was better than it had been in thirty years. And best off all, he could stand here and see all the way south along the length of the harbor to downtown Monroe. He didn't like to think about what had been in that mug Kob had handed him, but in the ten days since he had swallowed it down he had come to feel decades younger.

He wished he had some more of it.

"Still can't get over how lucky you were to find him laying in the grass over there," Bill said, glancing across the road. "Especially lucky he wasn't alive from what I heard about him."

"Guess so," George said.

"I understand they still can't explain how he died or why he was all dried up like a mummy."

"Yeah, it's a mystery, all right."

"So when you do get the fifty thou – what are you going to spend it on?"

"Make a few improvements on the old place, I guess. Get me some legal help to see if somehow I can get this area declared off-limits to developers. But mostly set up some sort of fund to keep paying the taxes until that comes to pass."

Bill laughed and let up on the mail truck's brake. "Not ready for the old folks' home yet?" he said as he lurched away.

"Not by a long shot!"

I've got responsibilities, he thought. And tenants to keep happy.

He shuddered.

Yes, he certainly wanted to keep those little fellows happy.

PELTS

People have asked what "Pelts" has to do with the Secret History. Good question.

Well, the ebony spleenwort growing in straight, wide rows on Zeb Foster's property in the Pine Barrens is the first clue. It flourishes only over old foundations, and its presence signals that buildings – big ones, in this case – once stood here in ancient times. Could it be that the humans aligned with the Otherness during the First Age built here – temples where they trapped Q'qrs and performed foul rites?

In the Repairman Jack Teen Trilogy, Weezy habitually springs leg-hold traps wherever she finds them. Most of these have been set by a younger Jeb Jameson. And Old Man Foster, who doesn't allow hunting on his land, is really Glaeken.

Satisfied?

"Pelts" is the only politically correct story I've ever written (also the goriest). I realized I was basing it on a trendy idea, but I wrote it anyway. It springs from the same values that fueled the very *incorrect* "Buckets" (in *Soft & Others*). I knew a dozen anthologies that would take it but I wanted something special for this story. I settled on publishing it as a chapbook from Bill Munster's (yes, that's his real name) Footsteps Press adorned with a wonderfully subtle cover illustration by Jill Bauman – a perfect showcase for "Pelts."

All royalties from the chapbook went to Friends of Animals.

And then, 16 years later, a screenwriter named Matt Venne calls and asks if he can adapt "Pelts" for the second season of Showtime's *Masters of Horror* (a series of one-hour horror films directed by "masters" such as John Carpenter, Stuart Gordon, John Landis and others). Like I was gonna say no? So Matt does a faithful adaptation and who decides he wants to direct it? The notorious / infamous and enormously talented Dario Argento. As I said, "Pelts" is the goriest thing I've ever written, but not gory enough for Mr. *Suspiria*. He upped the havoc and added generous dollops of sex along the way. But he stayed true to the spirit of the story. (I won't go into it here but you can read about our back and forth regarding my problem with his version of the script in *Ephemerata*.) The movie is available on DVD. Be prepared for nudity and avert-the-gaze mayhem.

Pelts

1

"I'm scared, Pa," Gary said.

"Shush!" Pa said, tossing the word over his shoulder as he walked ahead.

Gary shivered in the frozen predawn dimness and scanned the surrounding pines and brush for the thousandth time. He was heading for twenty years old and knew he shouldn't be getting the willies like this but he couldn't help it. He didn't like this place.

"What if we get caught?"

"Only way we'll get caught is if you keep yappin', boy," Pa said. "We're almost there. Wouldna brought you along 'cept I can't do all the carryin' myself! Now hesh up!"

Their feet crunched though the half-inch shroud of frozen snow that layered the sandy ground. Gary pressed his lips tightly together, kept an extra tight grip on the Louisville Slugger, and followed Pa through the brush. But he didn't like this one bit. Not that he didn't favor hunting and trapping. He liked them fine. Loved them, in fact. But he and Pa were on Zeb Foster's land today. And everybody knew that was bad news.

Old Foster owned thousands of acres in the Jersey Pine Barrens and didn't allow nobody to hunt them. Had "Posted" signs all around the perimeter. Always been that way with the Fosters. Pa said old Foster's granpa had started the no-trespassing foolishness and that the family was likely to hold to the damn stupid tradition till Judgment Day. Pa didn't think he should be fenced out of any part of the Barrens. Gary could go along with that most anywheres except old Foster's property.

There were stories...tales of the Jersey Devil roaming the woods here, of people poaching Foster's land and never being seen again. Those who disappeared weren't fools from Newark or Trenton who regularly got lost in the Pines and wandered in circles till they died. These were experienced trackers and hunters, Pineys just like Pa... and Gary.

Never seen again.

"Pa, what if we don't come out of here?" He hated the whiny sound in his voice and tried to change it. "What if somethin' gets us?"

"Ain't nothin gonna get us! Didn't I come in here yesterday and set the traps? And didn't I come out okay?"

"Yeah, but–"

"Yeah, but *nothin'*! The Fosters done a good job of spreadin' stories for generations to scare folk off. But they don't scare me. I know bullshit when I hear it."

"Is it much farther?"

"No. Right yonder over the next rise. A whole area crawlin' with coon tracks."

Gary noticed they were passing through a thick line of calf-high vegetation, dead now; looked as if it'd been dark and ferny before winterkill had turned it brittle. It ran off straight as a hunting arrow into the scrub pines on either side of them.

"Looky this, Pa. Look how straight this stuff runs. Almost like it was planted."

Pa snorted. "That wasn't planted. That's spleenwort – ebony spleenwort. Only place it grows around here is where somebody's used lime to set footings for a foundation. Soil's too acid for it otherwise. Find it growin' over all the vanished towns."

Gary knew there were lots of vanished towns in the Barrens, but this must have been one hell of a foundation. It was close to six feet wide and ran as far as he could see in either direction."

"What you think used to stand here, Pa?"

"Who knows, who cares? People was buildin' in the Barrens afore the Revolutionary War. And I hear tell there was crumblin' ruins already here when the Indians arrived. There's some real old stuff around these parts but we ain't about to dig it up. We're here for coon. Now hesh up till we get to the traps!"

*

Gary couldn't believe their luck. Every damn leg-hold trap

had a coon in it! Big fat ones with thick, silky coats the likes of which he'd never seen. A few were already dead, but most of them were still alive, lying on their sides, their black eyes wide with fear and pain; panting, bloody, exhausted from trying to pull loose from the teeth of the traps, still tugging weakly at the chains that linked the trap to its stake.

He and Pa took care of the tuckered-out ones first by crushing their throats. Gary flipped them onto their backs and watched their stripped tails come up protectively over their bellies. I ain't after your belly, Mr. Coon. He put his heel right over the windpipe, and kicked down hard. If he was in the right spot he heard a satisfying crunch as the cartilage collapsed. The coons wheezed and thrashed and flopped around awhile in the traps trying to draw some air past the crushed spot but soon enough they choked to death. Gary had had some trouble doing the throat crush when he started at it years ago, but he was used to it by now. It was just the way it was done. All the trappers did it.

But you couldn't try that on the ones that still had some pepper in them. They wouldn't hold still enough for you to place your heel. That was where the Gary and his Slugger came in. He swung at one as it snapped at him.

"The head! The head, dammit!" Pa was yelling.

"Awright, awright!"

"Don't mess the pelts!"

Some of those coons were tough suckers. Took at least half a dozen whacks each with the Slugger to kill them dead. They'd twist and squeal and squirm around and it wasn't easy to pound a direct hit on the head every single time. But they weren't going nowhere, not with one of their legs caught in a steel trap.

By the time he and Pa reached the last trap, Gary's bat was drippy red up to the taped grip, and his bag was so heavy he could barely lift it. Pa's was just about full too.

"Damn!" Pa said, standing over the last trap. "Empty!" Then he knelt for a closer look. "No, wait! Looky that! It's been sprung! The paw's still in it! Musta chewed it off!"

Gary heard a rustle in the brush to his right and caught a glimpse of a gray-and-black striped tail slithering away.

"There it is!"

"Get it!"

Gary dropped the sack and went after the last coon. No sweat. It was missing one of its rear paws and left a trail of blood behind on the snow wherever it went. He came upon it within twenty feet. A fat one, waddling and gimping along as fast as its three legs would carry it. He swung but the coon partially dodged the blow and squalled as the bat glanced off its skull. The next shot got it solid but it rolled away. Gary kept after it through the brush, hitting it again and again, until his arms got tired. He counted nearly thirty strikes before he got in a good one. The big coon rolled over and looked at him with glazed eyes, blood running from its ears. He saw the nipples on its belly – a female. As he lifted the Slugger again, it raised its two front paws over its face – an almost human gesture that made him hesitate for a second. Then he clocked her with a winner. He bashed her head ten more times for good measure to make sure she wouldn't be going anywhere. The snow around her was splattered with red by the time he was done.

As he lifted her by her tail to take her back, he got a look at the mangled stump of her hind leg. Chewed off. God, you really had to want to get free to do something like that!

He carried her back to Pa, passing all the other splotches of crimson along the way. Looked like some bloody-footed giant had stomped through here.

"Whooeee!" Pa said when he saw the last one. "That's a beauty! They're *all* beauties! Gary, m'boy, we're gonna have money to burn when we sell these!"

Gary glanced at the sun as he tossed the last one into the sack. It was rising brightly into a clear sky.

"Maybe we shouldn't spend it until we get off Foster's land."

"You're right," Pa said, looking uneasy for the first time. "I'll come back tomorrow and rebait the traps." He slapped Gary on the back. "We found ourselfs a goldmine, son!"

Gary groaned under the weight of the sack, but he leaned forward and struck off toward the sun. He wanted to be gone from here. Quick like.

"I'll lead the way, Pa."

*

"Look at these!" Pa said, holding up two pelts by their tails. "Thick as can be and not a scar or a bald spot anywhere to be seen! Primes, every single one of them!"

He swayed as he stood by the skinning table. He'd been nipping at the applejack bottle steadily during the day-long job of cutting, stripping, and washing of the pelts, and now he was pretty near blitzed. Gary had taken the knife from Pa early on, doing all the cutting himself and leaving the stripping for the old man. You didn't have to be sober for stripping. Once the cuts were made – that was the hard part – a strong man could rip the pelt off like husking an ear of corn.

"Yeah," Gary said. "They're beauts all right. Full winter coats."

The dead of winter was, naturally, the best time to trap any fur animal. That was when the coats were the thickest. And these were *thick*. Gary couldn't remember seeing anything like these pelts. The light gray fur seemed to glow a pale metallic blue when the light hit it right. Touching it gave him a funny warm feeling inside. Made him want to find a woman and ride her straight on till morning.

The amazing thing was that they were all identical. No one was going to have to dye these babies to make a coat. They all matched perfectly, like these coons had been one big family.

These was going to make one *hell* of a beautiful full-length coat.

"Jake's gonna *love* these!" Pa said. "And he's gonna pay pretty for 'em, too!"

"Did you get hold of him?" Gary asked, thinking of the shotgun he wanted to buy.

"Yep. Be round first thing in the morning."

"Great, Pa. Why'n't you hit the sack and I'll clean up round here."

"You sure?"

"Sure."

"You're all right, son," Pa said. He clapped him on the shoulder and staggered for the door.

Gary shivered in the cold blast of wind that dashed past Pa on his way out of the barn. He got up and threw another log into the pot-bellied stove squatting in the corner, then surveyed the scene.

There really wasn't all that much left to be done. The furs had all been washed and all but a few were tacked up on the drying boards. The guts had been tossed out, and the meat had been put in the cold shed to feed to the dogs during the next few weeks. So all he had to –

Gary's eyes darted to the bench. Had something moved there? He watched a second but all was still. Yet he could have sworn one of the unstretched pelts piled there had moved. He rubbed his eyes and grinned.

Long day.

He went to the bench and spread out the remaining half dozen before stretching them. Most times they'd nail their catches to the barn door, but these were too valuable for that. He ran his hands over them. God, these were special. Never had he seen coon fur this thick and soft. That warm, peaceful, horny feeling slipped over him again. On a lark, he draped it over his arm. What a coat this was gonna–

The pelt moved, rippled. In a single swift smooth motion its edges curled and wrapped snugly around his forearm. A gush of horror dribbled away before he could react, drowned in a flood of peace and tranquility.

Nothing unusual here. Everything was all right... all right.

He watched placidly as the three remaining unstretched furs rippled and began to move toward him. Nothing wrong with that. Nothing wrong with the way they crawled over his hands and wrists and wrapped themselves around his arms. Perfectly natural. He smiled. Looked like he had caveman arms.

It was time to go back to the house. He got up and started walking. On the way out the door, he picked up the Louisville Slugger.

*

Pa was snoring.

Gary poked him with the bat and called to him. His own voice seemed to come from far away.

"Pa! Wake up, Pa!"

Finally Pa stirred and opened his bloodshot eyes.

"What is it, boy? What the hell you want?"

Gary raised the bat over his head. Pa screamed and raised his hands to protect himself, much like that last coon this morning. Gary swung the bat with everything hc had and got Pa on the wrist and over the right ear as he tried to roll away. Pa grunted and stiffened, but Gary didn't wait to see what happened. He swung again. And again. And again, counting. His arms weren't tired at all. The pelts snuggling around them seemed to give him strength. Long before the fortieth swing, Pa's head and brains were little more than a huge smear of currant jelly across the pillows.

Then he turned and headed for the back door.

Back in the barn, he stood by the stretching boards and looked down at the gore-smeared bat, clutched tightly now in both of his fists. A small part of him screamed a warning but the rest of him knew that everything was all right. Everything was fine. Everything was –

He suddenly rotated his wrists and forearms and smashed the bat against his face. He staggered back and would have screamed if his throat had only let him. His nose and forehead were in agony! But everything was all right –

No! Everything was *not* all right! This was –

He hit himself again with the bat and felt his right cheek cave in. And again, and again. The next few blows smeared his nose and took out his eyes. He was blind now, but the damn bat wouldn't stop!

He fell backwards onto the floor but still he kept battering his own head. He heard his skull splinter. But still he couldn't stop that damn bat!

And the pain! He should have been knocked cold by the first whack but he was still conscious. He felt *everything!*

He prayed he died before the bat hit him forty times.

2

No one answered his knocking at the house – house, shmouse, it was a hovel – so Jake Feldman headed for the barn. The cold early morning air chilled the inexorably widening bald spot that commanded the top of his scalp; he wrapped his unbuttoned overcoat around his ample girth and quickened his pace as much as he dared over the icy, rutted driveway.

Old man Jameson had said he'd come by some outstanding pelts. Pelts of such quality that Jake would be willing to pay ten times the going price to have them. Out of the goodness of Jameson's heart and because of their long-standing business relationship, he was going to give Jake first crack at them.

Right.

But the old Piney gonif's genuine enthusiasm had intrigued Jake. Jameson was no bullshitter. Maybe he really had something unique. And maybe not.

This better be worth it, he thought as he pulled open the barn door. He didn't have time to traipse down to the Jersey Pine Barrens on a wild goose chase.

The familiar odor of dried blood hit him as he opened the barn door. Not unexpected. Buy fresh pelts at the source for a while and you soon got used to the smell. What was unexpected was how cold it was in the barn. The lights were on but the wood stove was cold. Pelts would freeze if they stayed in this temperature too long.

Then he saw them – all lined up, all neatly nailed out on the stretching boards. The fur shimmered, reflecting glints of opalescence from the incandescent bulbs above and cold fire from the morning light pouring through the open door behind him. They were exquisite. *Magnificent!*

Jake Feldman knew fur. He'd spent almost forty of his fifty-five years in the business, starting as a cutter and working his way up till he found the *chutzpah* to start his own factory. In all those years he had never seen anything like these pelts.

My God, Jameson, where did you get them and are there any more where these came from?

Jake approached the stretching boards and touched the pelts. He had to. Something about them urged his fingers forward. So soft, so shimmery, so incredibly beautiful. Jake had seen, touched, and on occasion even cut the very finest Siberian sable pelts from Russia. But they were nothing compared to these. These were beyond quality. These were beautiful in a way that was almost scary, almost...supernatural.

Then he saw the boots. Big, gore-encrusted rubber boots sticking out from under one of the stretching boards. Nothing unusual about that except for their position. They lay on the dirt floor with their toes pointing toward the ceiling at different angles, like the hands of a clock reading five after ten. Boots simply didn't lie like that...unless there were feet in them.

Jake bent and saw denim-sheathed legs running up from the boots. He smiled. One of the Jamesons – either old Jeb or young Gary. Jake bet on the elder. A fairly safe bet seeing as how old Jeb loved his Jersey lightning.

"Hey, old man," he said as he squeezed between two of the stretching boards to get behind. "What're you doing back there? You'll catch your death of–"

The rest of the sentence clogged in Jake's throat as he looked down at the corpse. All he could see at first was the red. The entire torso was drenched in clotted blood – the chest, the arms, the shoulders the – dear Lord, the head! There was almost nothing left of the head! The face and the whole upper half of the skull had been smashed to a red, oozing pulp from which the remnant of an eye and some crazily angled teeth protruded. Only a patch of smooth, clean-shaven cheek identified the corpse as Gary, not Jeb.

But who could have done this? And why? More frightening than the sight of the corpse was Jake's sudden grasp of the ungovernable fury behind all the repeated blows it must have taken to cave in Gary's head like that. With what – that baseball bat? And after pounding him so mercilessly, had the killer wrapped Gary's dead fingers around the murder weapon? What sick–?

Jeb! Where was old Jeb? Surely he'd had nothing to do with this!

Calling the old man's name, Jake ran back up to the house. His cries went unanswered. The back door was open. He stood on the stoop, calling out again. Only silence greeted him. The shack had an *empty* feel to it. That was the only reason Jake stepped inside.

It didn't take him long to find the bedroom. And what was left of Jeb.

A moment later Jake stood panting and retching in the stretch between the house and the barn.

Dead! Both dead!

More than dead – battered, crushed, *smeared!*

...but those pelts. Even with the horrors of what he'd just seen raging through his mind, he couldn't stop thinking about those pelts.

Exquisite!

Jake ran to his car, backed it up to the barn door, popped the trunk. It took him a while but eventually he got all the pelts off the stretching boards and into his trunk. He found a couple of loose ones on the floor near Gary's body and he grabbed those too.

And then he roared away down the twin ruts that passed for a road in these parts. He felt bad about leaving the two corpses like that, but there was nothing he could do to help the Jamesons. He'd call the State Police from the Parkway. Anonymously.

But he had the pelts. That was the important thing.

And he knew exactly what he was going to do with them.

*

After getting the pelts safely back to his factory in New York's garment district, Jake immediately went about turning them into a coat. He ran into only one minor snag and that was at the beginning: The Orientals among his cutters refused to work with them. A couple of them took one look at the pelts and made a wide-eyed, screaming dash from the factory.

That shook him up for a little while, but he recovered quickly enough. Once he got things organized, he personally supervised every step: the cleaning and softening, the removal of the guard hairs, the letting-out process in which he actually took a knife in hand and crosscut a few pelts himself, just as he'd done when he started in the business; he oversaw the sewing of the let-out strips and the placement of the thousands of nails used in tacking out the fur according to the pattern.

With the final stitching of the silk lining nearing completion, Jake allowed himself to relax. Even unfinished, the coat – *That Coat*, as he'd come to call it – was stunning, unutterably beautiful. In less than an hour he was going to be the owner of the world's most extraordinary raccoon coat. Extraordinary not simply because of its unique sheen and texture, but because you couldn't tell it was raccoon. Even the cutters and tackers in his factory had been fooled; they'd agreed that the length of the hair and size of the pelts were similar to raccoon, but none of them had ever seen raccoon like this, or *any* fur like this.

Jake wished to hell he knew where Jameson had trapped them. He'd be willing to pay almost anything for a regular supply of those pelts. What he could sell those coats for!

But he had only one coat now, and he wasn't going to sell it. No way. This baby was going to be an exhibition piece. It was going to put Fell Furs on the map. He'd bring it to the next international show and blow the crowd away. The whole industry would be buzzing about That Coat. And Fell Furs would be known at the company with That Coat.

And God knew the company needed a boost. Business was down all over the industry. Jake couldn't remember furs ever being discounted as deeply as they were now. The animal lovers were having a definite impact. Well, hell, he was an animal lover too. Didn't he have a black lab at home?

But animal love stopped at the bottom line, bubby.

If he played it right, That Coat would turn things around for Fell Furs. But he needed the right model to strut it.

And he knew just who to call.

He sat in his office and dialed Shanna's home number. Even though she'd just moved, he didn't have to look it up. He knew it by heart already. He should have. He'd dialed it enough times.

Shanna...a middle-level model he'd seen at a fur show two years ago. The shoulder length black hair with the long bangs, the white skin and knockout cheekbones, onyx eyes that promised everything. And her body – Shanna had a figure that set her far apart from the other bean-poles in the field. Jake hadn't been able to get her out of his mind since. He wanted her but it seemed like a lost cause. He always felt like some sort of warty frog next to her, and she treated him like one. He'd approached her countless times and each of those times he'd been rebuffed. He didn't want to own her, he just wanted to be near her, to touch her and once in a while. And who knew? Maybe he'd grow on her.

At least now he had a chance. That Coat would open the door. This time would be different. He could feel it.

Her voice, soft and inviting, came on the line after the third ring.

"Yes?"

"Shanna, it's me. Jake Feldman."

"Oh." The drop in temperature within that single syllable spoke volumes. "What do you want, Jake?"

"I have a business proposition for you, Shanna."

Her voice grew even cooler. "I've heard your propositions before. I'm not the least–"

"This is straight down the line business," he said quickly. "I've got a coat for you. I want you to wear it at the international show next week."

"I don't know." She seemed the tiniest bit hesitant now. "It's

240

been a while since I've done a fur show."

"You'll want to do them again when you see this coat. Believe me."

Maybe some of his enthusiasm for the coat was coming over the phone. Jake sensed a barely detectable thaw in her voice.

"Well...call the agency."

"I will. But I want you to see this coat first. You've got to see it."

"Really, Jake–"

"You've *got* to see it. I'll bring it right down."

He hung up before she could tell him no and hurried out to the work room. As soon as the last knot was tied in the last stitch he boxed it and headed for the door.

"What kind of coat you buy, Mister?" someone said as soon as he stepped out onto the sidewalk.

Oh, shit. Animal lovers. A bunch of them holding signs, milling around outside his showroom.

Somebody shoved a placard in his face:

The only one who can wear a fur
coat gracefully and beautifully
is the animal to whom it belongs.

"How many harmless animals were trapped and beaten to death to make it?" said a guy with a beard.

"Fuck off!" Jake said. "You're wearing leather shoes, aren't you?"

The guy smiled, "Actually, I'm wearing sneakers, but even if they were leather it wouldn't be for pure vanity. Cows are in the human food chain. Beavers, minks, and baby seals are not."

"So what?"

"It's one thing for animals to die to provide food – that's the law of nature. It's something entirely different to kill animals so you can steal their beauty by draping yourself with their skins. Animals shouldn't suffer and die to feed human vanity."

A chant began.

"Vanity! Vanity! Vanity...!"

Jake flipped them all the bird and grabbed a cab downtown.

3

Such a beautiful girl living in a place like this, Jake thought as he entered the lobby of the converted TriBeCa warehouse where Shanna had just bought a condo. Probably paid a small fortune for it too. Just because it was considered a chic area of town.

At the "Elevator" sign he found himself facing a steel panel studded with rivets. Not sure of what to do, he tried a pull on the lever under the sign. With a clank the steel panel split horizontally, dividing into a pair of huge metal doors that opened vertically, the top one sliding upward, the bottom sinking. An old freight elevator. Inside he figured out how to get the contraption to work and rode the noisy open car up to the third level.

Stepping out on the third floor he found a door marked 3B straight ahead of him. That was Shanna's. He knocked, heard footsteps approaching.

"Who's there?" said a muffled voice from the other side. Shanna's voice.

"It's me. Jake. I brought the coat."

"I told you to call the agency."

Even through the door he could sense her annoyance. This wasn't going well. He spotted the glass lens in the door and that gave him an idea.

"Look through your peephole, Shanna."

He pulled That Coat from the box. The fur seemed to ripple against his hands as he lifted it. A few unused letting-out strips fell from the sleeve, landing in the box. The looked like furry caterpillars; a couple of them even seemed to move on their own. Strange. They shouldn't have been in the coat. He shrugged it off. It didn't matter. That Coat was all that mattered. And getting past Shanna's door.

"Just take a gander at this coat. Try one peek at this beauty and then tell me you don't want to take a closer look."

He heard the peephole cover move on the other side. Ten

seconds later, the door opened. Shanna stood there staring. He caught his breath at the sight of her. Even without make-up, wearing an old terry cloth robe, she was beautiful. But her wide eyes were oblivious to him. They were fixed on That Coat. She seemed to be in a trance.

"Jake, it's...it's beautiful. Can I...?"

As she reached for it, Jake dropped the fur back into its box and slid by her into the apartment.

"Try it on in here. The light's better."

She followed him into the huge, open, loft-like space that made up the great room of her condo. Too open for Jake's tastes. Ceilings too high, not enough walls. And still not finished yet. The paperhangers were halfway through a bizarre mural on one wall; their ladders and tools were stacked by the door.

He turned and held That Coat open for her.

"Here, Shanna. I had it made in your size."

She turned and slipped her arms into the sleeves. As Jake settled it over her shoulders he noticed a few of those leftover fur strips clinging to the coat. He plucked them off and bunched them into his palm to discard later. Then he stepped back to look at her. The fur had been breathtaking before, but Shanna enhanced its beauty. And vice versa. The two of them seemed made for each other. The effect brought tears to Jake's eyes.

She glided over to a mirrored wall and did slow turns, again and again. Rapture glowed in her face. Finally she turned to him, eyes bright.

"You don't have to call the agency," she said. "I'll call. I want to show this coat."

Jake suddenly realized that he was in a much better bargaining position than he had ever imagined. Shanna no longer had the upper hand. He did. He decided to raise the stakes.

"Of course you do," he said offhandedly. "And there's a good chance you'll be the model we finally settle on."

Her face showed concern for the first time since she'd laid eyes on the coat.

"'A good chance'? What's that supposed to mean?"

"Well, there are other models who're very interested. We have to give them a chance to audition."

She wrapped the fur more tightly around her.

"I don't want anyone else wearing this coat!"

"Well..."

Slowly Shanna pulled open the coat, untied the terry cloth robe beneath it, and pulled that open too. She wore nothing under the robe. Jake barely noticed her smile.

"Believe me," she said in that honey voice, "this is the only audition you'll need."

Jake's mouth was suddenly too dry to speak. He could not take his eyes off her breasts. He reached for the buttons on his own coat and found the fur strips in his right hand. As he went to throw them away, he felt them move, wiggling like furry worms. When he looked, they had wrapped themselves around his fingers.

Tranquility seeped through him like fine red wine. It didn't seem odd that the strips should move. Perfectly natural. Funny even.

Look. I've got fur rings.

He pulled at his coat and shirts until he was bare from the waist up. Then he realized he needed to be alone for a minute.

"Where's your bathroom?"

"That door behind you."

He needed something sharp. Why?

"Do you have a knife? A sharp one?" The words seemed to form on their own.

Her expression was quizzical. "I think so. The paperhangers were using razor blades–"

"That'll be fine." He went to the work bench and found the utility knife, then headed for the bathroom. "I'll only be a minute. Wait for me in the bedroom."

What am I doing?

In the bathroom he stood before the mirror with the utility knife gripped in the fur-wrapped fingers of his right hand. A sudden wave of cold shuddered through him. He felt half-frozen, trapped, afraid. Then he saw old Jameson's whiskered face, huge in the mirror, saw his monstrous foot ram toward him. Jake gagged with the crushing pain in his throat, he was suffocating, God he couldn't breathe–!

And then just as suddenly he was fine again. Everything was all right. He pushed the upper corner of the utility blade through the skin at the top of his breast bone, just deep enough the pierce its full thickness through to the fatty layer beneath. Then he drew the blade straight down the length of his sternum. When he reached the top of his abdomen he angled the cut to the right, following the line of the bottom rib across his flank. He heard the tendons and ligaments in his shoulder joint creak and pop in protest as his hand extended the cut all the way around his waist to his back, but he felt no pain, not from the shoulder, not even from the gash that had begun to bleed so freely. Something within him was screaming in horror but it was far away. Everything was all right here. Everything was fine.

When he had extended the first cut all the way back to his spine he switched the blade to his left hand and made a similar cut from the front toward the left, meeting the first cut at the rear near the base of his spine. Then he made a circular cut around each shoulder – over the top and through the armpit. Then another all the way around his neck. When that was done, he gripped the edges on each side of the incision he had made over the breast bone and yanked. Amid sprays of red, the skin began to pull free of the underlying tissues.

Everything was all right...all right...

Jake kept tugging.

*

Where the hell is he?

Wrapped in the coat, Shanna stood before her bedroom mirror and waited for Jake.

She wasn't looking forward to this. No way. The thought of that flabby white body flopping around on top of her made her a little ill, but she was going through with it. Nothing was going to keep her from wearing this fur.

She snuggled the coat closer about her but it kept falling away, almost as if it didn't want to touch her. Silly thought.

She did a slow turn before the mirror.

Looking good, Shanna!

This was it. This was one of those moments you hear about when your whole future hinges on a single decision. Shanna knew what that decision had to be. Her career was stalled short of the top. She was making good money but she wanted more – she wanted her face recognized everywhere. And this coat was going to get her that recognition. A couple of international shows and she'd be known the world over as the girl in the fabulous fur. From then on she could write her own ticket.

In spite of her queasy stomach, Shanna allowed herself a sour smile. This wouldn't be the first time she'd spread to get something she wanted. Jake Feldman had been letching after her for years; if letting him get his jollies on her a couple of times assured her of exclusive rights to model his coat, tonight might be the *last* time she ever had to spread for anyone like Jake Feldman.

What was he doing in the bathroom – papering it? She wished he'd get out of there and get this over with. Then she could–

She heard the bathroom door open, heard his footsteps in the great room. He was shuffling.

"In here, Jake!" she called.

Quickly she pulled free of the coat long enough to shed the robe, then slipped back into it and stretched out on the bed. She rolled onto her side and propped herself up on one elbow but the fur kept falling away from her. Well, that was okay too. She left it open, arranging the coat so that her best stuff was displayed to the max. She knew all the provocative poses. She'd done her share of nudie sessions to pay her bills between those early fashion assignments.

Outside the door the shuffling steps were drawing closer. What was he doing – walking around with his pants around his ankles?

"Hurry up, honey! I'm waiting for you!"

Let's get this show on the road, you fat slob!

Suddenly she was cold, her leg hurt, she saw a boyish-faced giant looming over her with a raised club, saw it come crashing down on her head. As she began to scream she suddenly found herself back in her condo, sprawled on her bed with the fur.

Jake was shuffling through the door.

Shanna's mind dimly registered that he was holding something, but the red immediately captured her attention. Jake was all red – *dripping* red – his pants, the skin of his arms, his bare–

Oh God it was blood! He was covered with blood! And his chest and upper abdomen – they were the bloodiest. Christ! The skin was gone! *Gone!* Like someone had ripped the hide off his upper torso.

"I..." His voice was hoarse. A croak. His eyes were wide and glazed as he shuffled toward her. "I made this vest for you."

And then Shanna looked at what he held out to her, what drooped from his bloody fingers – fingers that seemed to be covered with fur.

It was indeed a vest. A white, blood-streaked, sleeveless vest. Between the streaks of blood she could see the wiry chest hairs straggling across the front... whorling around the nipples...

Shanna screamed and rolled off the bed, hugging the coat around her. She wished she could have pulled it over her head to hide the sight of him.

"It's for you," he said, continuing his shuffle toward her. "You can wear it under the coat..."

Whimpering in fear and revulsion, Shanna ran around the bed and dashed for the door. She ran across the great room and out into the hall. The elevator! She had to get away from that man, that *thing* who'd cut his skin into a –

The shuffling. He was coming!

She pressed the down button, pounded on it. Behind the steel door she heard the winches whir to life. The elevator was on its way. She turned and gagged as she saw Jake come through her apartment door and approach her, leaving a trail of blood behind him, holding the bloody skin out as if expecting her to slip her arms through the openings.

A clank behind her. She turned, pulled the lever that opened the heavy steel doors, and leaped inside. An upward push on the inner lever brought the outer doors down with a deafening clang, shutting out the sight of Jake and his hideous offering.

Clutching the coat around her bare body Shanna sank to her knees and began to sob.

God, what was happening here? Why had Jake cut his skin off like that? *How* had he done it?

"Shanna, please," said that croaking voice from the other side of the doors. "I made it for you."

And then the doors started to open! Before her eyes a horizontal slit was opening between the outer doors, and two bloody arms with fur-wrapped fingers were thrusting the loathsome vest toward her through the gap.

Shanna's scream echoed up and down the open elevator shaft as she hit the *Down* button. The car lurched and started to sink.

Thank you, God!

But the third floor doors continued to open. As she passed the second floor and continued her descent, Shanna's eyes were irresistibly drawn upward. Through the open ceiling of the car she watched the ever-widening gap, watched as the two protruding arms and the vest were joined by Jake's head and upper torso.

"Shanna! It's for you!"

The car stopped with a jolt. First floor. Shanna yanked up the safety grate and pulled the lever. Five seconds... five seconds and she'd be running for the street, for the cops. As the outer doors slowly parted, that voice echoed again through the elevator shaft.

"Shanna!"

She chanced one last look upward.

The third floor doors had retracted to the floor and ceiling lines. Most of Jake's torso seemed to be hanging over the edge.

"It's for–

He leaned too far.

Oh, shit, he's falling!

"–yoooooouuuuu!"

Shanna's high-pitched scream of "Noooo!" blended with Jake's voice in a fearful harmony that ended with his head striking the upper edge of the elevator car's rear wall. As the rest of his body whipped around in a wild, blood-splattering, pinwheeling sprawl, his shoed foot slammed against Shanna's head, knocking her back against the door lever. Half-dazed, she watched the steel doors reverse their opening motion.

"No!"

And Jake...Jake was still moving, crawling toward her an inch at a time on twisted arms, broken legs, his shattered head raised, trying to speak, still clutching the vest in one hand, still offering it to her.

The coat seemed to ripple around her, moving on its own. She had to get *out* of here!

The doors! Shanna lunged for the opening, reaching toward the light from the deserted front foyer. She could make it through if–

She slipped on the blood, went down on one knee, still reaching as the steel doors slammed down on her wrist. Shanna heard her bones crunch as pain beyond anything she had ever known ran up her arm. She would have screamed but the agony had stolen her voice. She tried to pull free but she was caught, tried to reach the lever but it was a good foot beyond her grasp.

Something touched her foot. Jake – it was what was left of Jake holding his vest out to her with one hand, caressing her bare foot with the one of the fur strips wrapped around the fingers of his other hand. She kicked at him, slid herself away from him. She couldn't let him get near her. He'd want to put that vest on her, want to try to do other things to her. And she was bare-ass naked under this coat. She had to get free, get free of these doors, anything to get free!

She began chewing at the flesh of her trapped wrist, tearing at it, unmindful of the greater pain, of the running blood. It seemed the natural thing to do, the *only* thing to do.

Free! She had to get *free!*

4

Juanita wasn't having much luck tonight. She'd just pushed her shopping cart with all her worldly belongings the length of a narrow alley looking for a safe place to huddle for the night, an alcove or deep doorway, someplace out of sight and out of the wind. A good alley, real potential, but already occupied by someone very drunk and very nasty. She'd moved on.

Cold. Really felt the cold these days. Didn't know how old she was but knew that her bones creaked and her back hurt and she couldn't stand the cold like she used to. If she could find a place to hide her cart, maybe she could sneak into the subway for the night. Always warmer down there. But when she came up top again all her things might be gone.

Didn't want to be carted off to no shelter, neither. Even a safe one. Didn't like being closed in, and once they got you into those places they never let you go till morning. Liked to come and go as she pleased. Besides, she got confused indoors and her mind wouldn't work straight. She was an outdoors person. That was where she did her clearest thinking, where she intended to stay.

As she turned a corner she spotted all the flashing red and blue lights outside a building she remembered as a warehouse but was now a bunch of apartments. Like a child, she was drawn to the bright, pretty lights to see what was going on.

Took her a while to find out. Juanita allowed herself few illusions. She knew not many people want to explain things to someone who looks like a walking rag pile, but she persisted and eventually managed to pick up half a dozen variations on what had happened inside. All agreed on one thing: a gruesome double murder in the building's elevator involving a naked woman and a half-naked man. After that the stories got crazy. Some said the man had been flayed alive and the woman was wearing his skin, others said the man had cut off the woman's hand, still others said she'd *chewed* her own hand off.

Enough. Shuddering, Juanita turned and pushed her cart away. She'd gone only a few yards when she spotted movement as she was passing a shadowed doorway. Not human movement; too low to the ground. Looked like an animal but it was too big for a rat, even a New York City rat. Light from a passing EMS wagon glinted off the thing and Juanita was struck by the thickness of its fur, by the way the light danced and flickered over its surface.

Then she realized it was a coat – a fur coat. Even in the dark she could see that it wasn't some junky fun fur. This was the real thing, a true, blue, top-of-the-line, utterly fabulous fur coat. She grabbed it and held it up. *Mira!* Even in the dark she could see how lovely it was, how the fur glistened.

She slipped into it. The coat seemed to ripple away from her for a second, then it snuggled against her. Instantly she was warm. So warm. Almost as if the fur was generating its own heat, like an electric blanket. Seemed to draw the cold right out of her bones. Must've been ages since she last felt so toasty. But she forced herself to pull free of it and hold it up again.

Sadly, Juanita shook her head. No good. Too nice. Wear this thing around and someone'd think she was rich and roll her but good. Maybe she could pawn it. But it was probably hot and that would get her busted. Couldn't take being locked up ever again. A shame, though. Such a nice warm coat and she couldn't wear it.

And then she had an idea. She found an alley like the one she'd left before and dropped the coat onto the pavement, fur side down. Then she knelt beside it and began to rub it into the filth. From top to bottom she covered the fur with any grime she could find. Practically cleaned the end of the alley with that coat. Then she held it up again.

Better. Much better. No one would recognize it and hardly anybody would bother stealing it the way it looked now. But what did she care how she looked in it? As long as it served its purpose, that was all she asked. She slipped into it again and once more the warmth enveloped her.

She smiled and felt the wind whistle through the gaps between her teeth.

This is living! Nothing like a fur to keep you warm. And after all, for those who of us who do our living in the outdoors, ain't that what fur is for?

THE SECRET HISTORY OF THE WORLD

Here are all the works in the Secret History listed in chronological order. (NB: "Year Zero" is the end of civilization as we know it; "Year Zero Minus One" is the year preceding it, etc.)

Scenes from the Secret History is FREE on Smashwords

The Past
"Demonsong"* (prehistory)
"The Compendium of Srem" (1498)
"Wardenclyffe" (1903-1906)
"Aryans and Absinthe"* (1923-1924)
Black Wind (1926-1945)
The Keep (1941)
Reborn (February-March 1968)
"Dat-Tay-Vao"* (March 1968)
Jack: Secret Histories (1983)
Jack: Secret Circles (1983)
Jack: Secret Vengeance (1983)
"Faces"* (1988)
Cold City (1990)
Dark City (1991)
Fear City (1993)

"Fix" (2004) with Joe Konrath and Ann Voss Peterson

Year Zero Minus Three
Sibs (February)
The Tomb (summer)
"The Barrens"* (ends in September)
"A Day in the Life"+ (October)
"The Long Way Home"+
Legacies (December)

Year Zero Minus Two
"Interlude at Duane's"+ (April)
Conspiracies (April) (includes "Home Repairs"+)
All the Rage (May) (includes "The Last Rakosh"+)
Hosts (June)
The Haunted Air (August)
Gateways (September)
Crisscross (November)
Infernal (December)

Year Zero Minus One
Harbingers (January)
"Infernal Night" (with Heather Graham)
Bloodline (April)
The Fifth Harmonic (April)
Panacea (April)
The God Gene (May)
By the Sword (May)
Ground Zero (July)
The Touch (ends in August)
The Void Protocol (September)
The Peabody-Ozymandias Traveling Circus & Oddity Emporium (ends in
September)
"Tenants"*

Year Zero

"Pelts"*
Reprisal (ends in February)
Fatal Error (February) (includes "The Wringer"+)
The Dark at the End (March)
Signalz (May)
Nightworld (May)

* available in *Secret Stories*
+ available in *Quick Fixes – Tales of Repairman Jack*

ALSO BY F. PAUL WILSON

Nightworld
Quick Fixes – Tales of Repairman Jack

The Teen Trilogy*
Jack: Secret Histories
Jack: Secret Circles
Jack: Secret Vengeance

The Early Years Trilogy*
Cold City
Dark City
Fear City

The ICE Trilogy*
Panacea
The God Gene
The Void Protocol

The LaNague Federation Series
Healer
Wheels Within Wheels
An Enemy of the State
Dydeetown World
The Tery

Other Novels
*Black Wind**
*Sibs**
The Select
Virgin
Implant
Deep as the Marrow
Sims
*The Fifth Harmonic**
Midnight Mass

Novellas
*The Peabody-Ozymandias Traveling Circus & Oddity Emporium**

*Wardenclyffe**
*Signalz**

Collaborations
Mirage (with Matthew J. Costello)
Nightkill (with Steven Spruill)
DNA Wars (formerly *Masque* – with Matthew J. Costello)
Draculas (with Crouch, Killborn, Strand)
The Proteus Cure (with Tracy L. Carbone)
A Necessary End (with Sarah Pinborough)
"Fix" (with Joe Konrath & Ann Voss Peterson)*

The Nocturnia Chronicles
(with Tom Monteleone)
Definitely Not Kansas
Family Secrets
The Silent Ones

Short Fiction
Soft & Others
The Barrens & Others
The Christmas Thingy
Aftershock & Others
*Quick Fixes – Tales of Repairman Jack**
Sex Slaves of the Dragon Tong
*The Compendium of Srem**
A Little Beige Book of Nondescript Stories
Ephemerata
*Secret Stories**

Editor
Freak Show
Diagnosis: Terminal
The Hogben Chronicles (with Pierce Watters)

Omnibus Editions
The Complete LaNague
Calling Dr. Death (3 medical thrillers)

* The Secret History of the World

ACKNOWLEDGE-
MENTS

"Demonsong" © 1979 by F. Paul Wilson. First published in *Heroic Fantasy* edited by Gerald W. Page (DAW #334 – 1979)

"Aryans and Absinthe" © 1997 by F. Paul Wilson. Revision © 2019 by F. Paul Wilson.
First published in *Revelations* edited by Douglas E. Winter (HarperCollins - 1997)
The author wishes to thank Charles Bracelen Flood for his remarkable *Hitler: The Path to Power* (Houghton Mifflin - 1989), the major source of historical data for this story.

"Dat-Tay-Vao" © 1987 by F. Paul Wilson. First published in *Amazing Stories* (March 1987)

"Faces" © 1988 by F. Paul Wilson. First published in *Night Visions 6* (Dark Harvest - 1988).

"The Barrens" © 1990 by F. Paul Wilson. First published in *Lovecraft's Legacy* edited by Robert Weinberg and Martin H. Greenberg (Tor - 1990).

"Tenants" © 1988 by F. Paul Wilson. First published in *Night Visions 6* (Dark Harvest - 1988).

"Pelts" © 1990 by F. Paul Wilson. First published in a Footsteps Press chapbook, 1990.

Made in the USA
Columbia, SC
12 April 2019